GW00359656

'*Ma pauvre, wh* doing to you?'

'N. . .nothing.' Held securely in his arms, Maryanne felt warm and protected and, at that moment, there was nothing she needed more.

'Nothing?'

Tears blurred Maryanne's vision as he took her chin in his big hand and tilted her face up to him. 'No one has even taken the tiniest liberty?'

'What do you mean?'

'This.' Before she could protest, he had bent his head and was kissing her.

Dear Reader

Despite an unavoidably long gap since JUST DESERTS, Elizabeth Bailey is back again with a beautiful and touching story set in Tunbridge Wells in the 1790s. AN ANGEL'S TOUCH gives us Verity, determined to do her best for the Marquis and his children. . . Mary Nichols returns with THE DANBURY SCANDALS, a marvellous love mystery where both the hero and heroine belatedly discover their connection to Viscount Danbury, and get into trouble because of it!

The Editor

Born in Singapore, **Mary Nichols** came to England when she was three, and has spent most of her life in different parts of East Anglia. She has been a radiographer, school secretary, information officer and industrial editor, as well as a writer. She has three grown-up children, and four grandchildren.

Recent titles by the same author:

DEAR REBEL

THE DANBURY
SCANDALS

Mary Nichols

All the characters in this book have no existence outside the imagination of the Author, and have no relation whatsoever to anyone bearing the same name or names. They are not even distantly inspired by any individual known or unknown to the Author, and all the incidents are pure invention.

All Rights Reserved. The text of this publication or any part thereof may not be reproduced or transmitted in any form or by any means, electronic or mechanical, including photocopying, recording, storage in an information retrieval system, or otherwise, without the written permission of the publisher.

This book is sold subject to the condition that it shall not, by way of trade or otherwise, be lent, resold, hired out or otherwise circulated without the prior consent of the publisher in any form of binding or cover other than that in which it is published and without a similar condition including this condition being imposed on the subsequent purchaser.

First published in Great Britain 1992 by Mills & Boon Limited

© Mary Nichols 1992

Australian copyright 1992 Philippine copyright 1992 This edition 1992

ISBN 0 263 77952 1

Masquerade is a trademark published by Mills & Boon Limited, Eton House, 18–24 Paradise Road, Richmond, Surrey, TW9 1SR.

Set in 10 on 10½ pt Linotron Times 04-9212-86134

Typeset in Great Britain by Centracet, Cambridge Made and printed in Great Britain

CHAPTER ONE

THE snow of the longest and hardest winter for centuries had gone at last and the snowdrops were nodding their delicate heads in the woods beside the lane and it would not be long before the daffodils were in bloom, carpeting the ground beneath the trees in a glory of gold. The first awakening of spring had never before failed to enrapture Maryanne, but today her thoughts were on other things, as the heavy family coach turned in at the gates of a huge estate and along a tree-lined drive.

Opposite her, James, Viscount Danbury, whose title seemed to sit uneasily on his upright shoulders, even after twenty-eight years, sat back in his seat, looking pensive. Lean and sinuous, he was in his early fifties, she judged, and still a handsome man, with a complexion which owed more to his time in the Navy than to his duties as the squire of Beckford, where he was a well-liked and respected figure. He had been married, though his wife had died many years before, leaving him to bring up a son and daughter alone.

All this Maryanne knew, but what had been puzzling her ever since her interview with him at Beckford Hall the previous day was what she had done to deserve his attention. They lived on a different plane entirely; he was so far above her as to seem god-like and yet he had asked to see her and then had startled her into agreeing to take his short journey with him, and unchaperoned at that. 'The reverend is in full accord,' he had said, when she protested.

So here she was, wearing her best—and only—silk gown, a warm cloak and a plain bonnet, on her way to goodness knew where and he alone knowing why. Except, perhaps, her guardian, the Reverend Mr

Cudlipp; he had come away from the interview looking
thoroughly pleased with himself.

She looked up suddenly to find his lordship's brown
eyes on her, and smiled nervously, then sat forward in
her seat with a gasp of surprise as the vehicle rounded
the bend which brought the mansion into view. But it
was not the graceful lines of the building, its great
length and height, nor its myriad shining windows
arranged in rows either side of a huge portal of marble
columns, which caused her surprise. It was the feeling,
so strong she could not believe it anything but fact,
that it was not the first time she had been there.

'What is this place?' she asked him. 'I'm sure I have
been here before.'

'You have?' He sounded surprised. 'When was that?'

Maryanne teased her memory, trying to pin-point
the occasion. As a child she had seen very little of her
father, who had been a sea captain and rarely at home.
It was why they had lived at Portsmouth, why they had
had no real home of their own, but lived with Benjamin
Paynter, her father's uncle. It was Uncle Ben who had
brought her here. He had been a seaman himself and
was gnarled and weatherbeaten, but he had the kindest
heart of any man she had ever known. She remembered
how he'd used to hold her on his knee to tell her stories
of his adventures in foreign places and show her
pictures of the ships he had served on. After her father
had been killed in the Copenhagen action of 1802, she
and her mother had continued to live with Uncle Ben,
existing on a small naval pension bought with her
father's share of the prize money. Her great-uncle had
been her only comfort when her mother, too, had died.

Even now, she could easily recall the feelings of
desolation, of bewilderment, she had felt then. She
remembered the people standing at their street doors
as the hearse passed, drawn by four black horses with
huge black plumes and shining harness, and followed
by a very few mourners on foot. It had poured with
rain while they stood at the graveside; everything,

including the sky, had looked black or grey, everything except the shining oak coffin and its brass handles. When they started piling earth on top of it, she had screamed aloud, so that one of the black-clad figures had led her away until she quietened down. Who had they been, those people at the graveside? As far as she was aware, she had never seen them before or since.

She had been too young to realise that it was a far grander funeral than a poor family like hers could afford and it had not, at the time, occurred to her to wonder who had paid for it. It had been easy to accept it without question, assuming that Uncle Ben had arranged it or that her mother had had enough savings to cover the expenses.

Uncle Ben, she remembered now, had hired a chaise to bring them up from Portsmouth, a trip which at any other time would have delighted her, especially in his company, but on that occasion he had been silent and thoughtful. When the coach stopped at the lodge, he had been obliged to spend several minutes persuading the lodge keeper that his business was important enough for him to be admitted without an appointment. Eventually he had succeeded, the huge gates had been opened and they had proceeded up the long drive through an avenue of trees to the front door of the house, when her view of it had been exactly as it was now. Her great-uncle had left her sitting in the chaise while he went to the door. He had not been admitted, although the footman had gone off with a message to someone, who had declined to see him. When he returned to the coach he had been almost purple with rage and uttering imprecations under his breath which had startled her.

Soon after that, she had been taken to live with the Reverend Mr Cudlipp and his wife. She remembered her arrival at Beckford, how bereft she had felt, how she had cried into her pillow night after night, cried for her mother and Uncle Ben, who had cruelly left her there. At the time she had not been able to understand

why it was out of the question to allow a growing girl
to be brought up by an old bachelor. The tears had
dried at last and since then she had hardened herself to
be indifferent to mental anguish; she had not wept
since. Tears changed nothing. She had settled down in
her new life and had learned to curb what her guardian
referred to as her 'wilful ways', although deep inside
her was a defiant streak born of a longing for something
different, a restlessness which the oppressive atmosphere of the rectory did nothing to assuage.

'My great-uncle brought me here,' she said, bringing
herself back to the present to reply to his question. 'It
was just after Mama died.'

He looked surprised. 'Whom did you see?'

'No one. Neither did he. We were turned away.'

'I am sorry,' he said softly. 'Did he say why?'

'No. I never knew.' She turned to him, her huge
eyes troubled. 'What is this place?'

'Castle Cedars, the country home of the Duke of
Wiltshire. We are going to see the Dowager Duchess.
She is my aunt, you know.'

'No, I didn't know.'

'You will not be turned from the door this time,' he
said softly.

Any questions she might have had were cut short
because the carriage had stopped and the groom had
jumped down to open its door and let down the step.
She was aware, as she stood hesitantly on the gravel of
the drive, that their arrival had been anticipated and
the great oak front entrance had been opened by a
liveried footman in yellow satin and white stockings.

She wondered if she was going to be offered a post,
perhaps as a maid or companion to the old lady, but
she dismissed that idea as being nonsensical; Her Grace
was unlikely to employ someone she did not know and
who had no experience of the duties expected of her.
Had her mother once worked in this great house? Was
that why Uncle Ben had brought her here, hoping for
a little charity, for the ten-year-old orphan? Charity!

Was that all it was? His lordship took her arm and escorted her up the steps and into a large high-ceilinged hall, where they were met by the house steward. 'Good afternoon, my lord.'

'Good afternoon, Mr Fletcher. How is Her Grace today?'

'She rallied a little this morning, my lord, and was able to direct her affairs.' This was said with a conspiratorial smile, as he took Maryanne's cloak and bonnet and his lordship's hat. 'Mr Mark and Miss Caroline are already with Her Grace, my lord. She gave instructions you were to be shown straight up.'

'Then let us go to her.' His lordship smiled at Maryanne, 'Come, my dear, you will not be kept in suspense any longer.'

She followed him up the grand staircase and along a gallery whose thick carpet deadened their footsteps, to a room at the end, where he knocked on the door and ushered her inside.

The curtains were almost fully drawn across the big windows and the room was in semi-darkness, so that it was a moment or two before Maryanne's eyes became accustomed to the gloom. She could not see the occupant of the bed, because the doctor's broad frame was in the way. On one side stood a young man in his late twenties, a handsome man, tall and upright, unsmiling. He was so like Lord Danbury that she guessed he must be his son, the Honourable Mark Danbury. The young lady sitting on the other side Maryanne knew to be the Honourable Caroline because she sometimes came to Church with her father and could be seen occasionally riding out in one or other of the family carriages, or galloping across the downs with a groom endeavouring to keep up with her. Today her fashionable pink-striped open gown over a satin petticoat in a darker shade made Maryanne feel dowdy and out of place.

'I do not think this is a good idea at all, Your Grace,' the doctor was saying, as he moved round to take the patient's wrist in his hand, allowing Maryanne a view of the tiny figure in the bed. 'You should not become excited.'

The Duchess's white hair, under a snowy cap, was spread about an equally snowy pillow, making her lined face look even greyer than it really was. She lay so still that, for one shocked moment, Maryanne thought she was dead. But then her eyes flickered open and they were as clear and blue as forget-me-nots.

'Tarradiddle, you old fool! I shall become more excited if I am thwarted, as you well know.' She turned her head slowly and looked directly at Maryanne. 'Come forward, child.'

Maryanne moved slowly towards the bed, conscious of everyone's eyes watching her, the young man with curiosity, his sister with disdain.

The old lady attempted to sit up and Lord Danbury hurried forward to plump up the pillows behind her. Once she was settled, Maryanne was subjected to a scrutiny which made her feel like a farm animal at market. No one spoke and Maryanne, self-conscious and uncomfortable, swallowed hard and resisted the temptation to speak first and shatter the silence.

'The likeness is there,' the old lady said at last, to the room in general, and then to Maryanne in particular, 'I am sorry, my dear, so very sorry.' She stretched out her hand and Maryanne moved forward to take it and drop a curtsy.

'Sorry, Your Grace?' she asked.

But the Dowager Duchess did not appear to hear. She dropped her hand and turned to her nephew. 'James, you must make. . .amends. . .'

'Yes, Aunt.'

'And don't leave it to Henry; you know what he is like.'

'It will be my pleasure to look after her myself, Aunt,' he said.

The old lady smiled. 'You always did have a soft spot in your heart for Helena, didn't you? When we condemned, you connived. . .' She sighed. 'But then we could hardly expect anything else from you, could we? Baked in the same mould, the pair of you.'

'Aunt. . .'

'Oh, do not try to hum your way out of it. It is of no consequence now. Just make sure she is brought out and makes a good match. Now, I am tired.' She turned to Maryanne. 'I'm glad to have met you, my child. Go now, I must sleep. . .' The voice was weaker, breathless. Her head sank back into the soft pillow. 'We will talk again when I feel stronger.' Her last words were almost inaudible and the doctor brushed Lord Danbury aside to go to her.

Maryanne felt herself being taken by the arm, turned and propelled towards the door. Once outside, she turned to look at the young man who had escorted her from the room. He smiled easily, although behind his smile was a certain wariness.

'I am sorry you had to be subjected to that, but once Her Grace gets an idea into her head there is no gainsaying it.'

'But I don't understand. Why am I being treated like some prize horse? I thought someone would ask to inspect my teeth next.'

He chuckled. 'I've no doubt my father will enlighten you shortly. I'm Mark Danbury, by the way.' He escorted her down to a small reception-room and turned to smile at her. 'Please wait in here; my father will come to you soon.'

'Mr Danbury,' she said, turning on him with anger flashing in her violet eyes. 'I insist on being told why I have been brought here and inspected just as if I were some chattel to be bargained for. I am me, Maryanne Paynter, and no one's property.'

'Of course, But you *did* agree to come.'

'Did I have a choice?'

'You could have refused.'

She smiled. 'I can just imagine what my guardian would have said if I had tried that, and besides. . .'

'You were curious.' He chuckled. 'Now admit it.'

She found herself laughing. 'Perhaps, but now I have had enough and I want to go home.'

'And if this were your home?'

She looked up at him, startled. 'I don't understand; am I to be offered a post here?'

He laughed aloud. 'I doubt that was in Her Grace's mind, though since she's been ill she has been a bit queer in the attic. Please wait until my father comes; he will tell you.' He smiled easily. 'Now, I must go back to the family. I shall look forward to seeing you again later.' He turned and left her, shutting the door behind him.

She stood quite still, listening to the sounds of the house: scurrying footsteps, subdued voices, the soft shutting of a door. She moved slowly to the window and looked out. Because the house was built on a hill, the room had a fine view over the surrounding country-side. Beyond the wood, she could see a village nestling in the valley, a row of cottages, the inn and the church; it reminded her of Beckford. Why was she standing here, alone and bewildered? Why was she not in her safe little world at Beckford Rectory, teaching the village boys their letters?

Her Grace had instructed Lord Danbury to find a good match for her. Did they intend to marry her off without so much as asking her what she had to say about it? Once she had overheard her guardian talking to his wife on the subject. 'How it is to be brought about, I cannot imagine,' he had said. 'She cannot marry into the gentry—no one will have her with her background—and yet she is too genteel to become the wife of a commoner.' He had sighed. 'I had done better not to have taken her in, but there, I have a soft heart. . .' Maryanne's mother had been a gentlewoman in the best sense of the word—anyone with eyes in their head could have seen that—so why had he made it sound like a barrier? And why had he involved Lord Danbury and the Dowager Duchess? If that was what

they were about, then they were going to find her
outward meekness hid a will of iron; she would not be
mated like some farmyard animal. She would live in
poverty first. And she would not wait on their con-
venience a moment longer. She went and flung open
the door.

There was no one about except a footman standing
beside the front door; she stopped, wondering if he
had instructions to prevent her leaving. She turned and
went back along the corridor, intending to find another
exit, but was brought up short when she heard her own
name being spoken by Caroline Danbury on the other
side of a closed door.

'Send her back where she came from—no one will
ever know the truth.'

'I cannot—the Reverend Mr Cudlipp is not expecting her to return.' This was Lord Danbury. 'And,
besides, I do not want to; she has been ill-used enough.
All I ask is that you be kind to her. . .'

'Kind to her!' The girl's voice was a squeak of
outrage. 'She's one of your by-blows, isn't that it?
Papa, how could you insult us by bringing her here?
And taking her up to Her Grace. I can't think what
Great-Aunt was thinking of to allow it. It's enough to
make Mama turn in her grave.'

Maryanne did not wait to hear more. She turned and
ran towards the front door. The startled footman
sprang to open it and she hurtled down the steps and
away across the lawn.

Her flying feet took her across the park between the
tall cedars which gave the mansion its name, to the
wall which enclosed the immediate grounds, where she
found a small gate which led into the woods. Here it
was quiet and cool and she stopped running to catch
her breath. She did not know where she was going; all
she wanted was to get away from that great house and
people who made hateful insinuations which made her
blood boil.

But she could not help remembering a titbit of gossip

told to her by the housemaid at Beckford Rectory. 'They say 'is lordship left his wife and ran off with a kitchen maid. They say he went abroad with 'er, but 'e came back a year or two later all by 'isself and settled down as if nothing 'ad 'appened. Though they do say there was a bebby. . .'

She had scolded the girl and dismissed it as nonsense, but could there have been some truth in it after all? She remembered, too, that when she first came to Beckford as a ten-year-old there had been some gossip about her which concerned her mother, but her guardian had soon silenced it and she had never learned what it was. He always referred to her mother, when he spoke of her at all, as 'that poor misguided lady' and that in condescending tones which infuriated Maryanne. There couldn't be a connection, could there?

She stumbled on, with her head in too much of a turmoil to notice where her feet were taking her, unaware of anyone else on the path until she found herself imprisoned against a broad chest. She let out a squeal of terror and began to struggle.

Six feet and more of bone and rippling muscle, he held her in a grip so powerful that she could not pull herself away, until he chose to release her. 'Let me go!' she shouted, trying to beat on his chest with her fists. 'Let me go!'

He put her gently from him, but still retained her hand. 'Your pardon, *mam'selle*.'

Startled by his accent, she looked up at his face. His hair was thickly curled and he had a small scar over his left eyebrow which made it look as if it was lifted in a permanent expression of doubt, but it was his eyes she remembered most of all; fringed with enviably long dark lashes, they were like brown velvet with a sheen of gold and now regarded her in a way which made her blush to the roots of her fair hair. 'Why, it's you. . .the gypsy. . .the poacher. . .man I saw. . .' She stopped suddenly, wondering why she had been such a ninny as to let him know she remembered him.

She had encountered him only three days before on her way back from a walk across the downs, when she had been taking a short cut through Lord Danbury's woods. Unlike today, when he was dressed in riding breeches, he had been wearing a rough labouring coat and had no collar or cravat, except a spotted neckerchief, tied flamboyantly beneath a firmly jutting chin. Strangers in Beckford were a rarity, and until the interview with Lord Danbury had driven everything else out of her mind she had been much occupied wondering where he had come from and what he was doing in Beckford woods. He could have been a poacher or one of the gypsies who were camping on the downs. On the other hand, when he had bidden her good-day, he had sounded French. She had wondered if he was a spy or had escaped from one of the many French ships which had been captured and brought to Portsmouth as prison hulks. But he had not been doing any harm, and the war was so nearly over, it hardly mattered. If the reports from the Continent could be believed, the Prussians, Russians and Austrians had, at last, decided to work together and Napoleon was near to defeat. She had said nothing of the encounter to anyone, but now she wondered if she had been right not to do so. To meet him twice and both times on land belonging to the Danbury family seemed more than coincidental.

'Why, it is *ma petite duchesse*,' he said, with an imperceptible twitch to the corner of his mouth and a slight lifting of the tiny scar above his eye.

'I am not a duchess,' she retorted. 'And you must know that or you would not be so forward. Please release me.'

He smiled, but showed no sign of doing as she asked. '*Eh bien*! It is not often a beautiful young wood nymph throws herself into my arms.'

'I did nothing of the kind. Please let me go.'

'If you tell me your name.'

'Maryanne Paynter.' Why had she answered him? She should have put her nose in the air and insisted on being allowed to pass, but it was difficult to stand on her dignity with her eyes full of unaccustomed tears.

He looked down at her small hand imprisoned in his and noted the absence of a ring. 'Mam'selle Paynter, I am *enchanté* to make your acquaintance.' He lifted her hand to his lips and added, in a voice that was surprisingly warm and without a trace of an accent, 'Forgive me, I did not mean to make you cry.'

'I am not crying. I have some dust in my eye.'

'Then let me remove it for you.' He took her face in his hands, tipping it up towards him. His eyes, searching hers, were like soft brown velvet, belying his strength and masculinity. She could feel his warm breath on her cheek, and she shivered involuntarily.

'Tip your head up,' he commanded, taking a handkerchief, which was miraculously clean and soft, from his pocket. 'Which eye is it?'

She blinked and a tear slid slowly down her cheek. Gently, he brushed it away.

'I think it's gone now,' she murmured, but, try as she might, she could not banish the tears, nor could she stifle the little sob which escaped her. If only he would go away; she did not like anyone to see her in such a weak state. She tried to turn from him, but found herself, once again, imprisoned against his chest.

'*Ma pauvre*,' he murmured. 'What have they been doing to you?'

'N. . .nothing.' Held securely in his arms, she felt warm and protected and, at that moment, there was nothing she needed more. No one, since her mother's death, had attempted to embrace her; neither the Reverend Mr Cudlipp nor his strait-laced wife would even have considered an affectionate hug let alone a kiss. No one had told her they cared for her. Not that he had said anything of the sort, nor did she expect it but, with her head lying snugly against his shoulder, it was a delicious self-indulgence to dream.

'Nothing?'

Tears blurred her vision as he took her chin in his big hand and tilted her face up to him. 'Nothing? No one has even taken the tiniest liberty?'

'What do you mean?'

'This.' Before she could protest, he had bent his head and was kissing her in a way which sent a tremor of delicious anticipation through her body. It was like nothing she had ever experienced before and she did not understand it. Unversed in the ways of flirtation, she allowed it to continue.

Suddenly coming to her senses, she wrenched herself out of his grasp and stood breathlessly facing him, like a young fawn catching the scent of the hunt and ready to bolt, he later described it. It was her expressive violet eyes which gave her away; they were wide and bright with a kind of knowing innocence. She was every inch a woman, but she still had an aura of childhood about her, seemed untouched by the tawdry world of those who lived in that great house, and yet she had come from there. But perhaps she was not one of them, and, if that were so, he had committed an unforgivable sin. He put out a hand to her, intending nothing but to reassure her, but she misunderstood him and tried to push past him, tripping over a tree root in her haste. He caught her as she fell.

'A thousand pardons, *mam'selle*,' he said, steadying her. 'But I am not a man to resist temptation, and when it is overwhelming. . .'

It was really much too late to pretend to any hauteur, but the whole encounter was getting out of hand. She lifted her chin and faced him squarely. 'Please allow me to pass, Mr. . .'

'Daw,' he finished for her. 'Jack Daw.'

She stared at him for a moment and then laughed shakily. 'I don't believe you. I don't believe anyone could be given such a preposterous name. You've made it up.'

He laughed, throwing back his fine head so that she was aware of the strong arch of his neck and the breadth of his chest. 'I assure you, that is the name I am known by.'

'What are you doing here? Are you a French spy?'

'Do you think I would tell you if I were?'

'No, I suppose not,' she admitted. 'At first I thought you were a poacher or a gypsy, but you are not like any gypsy I have ever met.'

'And have you met many gypsies?' he asked, with a smile and a lifting of his brows which made the little scar more obvious. 'I would never have guessed. . .'

'No, of course not.'

'Nor French spies?'

'Now you are laughing at me. It is very uncivil of you.'

'I'm sorry.' He was chuckling openly now. 'But you would hardly expect a gypsy or a spy to deal in civilities.'

'Who are you, then? What are you doing here?'

'You are an inquisitive young lady, are you not? What is it they say—"Curiosity killed the cat"? Beware of too much curiosity.'

Being curious about other people was one way to stop Maryanne thinking of her own bewilderment and insecurity, but suddenly it all came flooding back. A tear slid down her cheek, followed by another and then another and she, who, until today, had prided herself on her self-control, could do nothing to stop them.

He smiled and handed her his handkerchief. 'More dust?'

'N. . .no. Please let me pass.'

'If you tell me where you were going in such haste.'

'To Portsmouth,' she said suddenly. 'To visit my uncle.'

'Without bonnet or cloak? I know that spring has

come but we are not yet at high summer. And how were you expecting to arrive there?'

'By stage,' she said, saying the first thing that came into her head. 'From the village inn.'

'Forgive me, my dear Miss Paynter, if I do not believe you. Why are you so desperate you must run away? Have they been unkind to you?'

'Who?'

He jerked his head in the direction of the big house. 'The people up there. The Danburys.'

'What do you know of them?'

'Very little,' he said laconically. 'But they seem to have a talent for making people unhappy. The man you came with in the coach—who was he?'

'Came with? How do you know how I came?'

'I saw you arrive. Tell me, was that the Duke of Wiltshire?'

'No, it was his cousin, Viscount Danbury.'

'So *that* was Lord Danbury.'

Something in his tone made her look up sharply. 'Why are you so interested?'

He pretended indifference, though she was not deceived. 'If he made you cry. . .'

'It wasn't him, it was. . .' She stopped, uncomfortably reminded of the conversation she had overheard. She forced herself to speak brightly. 'It was my own foolishness and nothing you need concern yourself with.'

'Oh, but I do,' he said softly. 'When I saw you in that coach, you looked so. . .' He paused. 'So anxious—big troubled eyes and furrowed brow. You know, you should not frown, it spoils your looks.'

'You are insufferable,' she said, frustration making her forget her tears. 'What do you know of him, or me, or anything at all?'

'I know you are unhappy,' he said softly. 'And it distresses me to see someone so young and beautiful in tears.'

'If I am in tears it is because I am so angry,' she said.

'With me?' he asked softly.

'No, no, not with you,' she said, then laughed. 'Though I don't know why not. You are not behaving like a gentleman.'

'Perhaps it's because gypsies and poachers are not gentlemen,' he said. 'And I am loath to part with you.'

'Mr Daw, if that is your name, I have had outside of enough to contend with today and I would beg you not to add to it. Take your hand from my arm and allow me to pass.'

He laughed. 'Now I know you are a duchess! No one else would be so toplofty.'

She laughed in spite of herself. 'Where did you learn that word?'

'At my mother's knee; she was. . .' He faltered, suddenly remembering *Maman* as he had last seen her, outlined by the keyhole through which he, a terrified twelve-year-old, had been peering, being dragged away by two armed *gendarmes*. 'She was English.'

Her laughter faded. 'Was?'

'She died.' He spoke flatly, but she saw the pain behind his brown eyes.

'I am sorry.'

'It was a long time ago now.' He paused, as if mentally brushing himself down. 'Would you like me to take you to Portsmouth? I could, you know.'

'Certainly not!' she said sharply.

'But you do not want to go back to the house? Why not?'

'I. . . I was confused. I didn't know why I had been brought here, and things were said. . .'

'To you?' The scarred eyebrow lifted.

'No, something I overhead, but it's of no consequence.'

'It most certainly is, if it was bad enough to make you run away.'

'I was not running away and it is unkind of you to remind me. . .'

'I beg your pardon.' He smiled. 'But I'll wager you

are no coward, so why not go back and face them? Stand up to them, don't let them see you are afraid.'

'I'm not afraid, I wish only to be left in peace.'

'Peace,' he said softly. 'You do not wish it any more than I do.' He took her arm and turned to walk beside her.

She did not know what to do. Neither his words nor actions were those she would have expected a gypsy to use, nor, for that matter, a gentleman, and she was thoroughly nervous. Although he seemed to be relaxed, there was a certain tension about his shoulders and the way he held his head, as if he was watching for something or someone, and needed to be constantly alert. Occasionally his right hand strayed to the handle of the small dagger held in his belt, as if to reassure himself it was still there.

When they reached the edge of the wood, he stopped. 'Better you go on alone,' he said. 'I don't want to cause you more grief. I would be obliged if you told no one of our meeting.'

'Why not? Have you something to hide?'

'Not at all,' he said blandly. 'But it would hardly do, would it? We have been alone for some time and I believe the English are decidedly strait-laced on such matters.'

She smiled a little wanly, dreading what his lordship would have to say on her return. 'Goodbye, Mr Daw.'

He bowed and kissed her hand. '*Au revoir*, little wood nymph.'

She had to face the future. She took a deep breath and set out across towards the house. She did not look back but somehow she knew he was standing in the shadow of the trees, watching her. Was he hiding? And, if so, from whom? She refused to believe his name was really Jack Daw and she doubted he was a gypsy; she had a feeling that he was dangerous to know and she had better try to forget him. It would be difficult while the memory of that kiss lingered but it would fade as time passed, just as childhood recollections faded; happiness and misery both received the same treatment from Father Time.

Her hope of returning to the room she had left without being seen was dashed when she saw Caroline standing in the hall, dressed for outdoors and tapping her foot impatiently on the floor. She whirled towards Maryanne. 'Just where do you think you've been?'

'I went for a walk.'

'You know, of course, that you have missed luncheon and delayed our departure. Papa would not leave without you.'

'I am sorry. I missed my way. Where is his lordship?'

'Gone looking for you and decidedly cross. One does not keep a Viscount waiting.'

'I have said I'm sorry, Miss Danbury. If I had not been kept waiting myself, I would not have gone out. . .'

'Such impudence! Who do you think you are?' She turned as Lord Danbury came in through the front door. 'She's back, Papa, and has the effrontery to say *we* kept her waiting.'

'So we did,' his lordship said calmly, then to Maryanne, 'You must forgive us—my aunt was taken suddenly worse.'

'Oh, I am sorry.'

'It was the excitement, I think, but she is comfortable again now and we can all return to Beckford. Where is Mark?'

'Gone to the stables,' Caroline told him. 'He don't trust his precious rig to His Grace's grooms.'

His lordship smiled at Maryanne, trying to put her at her ease. 'Caroline came with her brother in his curricle—she enjoys being frightened to death by his driving. Our coach may be slow and cumbersome, but at least one can have a civilised conversation in it, and I want to have a long talk to you.' Hearing the rumble of the vehicle at the door, he smiled at Maryanne and beckoned to the footman to help her on with her cloak. 'Come, my dear.'

Maryanne, taking a deep breath to calm herself, followed him out of the front door and into the coach and in a few minutes Castle Cedars had been left behind and the horses were trotting at a sedate pace along the roads they had traversed that morning. Maryanne, sitting with her hands clasped nervously in her lap, found herself going over the last two days in her mind. Everything about the Danburys seemed to be cloaked in mystery, even down to trespassers and gypsies who were not really gypsies at all, and men with accents which disappeared when they had something serious to say. And she was part of it, part of something she did not understand. She turned to his lordship. 'You said we would talk. . .'

CHAPTER TWO

LORD DANBURY smiled, trying to put Maryanne at her ease. 'I must apologise for keeping you waiting so long for an explanation, but it all depended on what the Dowager said when she saw you. I did not doubt she would acknowledge you, but. . .'

'I am not who I seem, is that it?' Maryanne said; that much she had been able to surmise. 'But if you are going to scandalise my mother, then I do not wish to hear it.'

'Scandalise your dear mother! Oh, no, Maryanne, that is the last thing I would do.'

'But she was your. . .' She could not bring herself to say the word 'mistress'. 'I overheard Miss Danbury say something about. . .'

'You *did* hear that—I thought you might have. Is that why you ran away? The footman saw you fleeing as if all the demons in hell were after you.'

'I. . .'

'Do not say another word until you have heard me out. You want to know if you are my daughter, isn't that so? Well, you may set your mind at rest. I would dearly love you for a daughter but, regrettably, you are no closer related than second cousin.'

'Second cousin? I am your second cousin?'

'Yes, my dear. Your mother was my cousin Helena. She was also the daughter of the fifth Duke of Wiltshire, who was my father's brother. The present Duke is her brother.'

'But I don't understand.'

'Your mother never told you?'

'No, never. Why didn't she?'

'Because her parents, my aunt and uncle, disowned her. She wanted to marry your father and they disapproved. In fact, they forbade it, and, to avoid being forced into a marriage she abhorred, she ran away with your father.' He smiled suddenly. 'I was blamed at the time and I doubt if Her Grace will ever truly forgive me.'

'Why?'

'Because I introduced John to your mother. That was in the days when we were both serving as naval lieutenants on a three-decker, before I inherited the Beckford estates. They fell in love.'

'They stayed that way until death parted them,' Maryanne said softly. 'And I loved them both.'

'I loved them too. After you were born, I tried more than once to persuade the old Duke to recognise you, but he refused. And even after he died, my aunt, your grandmother, still held out against it. Until a week ago.' He turned to take her hand in his. 'Do not be too hard on her, Maryanne. She is dying and wishing to make amends.'

Maryanne's head was whirling and she could not think clearly. She was the granddaughter of a Duke; her mother had come from one of the foremost aristocratic families in England. It was too much to take in all at once.

'What exactly do you intend to do?' she said. 'Nothing is really changed. I am still me, Maryanne Paynter, and I think no differently of my parents, except to love them even more, if that were possible. I pray they have been reunited in heaven.'

'I am sure they have. But there must be some changes. You will have a home with me until you marry.'

'Suppose I never do?' Somewhere, deep inside her, was welling up a storm of rebellion. It was not ready to burst yet because she still felt too confused, but it was there, beneath the surface of her mind, waiting for something, or someone, to set it off.

He smiled. 'You are too beautiful to remain single, my dear, and I hardly think you wish it. As soon as you are brought out into Society, you will have a flock of suitors, you can be sure.'

'And no doubt I'll give the gabble-grinders something to talk about as well. I do not care to be the subject of scandal.'

'A nine-day wonder.' He chuckled. 'As far as the beaux are concerned, it will give your undoubted attractions an added piquancy.' He was suddenly serious. 'If your mother could rise above the tattlemongers, then I am sure you can.'

'Have I a choice?'

He grinned. 'You can try to live in obscurity if you wish, but I doubt if you will be allowed to, once the news is out. A beautiful new heiress on the scene is bound to cause a stir.'

'Heiress?'

'You have a little inheritance coming to you which should have been your mother's. . .'

'Then why did she have to live in poverty?' Maryanne was close to anger on behalf of her beloved mother, who had scraped along, barely making a living.

'It was held back—quite legally, I may add. Her parents hoped to make her see reason.'

'You mean abandon my father and return to the bosom of an unfeeling family,' she said sharply. 'I am glad she did not.'

'The money is yours now, or it will be when you reach your twenty-first birthday in a few months' time. Until then, you will make your home at Beckford Hall. Caroline will be pleased to have a companion.'

Maryanne doubted that; Caroline had displayed no friendly feelings towards her. 'Does she know. . .?'

'She does now. So does my son. You will be welcomed by them both.' He smiled. 'We are all to move to our London house for Caroline's coming out this summer. There will be any number of receptions, balls, visits to the opera, clothes to be bought. . .'

'I shall not be expected to go, shall I?'

'Of course, my dear. I intend that you shall be

brought out along with Caroline, and I mean to ask my sister, Mrs Ryfield, to see that all goes smoothly. She has the "in" to every drawing-room in London, not to mention Almack's. You will like her, I am sure.'

It was not Mrs Ryfield who occupied Maryanne's thoughts, as they continued towards her new life, but what Caroline thought about sharing her coming out with a second cousin whom she had never heard of until that day, and one she had no high opinion of either. It would all be acutely embarrassing. In fact, the idea struck her as so absurd that she began to laugh hysterically.

His lordship looked at her in alarm and took her hand to reassure her. 'It has all been a great shock to you, I know.'

She stopped laughing suddenly. 'I am glad I know about my mother, of course, but it makes no difference to the way I feel about myself. Can't I stay at the rectory, where I can make myself useful? The Reverend. . .'

'The rector is not expecting you back, Maryanne, not now you have been recognised by Her Grace. Your old life is behind you and a new one ahead. Do you not like the idea of living with us?'

'You are a very kind man, I know that, and it is not ingratitude which makes me reluctant. . .'

'You are not sure how you will go on, is that it?' His gentle features broke into a smile and he patted the hand he held. 'Have no fear, my dear, you will deal admirably with them all, I guarantee it.'

Not until she moved into Beckford Hall, smaller than Castle Cedars but nevertheless a substantial residence, did Maryanne realise quite what the changes to her way of life would mean to her. She could no longer teach at Sunday school, she had to give up her classes for the local boys, and, when she went sick visiting, instead of the warm, homely atmosphere she had always encountered before, she was greeted with uncomfortable stiffness. Worst of all, she could no longer enjoy solitary walks across the downs. The luxuries of her new position did not compensate for the restrictions on her freedom. She found herself almost envying the gypsies who camped on the downs.

They reminded her of the man who called himself Jack Daw. She had not seen him since that day at Castle Cedars and she assumed that whatever had brought him to Hampshire had taken him away again. It was extraordinary that the two places she had encountered him had both been on Danbury land and yet a good fifteen miles apart. Ought she to have told his lordship about him? If he was French, was he an *émigré*, son of an aristocrat who had fled the Revolution, or was he a Bonapartist, a prisoner of war, or a spy? But the war had been over since the beginning of April—there was no longer any need for him to hide.

Ever since the news had broken, the whole country had been celebrating. The flags of the Bourbons flew on every building and hawkers selling fleurs-de-lis and white cockades were doing a roaring trade, and wherever crowds gathered there were pie sellers and pedlars of ballads and news sheets, which told of the last days of Napoleon's reign. Marshal Marmont, left behind to defend Paris while Boney himself went to make a last attempt to repel his enemies, had surrendered the capital to the victorious Prussian troops, and not even Napoleon's faithful generals would continue fighting after that. Their Emperor had abdicated and agreed to retire to the island of Elba with an army of fewer than a thousand men and a navy which consisted of a single frigate. The news had arrived in England a few days later, almost before it could reach the Duke of Wellington, down in the south of France, preparing to take Toulouse.

There were balls and receptions everywhere in honour of this or that dignitary or valiant officer, and in London Louis, restored to the throne of France, held a levee at Grillons, to which everyone of importance was invited.

Hearing all this, nothing would satisfy Caroline but they must bring forward the date of their removal to London, so as not to miss a single minute. 'King Louis is bound to leave for Paris soon,' she said after supper one evening, when her father and Mark joined the girls in the drawing-room. 'Wellington is there already and, unless I miss my guess, half the world will follow suit.'

'If you mean the aristos, who think they can walk back on to their estates and take up their old privileges, just as if nothing had happened, they are no loss,' Mark said.

'I was not referring to them. I mean the *haut monde.* Paris will be fashionable again, you see.'

'There will be plenty of young bloods left behind,' her father said. 'I'll wager London will be in an uproar the whole summer long.'

Caroline pouted. 'I want to go now. What is there to keep us here? Nothing ever happens in Beckford.'

His lordship smiled at Maryanne, who was sitting beside him on the sofa, sewing and taking no part in the conversation; indeed, in the few weeks she had been at Beckford Hall she had learned to keep her own counsel over Caroline's whims. 'And what about you, Maryanne? Is that your wish too?'

If Maryanne could wish for anything, it would be to return to the life of a nonentity, but that was denied her and because she had to make the best of her situation she stayed in the background as much as possible, allowing Caroline to shine, but sometimes Caroline's tactless tongue cut her to the quick and she had to bite off the retort that came to her lips. When she came into her inheritance and was no longer dependent on Lord Danbury, she would leave and take up some occupation where she could be useful and not have to think constantly of her position.

'Please, don't take me into account,' she said, lifting

her eyes from her sewing. 'If you wish to go to London, I shall be quite content to remain here.'

'There you are, Papa.' Caroline sat back on the sofa with a smile of satisfaction. 'Maryanne does not want to come, and, besides, who will escort her?'

'I will,' said Mark, beaming at Maryanne over the newspaper he was reading. 'I have promised myself a little of her company.'

Maryanne, threading a needle, did not see the look which passed from father to son, but if she had she would not have known how to interpret it. Only Mark understood its warning and it tickled his fancy that he could put his father out of humour simply by paying court to his cousin. She was as demure as a whore at a christening, but he suspected that underneath that quiet countenance was an independent spirit and a fire which once set alight would be difficult to extinguish. If he could make it burn for him, then some of his difficulties might be overcome.

'The Duchess is still very ill,' James said. 'We can hardly go if His Grace thinks it inappropriate.'

'Like everyone else, he has already gone,' Caroline said. 'I had a letter from Georgiana Halesworth. She was at Louis's reception and saw the Duke there.' She giggled. 'She said the French King is even fatter than the Prince.'

Mark laughed and began to sing.

   'And France's hope and Britain's heir
Were, truth, a most congenial pair;
Two round-bellied, thriving rakes,
Like oxen fed on linseed cakes.'

Caroline laughed. 'Oh, capital! Where did you hear that?'

'It's all the crack,' Mark said. 'There's more. . .'

'Enough!' said James sternly, though there was a twinkle in his eye. 'Mark, that is hardly a drawing-room ballad.'

'Can we go?' Caroline persisted. 'I know for a fact

Lady Markham is holding a ball at the end of the month and we won't be invited if we're not even in town.'

'I shall have to write to your aunt Emma to find out if it's convenient for her,' her father said. 'And I must ride over and see how my aunt progresses.'

'You mean we can go?' cried Caroline, getting up to throw her arms round her father's neck. 'I shall have to have a new ballgown. In fact, Papa, I shall need. . .'

He smiled and disengaged himself. 'I know, a whole new trousseau.'

'But it *is* my coming out.'

'And Maryanne's,' he said, getting up to go and write his letter. 'Do not forget your cousin.'

'I do hope Her Grace holds out until the end of the season,' Caroline said, as the door shut on him. 'I should hate to have to spend the rest of the summer in black gloves, and if I have to wait another year for my coming out I shall be at my last prayers.'

'Don't be a ninny, Carrie,' Mark said. 'You're only eighteen—plenty of time yet.'

'Most of my friends are already spoken for and I have not even been introduced to anyone I half like,' his sister went on. 'And I should like a title. You will be a Viscount one day, but unless I marry one. . .'

'Oh, I have my eyes on more than that,' the young man said airily. 'If Cousin Henry don't have an heir, Father will become Duke of Wiltshire and I will be a Marquis and next in line for the dukedom. And you will be Lady Caroline in your own right.'

'Should you be speaking so about the Duke?' Maryanne asked mildly. 'It is only natural he should want an heir.'

'You don't know him, Maryanne,' Mark said. 'He's fat and drinks too much and no pretty girl is safe anywhere near him. I can't imagine anyone wanting to marry him.'

'Cousin Jane did,' Caroline said.

'Yes, poor dote, but that was before she knew what her portion was—the life of a brood mare. How any girl could contemplate that I can't imagine.'

'Oh, I don't know,' Caroline said with a laugh. 'With money and a title, most things can be endured and a wealthy wife can always take a handsome lover.'

'I say, Sis, *you* wouldn't marry him, would you?' he said anxiously. 'You don't fancy being the next Duchess of Wiltshire? You'd end up like Cousin Jane, in your grave, alongside half a dozen dead babies.'

'Do you think His Grace will allow us to have our own reception at Wiltshire House?' she said, ignoring his question. 'Oh, that would be bang up!'

He shrugged. 'If he thought it would find him another wife, I fancy he might.'

'Then I shall suggest it.' She turned to Maryanne. 'Wiltshire House is much grander than Danbury House—almost a palace—and it has the most elegant ballroom. We must have an orchestra and a tenor to sing the latest ditties.' She whirled round in excitement. 'And there must be flowers everywhere and piles of exotic fruit. There will be no difficulty now the war is over and all those horrid blockades are done with.' She sat down at the escritoire and drew some sheets of paper towards her. 'Mark, you must tell me the names of all the handsome young officers back from the campaigns. Some of them come from good families, don't they?'

'If you are looking for plump pockets, you'll not find many in the army,' he said laconically. 'You should be considering a nabob or a merchantman, someone who has grown rich by the war.'

'Mark, what nonsense you talk! I wouldn't dream of such a thing. When I marry it will be someone of breeding as well as wealth.'

'I can see you are going to be difficult to please,' he said, then, turning to Maryanne, 'What about you, Maryanne? What do you look for in a husband?'

'Me?' she said, feeling the warmth flood into her face. 'A man I can love and one who loves me.'

'And must he also be rich and handsome?'

'No, just good.'

'Good?' queried Caroline with a squeal of laughter. 'I have yet to meet a man I could describe in those terms, and, besides, how dull life would be.' For the first time she noticed what Maryanne was doing. 'What have you got there?'

'It's a hassock cover from the church. I hate to be idle and I have so much spare time nowadays, I thought I would repair all the hassocks. I brought this one home last Sunday.'

'The village women do that sort of thing. You should not stoop so low, Maryanne.'

'I do not call beautifying the church stooping, Caroline.'

'Oh, spare me the sermon, Maryanne. What will you wear for Lady Markham's ball?'

'I do not dance, so I haven't given it a thought.'

'Don't dance!' Caroline exclaimed, then, 'No, of course not; the Reverend Mr Cudlipp would hardly consider dancing a suitable pastime, would he? How dreary for you to have to stay at home when we go.'

'She will not stay at home,' Mark said. 'I shall teach her the steps, including the waltz. She will not be left out.'

'It is very kind of you,' Maryanne murmured. 'But really I would rather not put you to the bother.'

'Stuff!' he said. 'It will be my privilege. I will not hear of your being left behind. And, to be sure, I shall be hard pressed to cut out all the suitors who will doubtless be dangling after you.'

'Oh, Mark, what humbug you do talk,' Caroline said. 'One would think you intended to offer for her yourself.'

'If you want to talk about me as if I were not here,' Maryanne said, getting up from her seat abruptly, 'I will make it easy for you and take my leave. Goodnight

to you both. She collected up her sewing in the
surprised silence that followed and left them.

She ran up to her own room and shut the door
behind her. Caroline was the outside of enough! If it
were not for her determination to keep the peace and
her complete indifference to the heirarchy of Society
she would show that spoiled young miss just how a lady
should behave. Not that she agreed with the half of it;
it was all a sham, this business of bringing out young
ladies and parading them in front of all the eligible
young men, like so many animals at market. She fully
intended to hold herself aloof from it. They would call
her toplofty, as Jack Daw had done, but she didn't
care.

She crossed to the window and drew aside the
curtains so that she could look out on the starlit night.
Sitting in the window-seat, she leaned her head against
the wall, a smile hovering round her lips. She wasn't
against balls and if the man of her dreams were to
arrive at one and ask her to dance, then she would not
turn him away. The man of her dreams. Who was he?

She found her thoughts wandering to the handsome
stranger she had first met in Beckford woods; thinking
about him took her mind off Caroline's ungracious
behaviour. In the privacy of her room she could weave
romantic stories about him, and it didn't matter in the
least how fanciful they were because she was unlikely
ever to discover the truth about him. Even so, her
cheeks still burned when she thought of that kiss; how
could she have been so unthinking as to let it happen?
And the worst of it was, she had liked it.

Almost as if conjuring him up, she saw a dark figure
cross the park down by the lake, and leaned forward in
her seat to see the better, conscious of the quickening
of her heartbeat. He was striding quite purposefully
towards the bank of trees which began a little above
the water to her left. When he reached them, he paused
and turned to look up at the house. She shrank back
into the shadows and peered out at him from behind

the curtains. What was he looking at? Had he seen her? Did he mean to harm anyone in the house? Again she wondered if she ought to tell his lordship or Mark about him. If she did, his lordship would ask a great many questions about when she had seen him before, why she had not mentioned it and why she thought a man doing nothing in particular constituted a threat. Was he a threat? She wasn't sure. If they hunted him down, he would be dragged up before a magistrate, and what harm had he done, except hold her in his arms and kiss away her tears?

Out of humour with herself for being such a ninny as to remember a kiss he had undoubtedly forgotten, she twitched the curtains across and turned back into the room to prepare for bed, forgetting, as she so often did, to ring for her maid to help her. The man was probably poaching, and, though she ought not to condone that, she didn't see how his lordship could begrudge an odd rabbit now and again; he had certainly not complained that poaching was any great problem. Besides, they would all leave for London in a few days and she need think no more of him and what he was up to. She climbed into bed and blew out the candle.

The next morning was warmer than any day of the year so far and Maryanne dedcided to walk to the church to return the newly repaired hassock and fetch another. His lordship had ridden out to Castle Cedars; Caroline, never one to rise early, was still abed, and Mark had gone out to the home farm, which was his particular responsibility, so she set out alone, taking the path across the park and round the lake. She was alert for Jack Daw, telling herself that she would not let him surprise her for a third time with his sudden appearance, but she reached the village street without seeing any sign of him and let herself into the church, wondering why she felt so downcast.

It was dim and cool and she shivered slightly as she replaced the hassock in his lordship's pew and selected another for her attentions. Turning to leave, she noticed the vestry door was open and, wondering at the rector's being so careless, moved over to shut it. Jack Daw was standing at the table with the parish register open in front of him, running his finger down the page as he scanned it.

'Mr Daw!' She could not say his name without smiling, however hard she tried. 'What are you doing here?'

He whirled round to face her, his hand reaching for the dagger in his belt, but when he saw her his belligerent attitude changed suddenly to an elegant bow accompanied by a broad smile. 'Good morning, Mam'selle Paynter; a fine morning, is it not? You, too, like to be up betimes, I see.'

'I asked you a question,' she said, determined to keep cool and not allow her swiftly beating heart to betray her. 'What are you doing?'

'Looking for a past.'

'Whose past? Yours? Lord Danbury's?'

He looked at her sharply and the humour went from his eyes; they became hard and unrelenting. 'Why did you mention Lord Danbury?'

'No reason, except that whenever I see you, you are on Danbury land. I have a mind to speak to his lordship about you. . .'

'Do you mean you have not already done so?' he asked in surprise.

She coloured. 'You asked me not to.'

He took a step towards her and laid a hand on her arm. 'Is that reason enough, when you so obviously think I am up to no good?'

'I didn't say that.'

'A poacher or a spy, I think you said.'

'The war is over.'

'For the moment,' he said, and there was a grim sound to his voice which made her look up at him sharply.

'What do you mean? Napoleon has capitulated.'

'He does what is expedient at the time, as any good general does; it is dangerous to be complacent.'

She gasped. 'You do not think he is beaten?'

He shrugged. 'Who can tell? He has promised to return with the violets.'

'Are you a spy?'

He laughed suddenly. 'An I were, why come here? There is nothing here to interest Napoleon Bonaparte. And that leaves only the poaching.' He took her chin in his hand and tilted her face up to his. 'Do I look like a poacher?'

His eyes were burning into hers, searching out her deepest thoughts, and that embarrassed her because at that moment she was thinking of that kiss and wondering if he was going to repeat it, and what she would do if he did. Her limbs were trembling, but she met his gaze steadfastly. 'I do not know that poachers have anything in their looks to make them stand out. If they did, there would be many more arrests.'

'*Touché*!' He laughed and she realised that it was his light-heartedness which she found so attractive. He made her feel happy.

'You have not answered my question,' she said. 'What are you doing in Beckford?'

'Where else can I feast my eyes on such loveliness?'

She drew herself up to her full five feet four. 'Mr Daw, I do not find your remarks amusing.'

He chuckled. 'I can see through your bravado, you know. You are standing there affecting to be unafraid but really quaking in your shoes lest I try and take liberties again.'

'How arrogant you are!'

'No, honest.' His voice dropped until it was little more than a whisper. 'Are you afraid of me?'

'No.'

'Why not? Anyone else would have been swooning or screaming for help by now.'

'I am made of sterner stuff,' she said, clasping her hands round the hassock so that he would not see them trembling. 'If you meant to harm me, you would have done so before now.'

'Of course I won't harm you—why should I? But I won't promise not to kiss you again.' He paused and lifted a hand to touch her cheek with a gentle finger. Startled by the sensations that evoked, she stepped back out of his reach. 'You are different from the others. . .'

'Have there been many others?' she asked before she could stop herself. 'I should not like to be counted one of many.'

'You are unique,' he said, laughing. 'But I was referring to other young ladies of fashion, like the Honourable Caroline Danbury.' He turned his head on one side to survey her from her brown kid boots to her plain straw bonnet, tied on with ribbon which exactly matched her candid blue eyes, from small strong hands to pink cheeks now flaming with colour. 'Could it be the difference between a hot-house bloom and an English rose?'

'Oh, and which do you prefer?' She shouldn't be having this conversation with him, she told herself; it was almost flirting, and it could lead to. . .oh, anywhere, and she was playing with fire.

'They both have their place,' he said solemnly, but there was laughter in his brown eyes, as if he was enjoying teasing her. 'But at this moment I have eyes only for the English rose.'

She felt herself colour under his scrutiny and turned away. 'I must go back. . .'

'Back?'

'Home, to Beckford Hall. Where else?'

'Oh, dear, that has the sound of hopelessness about it. Surely a young lady as young and beautiful as you are has plans for her future?'

'Perhaps I have.'

He smiled. 'But they are secret? Ah, well, I don't expect you to tell me. Keep your pride, it is your best defence.'

'Against what?'

'Life's little set-backs. The disappointments, the dreams that fade, other people's censure.'

It was as if he knew all about her without having to be told, and it was most disconcerting. 'How do you know so much?' she asked.

He answered her with another question. 'Are you happy there?'

'Yes, of course. They are very kind.'

'Kind! Is that all you ask, that people be kind?' His voice softened. 'You deserve more than kindness, little one.'

'You, sir, are impertinent.'

'Your pardon.' He sighed melodramatically and bent over her hand. *'Au revoir, mam'selle,* until the next time we meet.'

'There will be no next time. We are all leaving for London very soon. Caroline is coming out.'

'And what about you?'

'Me too.'

'You are to be put on the marriage market, are you? How do you feel about that?'

'How I feel is nothing to do with you.' His prying was annoying her because he seemed to be able to dig deep into her innermost thoughts, to unearth her anxieties and lay bare her secret dreams.

'Do you think that is the best way to find the love of your life?'

'And what do you know of it? It is the custom and usually it works very well.'

'Perhaps for the Miss Danburys of this world, but not for you. I would have expected you to be more independent.' Before she could think of an appropriate retort, he went on, 'Tell me, what connection is that young lady to you?'

'Her father and my mother were first cousins.'

'Cousins? I hadn't realised you were truly one of the family. I thought. . .'

What had he thought? That she was a governess or

companion? She drew herself up to her full height and
tilted her chin. 'Mr Daw, I will have you know that the
Duke of Wiltshire is my uncle. . .'

'Then my condolences, ma'am.' The teasing look left
his eyes as he bowed to her. 'I bid you good-day.'

She watched him stride away, with a feeling of deep
disappointment in the pit of her stomach. They had
been enjoying a bantering light-hearted flirtation which
had been perfectly harmless and then all of a sudden it
had turned sour, and all because her pride had been
dented and she must boast of her breeding. 'Buffle-
head!' she scolded herself.

He did not like the Danburys; the more she saw of
him, the more convinced she became of it. What had
he against them? If anyone had cause to be resentful,
she had, because of her mother, but had he also
suffered at their hands? Could he be bent on revenge?
Who was he? His name was not Jack Daw, of that she
was certain, and he was certainly not a gypsy. If Lord
Danbury had not insisted on her accompanying them
all to London, she would have tried to find out more
about him. As it was, he would have to remain a
mystery, unless, of course, he was still in Beckford
when they returned in the autumn.

She was so engrossed in her thoughts that she did
not hear the sound of footsteps, until a shadow fell
across the stone floor at her feet. Startled, she looked
up, thinking he had returned, but it was Mark.

'Who was that fellow I saw leaving?' he asked, using
his crop to indicate the open door.

Maryanne had stepped across to look at the register
the Frenchman had been scrutinising and was surprised
to see the page open at the year 1787. The name Mark
James Danbury leapt out at her. Without knowing why
she did it, she shut the book before Mark could see it
and turned, with as much composure as she could
muster, to answer him. 'I have no idea who he was. He
was in the church when I arrived. We exchanged
greetings and he was perfectly civil.' She had missed

the opportunity to tell him of her suspicions, and now it would be even more difficult to do so.

'It is not only unseemly, but dangerous to speak to strangers, Maryanne.' He took her arm. 'I think I had better tell the Reverend Mr Cudlipp to keep a watch on the church plate. And it would be better if you did not walk out alone again.'

'Why not? I surely do not need an escort to come to the village, where everyone knows me. I don't suddenly stop being the parson's ward just because the Dowager Duchess of Wiltshire takes it into her head to recognise me after all these years.'

He opened his mouth to scold her, changed his mind and his tone softened. 'Maryanne, you are already very dear to me and I would never forgive myself if anything happened to you.' He was infuriatingly confident as he took her hand and tucked it in the crook of his arm and turned to leave.

'I told you, we hardly spoke. You are making something of nothing.'

'Your well-being is not nothing, Maryanne. I do not think you realise how important it is to me.' He shut the lych-gate behind them and took her arm again. 'I went home to ask if you would like to ride out, but you were nowhere to be found. You told no one where you were going.'

'How did you know where to look for me, then?'

'Your maid said you had taken the hassock with you, so it was not difficult to guess.' He smiled. 'Come, we will be back in time for luncheon, if we hurry, and perhaps Father will have returned home with the news that Her Grace remains tolerably well and we can all set off for London. I am looking forward to being your escort and the envy of the whole ton.'

She smiled at his compliment, and together they walked back to Beckford Hall, unaware that brown eyes watched their progress and the owner of the eyes was cursing his ill luck in voluble and colourful French.

CHAPTER THREE

As soon as they were all installed at Danbury House, in Piccadilly, Caroline, accompanied by a reluctant Maryanne, began a round of visits to friends who had also arrived in the capital, a pastime which was punctuated with receiving callers, shopping, carriage rides in the park and endless gossip. They were always chaperoned by Mrs Ryfield. Several years younger than her brother, Emma Ryfield was still a very handsome woman, with sleek dark hair and the Danbury brown eyes. James had told her to treat both girls alike and to make sure they were seen in the right places, spoke to the right people and were invited to the right gatherings, and she was to ensure that they were not plagued by the attentions of undesirables. Maryanne entered into the social whirl with rather less enthusiasm than Caroline, who spent much of her time speculating on the number of proposals she was likely to receive and looking daily for the longed-for invitations to Lady Markham's ball which arrived one morning when they were sitting over a late breakfast.

'A masked ball!' Caroline said, ripping hers open. 'And only a week away.' She turned to Maryanne, eyes alight with excitement. 'What shall I wear? Something striking, of course.' She got up and paced the room, waving the invitation in front of her face like a fan, while Maryanne watched from her seat. 'I think I shall go as Queen Elizabeth.' She turned to her cousin and surveyed her critically. 'What about you?'

'I will find something,' Maryanne said, but when she refused to divulge what she had decided on Caroline spent some time persuading her that if she had nothing suitable to wear it would be useless for her to go.

Mark would not hear of that. 'I shall be quite cast

down if you don't come,' he told Maryanne. 'I shall expect at least three dances, so that everyone will see what a handsome couple we make.' He sat down beside her on the chaise-longue where she was sewing, and added softly, 'We do, you know. I shall be the envy of the ton.'

By the time the carriages arrived at the front door on the Friday evening to take them to Bedford Row, even Maryanne had yielded to the excitement.

She took a last look at herself in the mirror and was pleased with what she saw, though she wondered if her dress might be too plain for a costume ball. It was one of her mother's which she had kept because the material was so fine, and because Mama had been very fond of it, though as far as Maryanne could remember she never had occasion to wear it. Its overskirt was of white Nottingham lace, trimmed with white satin ribbon and the underskirt of finest white silk, which draped itself into soft folds from a high waist. It showed her figure to perfection without being too daring. A wreath of greenery around curls dressed *à la Grecque* and a sash of twisted foliage across her shoulder and over her breast, together with a pair of silver sandals, put the finishing touches to her idea of what a wood nymph might look like. She smiled to herself remembering Jack Daw, who had given her the idea.

'Oh, Miss Maryanne, you look so pretty,' her maid said, opening the door for her. 'Bowl them over, you will.'

'Thank you, Rose. You need not wait up for me.' Trembling a little and with shining eyes, she went slowly downstairs.

Mark was already in the hall, dressed as a highwayman with a many-caped cloak and a large feathered hat. He turned from admiring himself in a long mirror and smiled up at her. 'My!' he said.

She smiled. 'Do you like it?'

'Like it?' He laughed and came forward to take her hand. 'I am speechless.'

'That certainly makes a change,' said his father, coming out of the library with Mrs Ryfield. He turned to Maryanne and for a moment looked startled. Then he smiled. 'You look charming, my dear—so much like your mother, I was quite taken aback.' There was a look of sadness behind his eyes which lingered for a while even after he had smiled and said, 'You will have them all by the ears. Now, where is Caroline?'

'I am here.' Caroline appeared, at the top of the stairs, regal as Queen Elizabeth, complete with red wig and a huge starched ruff. The family diamonds, with their hard white glitter, encircled a *décolletage* which was only just decent. She descended the stairs slowly, defying anyone to do anything but praise her, and although her father's brows rose a little his only comment was, 'A queen indeed.'

The press of carriages in the street outside Lady Markham's home meant that they were kept waiting in line for several minutes before they could reach the door and alight, but at last they found themselves in a brilliantly lit foyer, where a footman took their cloaks. Then they made their way along a wide corridor to where Lord and Lady Markham stood at the entrance to the ballroom, receiving their guests. His lordship had declined to wear costume, but her ladyship was dressed as Nell Gwynn. She was short and plump, with a mischievous smile and laughing brown eyes. She kissed Mrs Ryfield on both cheeks, dropped an imperceptible curtsy to James and held out her hands to the girls. 'How nice to see you. Now go on and enjoy yourselves; if you don't get handsome offers before the night is out, I shall want to know why.'

Mark took Maryanne's arm and they moved forward into the ballroom where they were just in time to join a cotillion. It was not until the dance had finished and he escorted her to a seat that she was able to look at her surroundings. The ballroom was enormous, with a high domed ceiling and long windows, draped with velvet curtains which were drawn back so that the light from hundreds of candelabra shone out on to a terrace and garden. An orchestra played on a dais at the end of the room and everywhere there were banks of flowers. The costumes delighted and amused her; kings, queens, Greek gods and goddesses, harlequins, coachmen and gypsy maidens abounded. And sprinkled among them were the scarlet, blue and green of dress uniforms.

In spite of their masks, Maryanne recognised many of the guests as people to whom she had already been introduced—young Lord Brandon in the full dress uniform of a captain of the Guards, plump, red-faced Lord Boscombe, and Caroline's particular friends, the Misses Georgiana and Henrietta Halesworth.

'Caroline is happy,' Mark observed drily, seeing his sister surrounded by an animated group of admirers. 'And while she holds court I can have you all to myself.'

'I am rather hot,' she said, wondering why she found this declaration unnerving. Mark's attentiveness had become more and more like serious courting since they had arrived in London and he was becoming a little possessive. 'Would you fetch me a glass of cordial, please?'

'Of course.' He went off on his errand, leaving her to look round at the glittering assembly. The noise of conversation and laughter buzzed all around her, almost drowning out the orchestra as everyone greeted everyone else and commented on their costumes. It died away as the musicians began to play a waltz and the men searched out their partners.

'Miss Paynter, may I present Mr Adam Saint-Pierre? He has asked particularly to meet you.'

Maryanne turned in surprise to find Lady Markham at her side, accompanied by another of her guests, who bowed low over her hand. Like Mark, he was dressed as a highwayman and was equally slim and dark-haired, but somewhat taller. She gave a gasp of astonishment when he lifted his head and she found herself looking into warm brown eyes flecked with gold. 'Mr Daw!'

'Mam'selle is mistaken,' he said in a heavy French accent, though there was the light of laughter in his eyes which totally mesmerised her. 'I am Adam Saint-Pierre. You geev me the *plaisir* of thees dance, *non*?' Before she could answer him, he had taken her hand, raised her to her feet and whirled her away.

'Mr Daw, I must protest. . .' Her heart was thumping against her ribs, and she was thankful for her mask because she knew she was blushing to the roots of her hair.

He looked down into her upturned face and smiled. 'How did you recognise me? I thought I was well disguised.'

'Your eyes,' she said. 'And that little scar.'

He brushed away her unconscious reminder of a time he would rather forget and smiled at her. Memories of the bloodshed at Salamanca did not belong in a London ballroom. 'Not my French accent?'

She laughed suddenly and allowed herself to relax. He danced well and she did not need to think about the steps as she followed his every move as if they were one being. 'You have no accent, so why pretend you have?'

'The ladies usually like it.'

'What are you doing here?'

'Dancing with the most beautiful girl in the room.'

'You know I didn't mean that. And why invent that ridiculous name?'

'Saint-Pierre or Jack Daw? They are both names by which I am known.'

'Why do you need more than one? Have you something to hide?'

He smiled. 'Do we not all have something to hide? Have you no secrets?'

'No.'

'Liar!' he whispered. 'You have told no one of our meetings; is that not a secret?'

'How do you know I haven't?' She was acutely aware of the staid matrons and chaperons sitting on the sidelines watching them with more than passing interest.

'You would be surprised what I know, *mam'selle*.'

'What do you know?' She should not have asked; it would only encourage him and he frightened her a little. Or was it herself she was afraid of? Was she afraid of her own emotions, afraid of where they might lead her?

'I know you are beautiful, that you have eyes like a summer sky, a clear, honest blue, that your lips are irresistibly inviting and just now. . .'

'Mr Saint-Pierre, I beg you, no!'

'No, I won't do it, not in front of all these people.'

'I am relieved to hear it.' Her voice was cool, but there was such a fire raging inside her that she thought everyone must be able to see it.

'No, you are too delightfully good to be the subject of gossip, too. . .' He stopped speaking suddenly, then went on softly, 'I should not have asked you to dance.'

'Why not? Do I dance so badly?'

'You waltz like an angel, on wings, nothing so ordinary as feet,' he said. 'I was thinking of what others might think.'

'Pooh to that,' she said, making him laugh. 'We are masked and there is more than one highwayman.'

'Indeed, yes, the Honourable Mark is similarly dressed. Could we be mistaken, do you suppose?'

'You are very alike, it is almost uncanny. One would almost think you were related, though his eyes are grey and yours are brown, and I do believe you are slightly taller. Your voice is very different, though, and as for your behaviour. . .' She laughed suddenly. 'He would not behave so disgracefully towards a lady.'

'Disgracefully? You mean because I stole a kiss?'

'And your familiar manner.' Why was it so difficult to be serious when she was talking to him? 'But you have still not said why you are here in London; the last

time I saw you, you said you were in Beckford looking
for a past. Did you find it?'

'Partly.'

'Tell me about it.'

'There are more important things to talk about. Are
you going to marry Mark Danbury?'

'Mark?' She was shocked into stumbling. He caught
her in his arms and whirled her round so that her feet
hardly touched the floor. Breathlessly she said, 'Such a
thing never entered my head and I am sure it has not
occurred to him.'

'Forgive me if I disagree. He has the look of a man
determined to keep you to himself, and if marriage is
not on his mind he is a greater rogue than I took him
for. . .'

'Rogue? How can you say such a thing? Mark is a
very kind man; he has been good to me ever since. . .'

'Kind? No more than that?' Why had he insisted on
Beth Markham introducing him? Why had he come to
the ball in the first place? Was it so that he could
observe Lord Danbury and Mark at close quarters?
Would it help him to make up his mind what to do? Or
was it because of the girl he was dancing with? Oh,
why did she have to be a Danbury? He was in danger
of being diverted from his purpose. His annoyance was
directed at himself, for his weakness, not her, who
could know nothing of what he had been through. He
found himself wanting to tell her, to try to explain, but
then he pulled himself together; she was simply a girl
who had fallen into his arms, nothing more, and it was
unfair to involve her. But she was involved, and if she
was going to marry Mark Danbury she had a right to
know the truth.

'I must see you alone,' he whispered against her ear.
'I have something to tell you.'

'Tell me now.'

'No, not here. We must meet later.' His hand,
gripping hers, tightened. 'Or are you afraid to be alone
with me?'

'You know I am not. But it would not be proper. People will talk.'

He grinned at her. 'Then it is as well they know nothing of our other meetings, don't you think?'

'They were accidental.'

'This could be accidental too. I must see you. I need to ask you something.'

Ask her something; surely he wasn't going to propose without even offering for her in the proper manner? Whatever would she do? She could not possibly entertain the idea. 'I cannot meet you alone, you know that, and you should not have asked. I have heard that Frenchmen can be very forward but you are in England now, Mr Saint-Pierre, and in this country. . .'

He laughed, drawing a click of disapproval from the matrons on the sidelines. 'It is no different from any other, except there's a deal more hypocrisy.'

They were dancing near the open french window and a cool breeze fanned her hot face. She wished she could go out into the cool darkness and be alone to think. It was so hot and noisy in the ballroom. 'It's out of the question,' she said.

'I could dance you straight out on to the terrace here and now.'

She looked up at him in alarm. 'You wouldn't. . .'

'Try me.'

'Is it really important?'

'I think so.'

'But how can I possibly manage it? Where and when and how can it be an accident?' It was unthinkable that she should even consider it and yet her questions implied that she would.

'At suppertime, when everyone is moving from room to room. Make some excuse and come to the garden-room. I'll meet you in there.'

'I don't know. . .'

The music was drawing to a close and they were back at their starting place, where Mark stood with the glass of lemon cordial he had fetched for her. His dark brows were drawn down in a deep frown.

'*Merci, mam'selle*,' Adam said, releasing her to her official escort. 'Perhaps you will do me the honour again?'

'She will not,' Mark said abruptly. 'Her dances are all taken, even the one you stole. . .'

Adam laughed. 'If that is all I have stolen, then I am no thief, for the lady came willingly.'

'Please,' Maryanne begged. 'Please don't quarrel over it.' She took the glass from Mark and sipped the cool drink appreciatively. 'Thank you, Mark.' She pretended not to see Adam leave, but she knew he had gone from behind her; his going left a kind of emptiness inside her. How could he have that effect on her, a stranger with two names and apparently two characters to go with them? And why had he and Mark taken such a dislike to each other? She needed to know and the only way to find out was to meet him as he asked. But that, she decided, she could not do.

She moved off on Mark's arm in a dream, hardly listening to what he was saying. Later they went into the supper-room, pushing their way through the crush to the laden tables. A servant carried their two plates of food to a table where Caroline and Mrs Ryfield sat, and she could do nothing but sit down with them and pretend to eat. In spite of her resolve not to do as Adam asked, she was preoccupied trying to think of a way of leaving the company without raising suspicions. She was mad, she told herself, completely off her head, to make assignations with a man she hardly knew. And she did not have to go; she could stay by Mark's side all evening and, though the gossips might have a good crack at that, at least it would not be considered beyond the pale.

'I saw you dancing with that mysterious Frenchman,' Caroline said, and made it sound like an accusation. 'Who is he? You seemed to be getting on remarkably well together.'

'Mysterious Frenchman?' Maryanne repeated, hardly hearing her. 'Do you mean Monsieur Saint-Pierre?'

'So that's his name! I had heard that he was handsome and prodigiously rich. He is certainly good to look at; I wonder if the other is true too.'

'I am sure I don't know,' Maryanne murmured, wishing Caroline would talk about something else; she was sure her flushed cheeks would give her away.

'I wonder if he is married?' Caroline went on. 'Maryanne, did you find out?'

'No, of course not. I should not ask such a personal question on so slight an acquaintance.'

'It didn't look slight to me,' Mark said, taking a good gulp from his wine glass. He had already had quite a lot to drink and Maryanne was afraid he was getting rather tipsy. One thing she was certain of; it had now become much too late to tell him, or anyone else, of her earlier meetings with the Frenchman.

'Why did you call him mysterious?' she asked Caroline, pretending she had not heard Mark's comment.

The other girl shrugged. 'That's what everyone is saying; he turned up out of nowhere as soon as the armistice was agreed, and no one knows a thing about his family.' She turned to Lady Markham, who had come to see if they had all they wanted. 'Do you know his background, my lady?'

'Whose?'

'Why, the Frenchman. Maryanne danced with him, though how she could do so I cannot imagine.'

'I introduced them,' Lady Markham said. 'So you may blame me.'

'Is he an aristo?' Caroline persisted. 'Does he have a title?'

'That I cannot say,' her ladyship said with perfect truth. 'He was brought up in France, though he speaks English well, and he is as forthright as most of his race, and used to having his own way. You would think that would deter the young ladies, but if anything the competition is fiercer.'

'I am not afraid of competition,' Caroline said. 'Will you introduce him?'

'If I can find him,' her ladyship said, looking round the crowded room. 'He seems to have disappeared.'

'You are surely not thinking of setting your cap at him?' Mrs Ryfield said, tapping Caroline's arm with her fan. 'He doesn't sound at all suitable to me.'

That was just it, Maryanne thought; he would not be considered suitable and the manner in which she had first met him made it even more impossible. She would not go to him; whatever he had to ask her would have to go unasked. She forced herself to concentrate on the conversation, thankful that the subject had moved on and the Frenchman was no longer the talking-point.

Supper was over and she and Mark were strolling back to the ballroom when a servant came to tell Mark he was wanted by his father in the gaming-rooms. He excused himself and left her to return to the ballroom with Caroline and Mrs Ryfield, who were walking a few paces in front. Maryanne hesitated; she would never have a better opportunity. She turned and walked back along the corridor and slipped into the garden-room, telling herself that he would not have waited and if he had she would tell him exactly what she thought of his manners, and then leave.

She shivered involuntarily as she crept forward. The room was made almost entirely of glass and was lit only by the light showing through from the ballroom windows. She almost stumbled over a couple sitting on a low bench with their arms entwined. The young man muttered an oath and the girl hid her face in her hands, as Maryanne hurried past them, eyes averted. Was that what Adam expected from her? How foolish she had been! Almost in panic, she turned to go back. Someone reached out from beside a huge tropical plant and pulled her behind it. She opened her mouth to shriek but it was immediately covered by a large hand.

'Be quiet, you little silly. It's only me.' He took his hand from her mouth.

'Let me go back,' she whispered. 'I wish I hadn't come. If anyone sees us I'll be ruined.'

'Why *did* you come, then, if you are so careful of your reputation? Intrigued, were you? Curious? I told you about curiosity killing the cat, didn't I?'

'I. . .I don't know. I didn't mean to, I just found myself here. . .'

'Found yourself here!' He laughed harshly. 'You are no different from the others, after all. You tantalise a man, lead him on and then your courage deserts you. . .'

'That's not fair! You said you had something to ask me. What is it? Ask it and let me go back to my friends.'

'Friends, are they? I wonder.' He shrugged, then smiled. 'Yes, I suppose they are more your style than an unknown Frenchman without a name.'

'You seem to have two names,' she snapped. 'Though I wonder if either of them is real?'

He looked at her sharply. 'I was wrong, I should not have asked you to meet me. I am sorry. Let me take you back.'

'I would rather go alone.'

'Yes, of course. *Adieu, ma petite.*' He bent over her and his lips, brushing her hand, sent a shiver through her. 'I doubt we will meet again.'

'No,' she agreed. Why did the prospect of never seeing him again fill her with such despair? She didn't want to leave him but she knew if she stayed there would be no repairing her tattered reputation. And he had changed; his voice and manner were rough, as if he could not keep up the pretence of being a gentleman any longer and must revert to his roots. What were his roots? She turned back towards him. 'Mr Saint-Pierre. . .'

He saw the bleak look in her eyes, felt her sway towards him and caught her in his arms. *Sacre Dieu!*

What had possessed him even to think of confiding in her? She deserved her comfortable little corner in the life of the Danburys, might even be happy as Mark's wife. If only he could be sure of that, he would go back to France and leave well alone. Now he realised the only way he could retrieve the situation was to make light of it, pretend to a flippancy he was far from feeling, make her think he had wanted her alone only to flirt with her. 'I shall be as my lady wishes,' he said. 'But first I intend to claim recompense. . .'

'Recompense?' Her voice was a thread of a whisper. What was the matter with her? Could she be falling in love—in love with someone she knew nothing about and, what was worse, a probable enemy of her family? The idea was preposterous.

'For losing you to another.' He took her in his arms and kissed her lips, gently at first, light as a butterfly, and like a butterfly her heart fluttered beneath his hand. The pressure of his mouth on hers grew harder, more demanding until her lips were forced to part. She tried to think coherently, but could not; she was drowning in a sensuous delight which took no heed of time and place, carrying her helplessly to heights she had never even dreamed of and depths she never knew existed. She rode a see–saw, a whirlpool, a carousel. She did not want it to stop.

Suddenly he was wrenched from her and Mark's voice, venomous with anger, hissed, 'Go back to the others, Maryanne, and leave him to me.'

She could not move and watched in horror as Mark let fly with a clenched fist. Adam put up a hand as blood poured from his nose, but he did nothing to defend himself. Mark stood with feet apart and hands raised in a belligerent attitude. 'Come on, man, fight if you have any guts. I demand satisfaction.'

Adam smiled. 'Here and now? Is that wise?'

'No!' Maryanne cried, trying to put herself between them. 'Please, don't fight.' She turned to Mark. 'It was truly nothing, please forget it.'

'Forget it? He has insulted you. I demand satisfaction.' He turned back to Adam. 'If you will not fight me now, name your seconds.'

'I have no quarrel with you,' Adam said, mopping up the blood with his handkerchief. 'And if the lady does not wish to shed your blood. . .'

'My blood!' Mark was puce with fury. 'It will not be my blood that is shed.'

'I assure you,' Adam said, with a calmness that only aggravated the other's anger, 'I can well take care of myself.'

Maryanne believed that. She tried once again to interpose herself between them. Adam took her arm and gently turned her aside.

'You will not fight?' Mark demanded.

'No.'

Mark was nonplussed. 'Have you no honour, sir? Are you content that everyone should call you coward?' It was unheard-of for a gentleman to refuse a challenge on his honour and yet Adam was clearly doing so. Why? Was he a coward? Maryanne did not believe that for a moment, but she was glad that there would be no duel; she did not want anyone killed or wounded on her account.

Adam's brown eyes turned dark and the scar on his forehead stood out with the tensing of his muscles as he fought to control his anger. He looked from Mark to Maryanne and bowed low to her. 'Your servant, ma'am.' Then he turned and walked away.

Standing miserably beside Mark, she watched him go. Was that the last she would see of him? Did it matter? Yes, she told herself, it mattered terribly. Underlying their light-hearted banter had been a seriousness which both had recognised and neither acknowledged. Whatever they had had between them was over before it had begun.

She pulled herself together and went over to take Mark's arm. 'Please, Mark, think no more of it. It was as much my fault as his and meant nothing.' She was aware of the untruth as she said it.

He shrugged her off. 'I told you to go back inside. What were you thinking of to come out here in the first place?'

'I was hot and I felt faint. . .'

He snorted. 'And a kiss like that was meant to cool you, I suppose.' He grabbed her arm. 'Good God, Maryanne, don't you know how this makes me feel? I must take that fellow's insult and do nothing because he is too much of a coward to stand up to me.'

'You should not have challenged him in the first place.'

'I had no choice. Finding you like that. . .' He was hustling her back into the ballroom as he spoke. 'Didn't you know I meant to propose myself?'

'No.' She was too agitated to stop and consider the meaning of what he had said. 'And that is hardly a romantic proposal.'

He laughed harshly. 'You did not give me the opportunity for that, did you?'

'And now you have changed your mind.' She turned to the attack. 'How fickle you are! But at least it will save me having to turn you down.'

He stopped in the doorway to stare down at her. 'Would you have turned me down?'

'I should certainly have thanked you for the honour you did me, but I would also have asked for time to think about it.'

'Hm.' He took her arm and led her through the couples who were forming a quadrille, smiling to right and left at acquaintances, pretending all was well. 'We must dance or the old gabblegrinders will have a field day.' He found a set wanting a couple and pulled Maryanne into it. 'Smile!' he commanded, bowing over her hand as the music began. 'We are in love, so play your part, if you ever want to hold your head up in Society again.'

She curtsied and smiled, danced up and down,

bowed this way and that, laughed and pretended to enjoy herself, but all the time she was asking herself, Where has he gone? What was he going to tell me? Why do I ache inside so much that I must hurt Mark, who loves me enough to protect me from scandal?

She had no answer and was glad when Mark said they could leave without comment being made, though it was still an hour or two before dawn. Caroline, who was flirting with half a dozen young men at once, all of whom had drunk more than enough, was understandably reluctant to leave.

'I had Cousin Henry eating out of my hand,' she said. 'He was on the point of agreeing to have a ball at Wiltshire House and now I shall have to sweet talk him all over again. . .' She followed reluctantly as they went to find their hostess to thank her.

Mark saw them all into the carriage, but instead of climbing in beside them he turned and went back into the house. He felt angry and let down, but, what was worse, his carefully laid plans looked set to be overturned. And for what? A no-good Frenchman. How long had Maryanne known him? It was the man he had seen leaving Beckford Church; he was almost sure of it. Who was he? Not a gentleman, that was certain, for he had not come out of the encounter with any honour. Well, the world would soon know about it; the tale would go round, though he must be careful not to tarnish Maryanne's reputation in the process, and the fellow would not dare to show his face again.

He went upstairs and into the card-room, where the gentlemen who did not dance could be found at the tables. The room was thick with cigar smoke and the smell of good French brandy which, with the end of the war, was coming into the country legally again, much to the chagrin of the smugglers. There was ribaldry and laughter, except at those tables where the play was too serious to admit of anything but the greatest concentration. Seeing the Duke of Wiltshire at one of these, Mark went over to him.

His Grace was corpulent to the extent of being gross; his tight coat of satin was stretched across a belly that was obviously confined by stays tight enough to make it almost impossible for him to bend. His purple waistcoat was heavily embroidered with gold thread and his frilled shirt was topped by a collar whose points threatened to scratch his cheeks whenever he moved his head. Beneath this, held by a jewelled pin, was a voluminous spotted cravat. He beamed at Mark. 'Come and join us, me boy. Hunter is just quitting.'

'Cleaned out, I'm afraid,' Lord Hunter said, rising from the table. 'Perhaps you'll have better luck.'

Mark sat down and a new game was started, but he was still too cut up to concentrate and had soon lost a great deal, and it was no good applying to His Grace, because he had lost even more. Lord Markham and Lord Boscombe sat with a growing heap of coins at their elbows.

'I'll have to give you a note,' His Grace said. 'Pockets empty. Didn't intend to gamble tonight. Got drawn into it by a fit of the blue devils. Not an eligible girl in sight, except me cousin Caroline.'

'Caroline!' Mark said in surprise.

'Why not? Seems to me she'll do very well.'

'You can't mean it.'

'Never more serious in me life. Young, healthy and willing. . .'

'I don't believe it.'

'Why not? She'll jump at the chance to be a duchess, 'specially if I don't keep her on too tight a rein. All I ask is discretion and care. Don't want to play parent to anyone else's by-blows.'

'Have you asked her?'

'Not formally, but I will. She wants to have a ball at Wiltshire House—well, so she shall—an engagement ball.'

Mark opened his mouth to protest, but decided against it, and they continued to play, but now he had something else to occupy his mind besides Maryanne.

Somehow he had to stop the Duke from marrying Caroline. If they married and she had a son, it would put paid to his own hopes of the dukedom. The problem concentrated his mind wonderfully and he was soon winning again, while His Grace found himself even deeper in debt and the two baronets were just breaking even.

'I'll make you a proposition,' Mark said, when it looked as though the game was coming to an end, because even the Duke realised he had gone as far as he dared; the spectre of his mother's wrath was large in his mind. 'Double or quits on a little race.'

'What kind of race?' the Duke asked guardedly.

Mark shuffled the cards, watching his face carefully. 'You've got a new rig, haven't you?'

'Yes, bang up, and the best cattle in the country.'

'Then I'll put my rig against yours over a measured five miles. If you win, your debt is cleared; if you lose. . .' he shrugged, as it it were nothing '. . .the debt is doubled.'

'Don't do it, Henry,' Lord Boscombe said. 'The young shaver is a first-class whip.'

'And so am I,' His Grace said. He turned to Mark. 'I'll take you on, young fellow, if you throw in the rigs as part of the stake.'

'Done.'

They shook hands and left the table together. 'Give you a ride home, me boy?' the Duke offered.

Mark laughed. 'Thank you, Cousin, it will give me a chance to see what I'll be getting when I win.'

'*If* you win, young fellow, *if*.' Arm in arm, they went downstairs and out of the front door. A footman offered to fetch his carriage, but His Grace waved him aside. 'Get it ourselves.'

As the two men reached the stables, a groom came out leading a riding horse, a great, restive bay which threw back its head as if wanting to rid itself of the hand that held the snaffle. 'Easy, easy, ol' fellow,' the groom soothed, then, seeing the Duke, he added, 'I'll have yours harnessed in a shake, Your Grace.' He tethered the horse and turned to go back to the stables, passing a man coming out.

Mark stopped in his tracks when he saw who it was. 'You!' he said, taking a step towards him. 'You dare to stay around here!'

'I have no quarrel with my hostess,' Adam said calmly, going to pass him. 'Nor yet with you, if you would but believe it.'

'You, sir, are a coward,' Mark went on. 'And if that will not make you fight I shall continue to say it all over the country until you do.'

'Hey, what's afoot?' His Grace asked, looking from one angry man to the other.

'It is a private matter,' Adam said.

The Duke laughed. 'Lady, was it?'

'This *gentleman*. . .' Mark's voice was heavy with sarcasm '. . .has insulted a lady for whom I have a high regard. I called him out, but he will not fight.'

'Strange, I would not have put him down for a coward,' His Grace said. 'Markham said he had served with distinction in the war.'

'Yes?' Mark sneered. 'In whose army?' He smiled suddenly as an idea came to him; there was a way to kill two birds with one stone. He turned to Adam. 'If you haven't the stomach for a fight, will you accept another kind of challenge?'

'I will accept any challenge which does not involve the unnecessary shedding of blood.'

'A race. Have you cattle and a curricle?'

'No, but I can get them.'

'Five miles,' Mark said. 'Where and when to be decided. Do you accept?'

Adam smiled. 'With pleasure. And I'll back myself to the tune of a thousand guineas. That should make it worth the effort.'

'Done,' said Mark, not daring to think what might happen if his plans went awry and he lost. 'Though you will understand if I prefer not to shake hands on it. You will learn time and place by letter.'

'You may contact me with the details at the home of my lawyer, Mr Robert Rudge, at Adelphi Terrace.' Adam bowed to the Duke. 'Your Grace.' Then he strode over to the bay, unhitched it and leapt into the saddle.

He did not feel like returning to Robert, with whom he was staying; he needed to think. He set off to ride on the heath until his anger cooled.

It was directed more at himself than Mark Danbury. He had been a fool to allow himself to get into a situation where he could not defend his honour, and all because of a girl. He smiled to himself. But what a girl! He hadn't meant to kiss her again but simply to talk to her, to try to explain his dilemma. Instead. . . *Sacre Dieu*! Why did she have to be a Danbury? Why, when he had almost decided to leave well alone and return to France, did he have to meet her? She made him feel light-hearted in a way he had not felt since his happy childhood had been shattered by the Terror. He forced himself to think about it, to remind himself of why he had come to England.

He remembered Louis Saint-Pierre, the only father he had ever known, pleading with *Maman* to take the boy to England. 'I have made provision for you there,' he had said. 'Go to Joseph Rudge and I will join you when I can.'

She had refused and then the Committee of Public Safety—what a misnomer!—had sent men to arrest them, and there had only been time to push the twelve-year-old Adam into a cupboard and exhort him not to come out until it was safe, before they were dragged away and the house ransacked. His secure, contented life had ended in that cupboard and he would bear the inner scars of it to his death. He had not dared to come out for hours and by then all the servants but old Henri Caronne had fled. The old man had urged him to leave

the area. 'They will be back for you,' he said. 'They
won't leave any aristos alive, you can be sure.'

But Adam could not tear himself away from home
and those he loved, and he had been beside the rough
guillotine when Louis Saint-Pierre was brought out to
his death. He had run and flung himself into his father's
arms, trying to hold him back, wrestling with the
guards, crying, 'No! No! No!' until *Papa* had made him
stand back.

'Go to England,' he had whispered. 'Find Mr Rudge.
Tell him what has happened.'

'And *Maman*?'

'I don't know. They separated us. Pray God they
were merciful.' Then he had been dragged up the steps
by his bloodthirsty captors and his head had been
severed from his body.

The memory of that terrible scene could never be
erased by anything that happened afterwards, however
appalling or however pleasant. Twelve years old and
alone in the world, he had set off for Paris, a city
teeming with beggars and orphans, as he soon discovered. Wary and untamed as a wild animal, he had
learned to live on his wits, to trust no one. He had
never allowed his emotions to get the better of him
since then—not until now—and no woman had held
his affection. Why should Maryanne Paynter be the
exception? Was she worth being called a coward for?

He could never have accepted Mark's challenge to a
duel; he was prepared to wager the young man had
never heard a shot fired in anger and had never faced
a rapier that wasn't cork-tipped. If he had agreed to
fight and killed him, the truth would have come out
and he would have been vilified the length and breadth
of the country and, what was worse, he would never
have been able to live with himself afterwards. And
not even the sparkling blue eyes and soft lips of the
only girl who had ever made his heart beat faster could
alter that. He should never have come to England,
never started to pry, never gone to Beckford or Castle

Cedars; it solved nothing. He smiled suddenly. Then he would never have met Maryanne and that he could not regret, even if it did increase his dilemma. But the curricle race would have to be his Parthian shot, so he had better win it.

CHAPTER FOUR

His lordship, clad in a full-length burgundy satin dressing-gown and with his dark hair brushed but not dressed, was sitting alone eating his breakfast when Maryanne went down next morning. She had always risen betimes and could not lie abed as Caroline did, not even after a late night. And, besides, she had not slept well; it was a relief when morning came and she could get up, though she knew she would have to face his lordship's displeasure. Mark had told him what had happened before they left the ball; he was too angry to keep silent on the subject and, in all fairness, his lordship had a right to know.

She hesitated in the doorway before taking a deep breath and moving forward to make her curtsy. 'My lord. . .'

'Good morning, Maryanne. Come and have breakfast with me. I want to talk to you.'

She sat down next to him but made no effort to help herself from the many dishes set out on a side table. 'My lord, I am sorry if I have disappointed you. . .'

He smiled. 'Mark flew into the boughs over nothing, is that what you were about to say?'

'It was all so silly. If Mark had not come along, I. . .' She hesitated, remembering that kiss and how she had lost herself in the pleasure of it. 'I could have dealt with him.'

'Who was he?'

'I don't know.'

'A stranger? Maryanne, you astound me.'

'He wasn't exactly a stranger. I had seen him before, several times.'

'Where and when?'

She told him everything, including her doubts, finish-

64

ing, 'I am sorry, my lord, I should have come to you before, but I could not see that he was doing any harm. I still don't think so.'

'Mark saw him in the village too?'

She nodded.

'That might account for his anger, don't you think? It was not just last night's indiscretion he objected to, was it?'

'I suppose not, but he had no right. . .'

'Come, Maryanne, you are part of our family and Mark is very fond of you, as I am; he was only protecting you. Thank goodness no one else saw you and he was able to cover up your absence.'

'I am grateful to him, of course, but if there had been a duel, as Mark wanted, it would have been all over London.'

'Yes, it would seem the young man had more sense than Mark on that score. You know his name?'

'At first he said it was Jack Daw.' She watched his mouth twitch in a smile. 'Oh, I am sure that is not his real name. Lady Markham called him Saint-Pierre. . .'

'Saint-Pierre!' His lordship almost dropped the cup of coffee which, at that moment, he was carrying to his lips. He set it down hurriedly. His face had gone very white and his hands shook a little, but his eyes were bright—with what? Fear? Hope? Anger? She could not tell. 'Where did he come from?'

Why had his lordship not heard the name before? she asked herself. But then, she reasoned, he did not often listen to gossip, nor had he been present when Lady Markham had introduced them. And last night Mark had referred to Adam as 'that damned Frenchman'. 'I don't know. No one seems to know; he just appeared. I believe he is French, but he speak English very well.'

'It can't be,' his lordship murmured. 'They are all dead.'

'My lord?'

He seemed to shake himself. ''Tis nothing. Where is he staying in London?

'I have no idea, but surely he will not stay in town after refusing a challenge? Not that I am sorry about that—I could not bear it if either of them were to risk arrest or be hurt on account of me. Please don't try to find him. I beg you, let sleeping dogs lie.'

'Let sleeping dogs lie,' he repeated softly. 'Can it be that easy?'

'I don't understand, my lord.'

He seemed to pull himself out of a daydream to answer her. 'No, of course you don't. Now, we will say no more about the matter; there is no need for anyone outside the family to know about it. It is an indiscretion I am sure you will not repeat; isn't that so?'

'Yes, my lord.'

She would not repeat it, she could not repeat it because she was sure the opportunity would not arise again. If Adam had any sense, he would leave the country, go back home to France and forget whatever it was he had come to England for. But he had left her emotions in a tangle and the more she tried to straighten them out, the more confused she became. Had she really wanted a complete stranger to kiss her like that? In the cold light of day and facing this gentle man who had loved her and befriended her all her life, even if she had not known of it, she could only look back in horror at her own weakness and stupidity. It must be, as Caroline so often said, that she did not know how to go on in a society which allowed flirting so long as it was conducted in the prescribed manner. It was looked on as a kind of game, but only for those who knew the rules, not young unmarried ladies at their first coming out.

Her confusion was not helped by Lord Danbury's reaction on learning the man's name. It had, for a moment, thrown him off balance, and sent him into another time, another place, and confirmed her suspicions that it was the Danbury family and perhaps his

lordship in particular who were the objects of the
Frenchman's curiosity. Or was it more than curiosity?
Hatred perhaps? She had no answer to that and now
she supposed she never would have. And mixed with
her feelings of shame and remorse for being such a
disappointment to his lordship were others of grief, of
having lost something beautiful, of joy stillborn.

She was in no mood to hear that it was not the end
of the affair and that the Frenchman had accepted
another kind of challenge, and that, far from leaving
town, he was still to be seen out and about. Not quite
in the highest circles, but certainly among those of the
ton who enjoyed a certain notoriety. He rode in the
park with Lord Markham, played cards with Lord
Alvanley, had Henry Luttrell to dine and even out-
dressed Sir Lumley Skeffington. All this came to
Maryanne by way of Caroline's gossip. He was, the
tattlers variously said, a French spy; a nabob; a highwayman whose costume had not been put on solely for
the benefit of Lady Markham's ball; a smuggler who
had become rich smuggling French brandy; a pro-
fessional gambler. And everyone brought their own
evidence to bear on their own theories. Far from
making an outcast of him, the stories only added to his
allure for all but the most staid of matrons.

The biggest talking-point of all was the curricle race
and that threatened to eclipse even the gathering of the
Congress of London as a subject of conversation. While
all the European heads of state gathered in the capital
with all the pomp and ceremony such as occasion
demanded, and with the populace going wild at the
imminent return of the Duke of Wellington, the ton
was speculating on the Frenchman and why he had
refused a challenge from someone who was considered
an indifferent swordsman, and why a fight to the death
should have been reduced to a curricle race.

Caroline, who would not let the matter drop until
she had inveigled the details from an irritable Mark,
never lost an opportunity to plague Maryanne about it.

'You would think you had been brought up in a whorehouse, not a rectory,' she said one morning about a week later, just when Maryanne was beginning to think no more would be said on the subject. 'But they say still waters run deep, don't they? And the demure ones are the most depraved.'

'Caroline, that was uncalled for,' Mrs Ryfield put in. 'And it would be better if you did not talk so freely about it, nor repeat the gossip you hear. After all, no one outside the family knows Maryanne is involved in the affair, and we must make sure it stays that way. Maryanne is wanting in conduct, that is true, but it behoves us to be charitable and I doubt the Reverend Mr Cudlipp taught her how to behave towards the less respectable gentlemen in Society.'

'He is not a gentleman,' Caroline said. 'Lady Markham introduced him into Society and must needs stand by him, though I'll wager she regrets her generosity. Everyone of any note will refuse him entry. I certainly hope he will not be at Almack's on Wednesday, for I should not be civil to him.'

'We are unlikely to meet again,' Maryanne said, her calm voice belying the misery and anger she felt; it did not help to have a verbal battle with Caroline, who could make life unbearable simply by constant and loud repetition of her supposed grievances. 'I would as lief forget the whole thing.'

'If the reason for the challenge gets out, you will not be allowed to forget and you will not be invited to any more functions.' Caroline turned to the mirror to put on her riding hat with its tall crown and raking feather, for she was off to the park with Lord Brandon to show off her new habit with its elaborate Polish frogging. 'You will be cut by everyone and I shall disclaim all connection with you, and so will Mark, if he has anything in the attic at all. Why Papa has not insisted on sending you back to Beckford I cannot imagine.'

'The last thing I want is to embarrass you,' Maryanne said. 'And I would return to Beckford if his lordship would allow it, but you know he will not. He says if Mark didn't prolong it by delaying the race it would all blow over in no time.'

'You can hardly have a race through the streets of London when they are so thronged with people that there is hardly room to walk, let alone drive,' Caroline said, referring to the fact that the streets had been almost impassable since the Prince Regent had entertained his illustrious guests to dinner at the Guildhall, a few days before, and staged an elaborate procession which had driven the populace wild with excitement. 'He has been persuaded to wait until the celebrations die down.'

'Why does it have to be in London? He could arrange it in the country just as easily,' Maryanne replied.

'And who would watch it? Mark needs witnesses to the Frenchman's defeat, if honour is to be satisfied. It will be the event of the season and already the wagers are reaching prodigious proportions.' She pulled on her gloves and picked up her crop.

Mrs Ryfield, torn between accompanying Caroline and leaving Maryanne to her own devices, sighed and decided her first loyalty was to her brother's daughter; she went out to the waiting barouche in which she intended to follow the riders.

Left to herself, Maryanne went to her room and fetched a book, which she took out into the garden. She had told herself to forget Adam Saint-Pierre, but how could she do that when everyone was talking about him, when Caroline grumbled endlessly about him and Mark could not bring himself to speak to her because of him? On the one hand, she wanted to clap her hands over her ears so she did not have to hear what was said about him; on the other, she was hungry for the tiniest scrap of information, the least morsel which would tell her he was not as black as he was painted. Her book could not hold her attention and she let it fall in her lap.

'Maryanne.'

She looked up to see Mark approaching her and smiled. She did not like quarrelling with him and if they could make it up she would feel a great deal better about everything.

'I want to talk to you.'

'I am listening, though I hope you are not going to scold. I have had enough of that from Caroline.'

'Maryanne. . .' He sat down on the bench beside her. 'I believe what happened was because of your innocence, your inexperience, and that is something I prize.' He took her hand. 'Tell me that is true, that you didn't understand what the man was about.'

'Oh, I knew what he was about—he was kissing me.'

He hid his annoyance. 'You misunderstand. I mean you did not know the man was a bounder.'

She smiled wearily. 'That is still true. I don't know that he is a bounder, only that you *think* he is.'

'Maryanne! How can you say that? He put his own honour and your reputation at risk; no gentleman would have behaved in that fashion.'

'I am sure it was done on impulse and meant nothing,' she said dully. 'I wish everyone would not go on about it. I was the victim, after all, not the perpetrator, and that should have made a difference.'

'Very little to Society,' he said laconically.

'But I am assured Society knows nothing of it.' She was beginning to feel angry with him for the first time since it had happened. 'Unless you have said something, or Caroline, perhaps? Your sister is not always careful of her tongue.'

'Certainly I have said nothing and I am sure Caroline has more sense than that. How do you think a scandal would affect her chances of a good marriage? My concern is that you seem to treat the matter so lightly.'

'What do you expect? Sackcloth and ashes? I have apologised to his lordship and that should be enough.' She stood up suddenly. 'I will not stay to hear any more.'

He stood beside her and laid a hand on her arm. 'I

am sorry, my dear, I did not mean to grumble. It is just that whenever I think of him touching you my blood runs hot and nothing would give me greater pleasure than to put a sword through his heart.'

'Why should you be so angry? What has he done to hurt you?' Nothing yet, she thought, but in the future, what of the future? Was Adam Saint-Pierre his enemy? Should she be concentrating on that and not worrying if she would ever see him again?

'It is what he has done to you that matters. I shudder to think of what would have happened if anyone but me had come into the conservatory and saw what I saw. You would have been branded a harlot and that didn't seem to have bothered him in the least. You can't possibly think that he cares for you?' She did not answer and he persisted. 'You don't, do you?'

'No.' She spoke softly, not daring to look into his eyes.

'Then why, Maryanne? Why?'

'I don't know, I didn't think. He said he had something to tell me.'

'And you believed him?'

'Yes.'

He smiled and took her hand. 'You silly little goose, what an innocent you are!'

'Your father says it will blow over as soon as you have held this race you are planning.'

'So it might, and I would have it tomorrow if I could be sure of a clear passage.'

'You are surely not intending to race through the streets? If you must indulge in such childish pursuits, then why not go to Hyde Park?'

'There is nothing childish about it, Maryanne, I assure you. And Hyde Park is being turned into a fairground. Every tavern keeper in London has set up a booth and moved there lock, stock and barrel. They are building pagodas and temples and heaven knows what else. There will soon not be a blade of grass to be seen.' He paused, then went on, 'You are turning me aside from my purpose, Maryanne. Please sit down again and I promise I will not mention the Frenchman.' He took her hand and lifted it to his lips. 'There are more pleasant topics of conversation.'

'What do you want to talk about?' she asked, as they seated themselves again. 'Have you read *Pride and Prejudice*?' She tapped the cover of the book she had been reading. 'It is very good.'

'No.' He did not want to talk about literature either.

'You should. It pokes fun at the pomposity of Society in a most amusing way.'

'Maryanne, I am trying to propose to you.'

'Oh.'

'Don't pretend to be surprised. After all, I have mentioned it before.'

'So you have, but I did not think you were serious.'

'I was never more serious in my life.'

'Even though I appear to have disgraced you?'

'It is not you who has been disgraced, nor will you be while I can protect you; it is that. . .' He saw her open her mouth to speak and stopped her with a finger on her lips. 'I know, I gave my word not to mention him.' He moved his finger from her mouth to her chin to tilt it up so that she was forced to look into his eyes. 'Tell me you will marry me. I am eminently suitable, one day I shall be Viscount Danbury, if nothing higher, and, though I am not exactly plump of pocket, I am not penniless and Father will see us right. We could go on very well together.'

'What does his lordship say about it?' she asked, avoiding a straight answer.

'Oh, I think I can safely say he will give us his blessing, not that you need it. In a few months' time you will be twenty-one and may choose whom you please.'

For a moment her mind left the young man beside her and flew to another who was uncannily like him in looks but so very different in every other way. Would he have been her choice? But he had not asked her to make a choice; he had simply kissed her. She shook herself. That was the most cork-brained thing she had thought of yet.

'I have already told you what I would say,' she said. 'Thank you for the honour you do me, but I need time to think about it.'

'How much time?' He took her hand in his. 'Please forgive my impatience, but I have been able to think of nothing else since you came to live with us. My thoughts are full of you, of a future that is bright and hopeful as May Day blossom.'

She laughed, wondering why his compliments did not ring so true as Jack Daw's, why she felt embarrassed by the one and delighted by the other. 'And as easily blown away by a puff of wind.'

'No, no, for blossom bears fruit; it endures in that.'

'Oh, I am to be a bearer of fruit, am I? I am not at all sure I like that.'

'You are teasing me, and all because I am so inept at putting my feelings into words.'

'That is the first time you have mentioned feelings.'

'They are too deep for easy expression.' She was laughing at him! This nobody who had risen from obscurity to an envied place in his father's household was making fun of him, and it rankled. He got up and bowed to her. 'I will come back when the influence of Miss Austen has worn off. Good-day, Maryanne.'

She sprang to her feet and took his arm. 'I am sorry, truly sorry. It is simply that a proposal that does not mention love is, to me, not worthy of the name. Oh, I know many couples exist quite happily without much affection, but, you see, my father and mother loved each other deeply and, as far as I am concerned, that is how a marriage should be.'

'You would be hard put to exist on love alone,' he said, picking up her book and tucking her hand beneath his arm to stroll with her along the path. 'The necessities of life demand more than that. I was merely pointing out. . .'

'That you have much in your favour. Yes, I am humbly aware of that, but, you see, it is not only that I want my husband to love me, I must also be in love with him. . .'

'You do not love me?'

'I have a very high regard for you. If it hadn't been for your kindness when I first came to Beckford Hall, I don't think I could have stayed, but my life is so different from what I expected it to be when I lived at the rectory that I am unsure of myself.'

He smiled and there was a light in his eye which could have been relief, but could equally have been triumph. 'Do you think it was simply kindness which made me escort you back to the ballroom and dance with you a second time? It was the only way to protect you from gossip and the only way to keep the family name untarnished. I shudder to think what the tattle-mongers would say if they had seen what I saw—a Danbury allowing herself to be manhandled by a perfect stranger. It was as well the fellow was also dressed as a highwayman; as far as the world is concerned, it was you and I in the conservatory and we were there for one reason only—that I might propose to you. If the public announcement of our engagement does not follow very shortly, not only will your name be murmured over the teacups, but mine as well.'

'Are you serious?'

'I do not joke about such things.'

'I need time, Mark, it is too soon. . .'

He sighed; if only he could make her agree before that confounded curricle race, he would feel much happier. 'I do not want to be kept dangling, Maryanne; I have my pride, you know. Do you want to make me—our family—a laughing-stock?'

'No, of course not, but. . .'

'Then it is settled. We are engaged?'

She felt trapped, like a wild bird caught to be caged and made to sing its master's tune. Was he right about the scandal? Even if she cared little about the gossip on her own account, was it fair that the rest of the family should suffer for something she had done? If she was in a trap, it was her own fault. And was the prospect of being married to Mark so distasteful? He seemed gentle, kind and attentive, and he professed to care for her, so why was she hesitating? Could it be because of a man who had thought nothing of her honour and reputation, a nobody who considered only his own pleasure? She should not even be thinking of him.

'And that is the best you can do in the way of a proposal?' She smiled up at him, teasing again, simply to lighten the atmosphere, to release the bands of tension which seemed to be strapped around her chest, preventing her from breathing. 'I am disappointed in you.'

He laughed with relief and caught her in his arms to kiss her. She did not resist, but neither did she respond with any enthusiasm, though he did not appear to notice that. 'Oh, my darling, we will do very well together.' He tucked her hand beneath his arm and grinned like a schoolboy. 'Shall we go to Westminster? The Duke of Wellington is due to arrive there soon and the world will be there to greet him.'

'Yes, I should like that, but Mrs Ryfield is using the barouche.'

'We don't need that. My cattle need an airing; I'll drive you in my curricle.'

'Without a chaperon? After all you have been saying?'

'We are cousins and as good as engaged; it wants only the announcement in *The Times*. Besides, we are unlikely to meet anyone who matters.'

The trap had closed; there was nothing more to be done. She smiled wryly to herself; so much for all her determination to marry only for love. But perhaps love would come; she was very fond of him and there was nothing about him to dislike. If only she could forget a pair of laughing brown eyes and a mouth which had claimed hers with such devastating effect. But she must forget.

She went up to her room to change and then joined Mark at the front of the house where two magnificent horses stood harnessed to his curricle. She smiled as he helped her up and climbed in beside her; she would learn to love him.

At first she was nervous that he might try and drive too fast for the prevailing conditions, but he was most careful and she began to relax and enjoy the outing, marvelling that so many people could be gathered in one place. Before they had come within half a mile of Westminster, the press was too great even for the curricle. They left it in an inn yard and walked.

'Hold on to my arm.' He smiled, tucking her hand beneath his elbow. 'I do not want to lose you.'

Somehow he managed to push his way through the throng and they were right at the front when the Duke's carriage came in sight, amid resounding cheers which went on and on and almost deafened her. She felt Mark tug on her arm and turned towards him. His mouth was moving, but she could not hear what he said. and, shrugging, gave up trying. She pushed her way forward, craning her neck for a glimpse of the great man. He was not particularly handsome and she could see why they called him Old Hooknose, but he had fine eyes and a way of looking about him which seemed to take in everything at a glance. His smile turned to a frown when the people brought the coach to a halt and began taking the horses from the shafts and vying with each other for the honour of pulling it.

The crowd surged forward, carrying Maryanne along with it. It was not until she turned to speak to Mark that she realised he was not behind her. She tried to turn and go back, but the press of the throng would not allow it; she had to let herself be carried along or be trampled underfoot.

Before long she lost a shoe but could not stop to retrieve it and then her bonnet came off and disappeared under the feet of the cheering mass who surrounded her. She was hot and near to panic, but if she fainted she knew no one would help her and she would be trampled to death. She hobbled along, no longer interested in the coach and its occupant, her only thought to keep upright until the crowd thinned out enough for her to stop and find some other way back to Mark.

The crowd grew thicker than ever and the roads were lined with even more spectators, cheering wildly; she could not even drop out to the side. Her shoeless foot was hurting her and she could hardly breathe. 'I must *not* swoon,' she told herself. 'I must not.'

'You all right, miss?' said a voice at her elbow.

She screwed her head round towards the speaker. He was dirty and scruffy but he seemed concerned for her. 'I . . . I. . .' She felt herself sliding down into a jumble of bodies and legs, heard the man beside her shout, and then nothing as darkness claimed her.

Adam, on the back of his great bay, surveyed the mass of bodies, looking for the glint of steel or the dark barrel of a pistol, for a stirring in the mass or someone creating a space about him, a movement which went against the tide. Others, in the body of the crowd, pretending to be part of it, were doing the same thing and he scanned the heads looking for their signal. He heard the shout and spurred his horse foward, but it was not the trouble he had been expecting. Maryanne's inert form, without bonnet or shoes and with hair tumbling about her shoulders, was being hoisted above the heads of the crowd and passed from hand to hand.

'Give her to me.' He urged the bay into the throng and reached down to take their burden from them. He propped her up in front of him, holding her inert body steady with one hand while he held the reins in the other. 'Keep alert,' he said to one of the men, a disreputable-looking individual who seemed to have forgotten that a moment before he had been hobbling along with the aid of a stick. 'I will rejoin you in a minute.'

Maryanne, in that grey dawn between sleeping and waking, thought she must be dreaming; she could have sworn the voice was Adam's. Her eyelids fluttered. 'I fainted.'

'Yes. Sit still.' It *was* Adam.

Her head lolled until it found something firm to lean against. It was comfortable there and though her feet were burning the pain in them had eased. In fact, nothing hurt her now and all she wanted to do was sleep in his arms. It was a ludicrous situation and she began to giggle weakly.

'I am glad you are in such good humour,' he said, attempting to be stern. 'You know you could have been killed?'

She stopped as suddenly as she had begun; considering all that had gone before, it really wasn't very funny after all. 'I know, and I was very frightened, and I'm truly grateful you came along to rescue me.'

'What were you doing in that crowd?'

'We went to see the Duke arrive.'

'We?'

'Mark and I. We were separated. He will be very worried about me.' She tried to turn towards him, and his grip tightened.

'Sit still.'

'But I must go back to him.'

'You'll not find him until the crowd has dispersed. *Mon Dieu*, the man is an *imbécile*. What possessed him to take you into that crowd on foot?'

'It wasn't his fault. I went forward and didn't realise he hadn't followed me. We left the curricle in an inn yard.'

'Which one?'

'I don't know its name, though if I saw it again I might recognise it.'

They arrived outside a tall narrow house in a new terrace facing the river. A tall, broad-shouldered man

about Adam's own age came out of the front door and
down the steps. Adam handed her down to him. 'The
young lady has been in a scrape with the crowd,' he
said, by way of explanation.

The man, who was actually a little older than Adam
and fair-haired, took her weight easily while Adam
dismounted. She struggled to be let down and he
chuckled. 'This is an unexpected pleasure but, I pray
you, do not wriggle so, or I shall drop you.'

'I'll take her now.' Adam held out his arms for her.
'I'd appreciate it if we might have the use of a room.
And perhaps a little brandy.'

'Of course.'

'This, by the way, is Miss Maryanne Paynter. And
once again she has intruded into my affairs.' His smile
belied the unkindness of his words.

'I assure you, sir, that I had no wish to do so,' she
said, but it was impossible to be dignified when she felt
like nothing so much as a rag doll. 'And you may put
me down, I am perfectly able to stand.'

'I think not. Your stockings are torn to ribbons and
your feet are bleeding.'

He carried her up the steps and into the house and
to her shame she ceased to struggle. She heard a voice
behind them say, 'Take her up to the blue room. I'll
ask Jeannie to bring some hot water. Miss Paynter will
need to wash and change her clothes.'

'Where am I?' she demanded. 'I must go back to
Mark. . .'

'He can wait,' Adam said grimly. 'And this is the
home of my good friend Robert Rudge.' He carried
her effortlessly up the stairs and into a well-furnished
bedroom, where he put her on a sofa and sat down
beside her.

She became suddenly aware of the pickle she was in.
Alone in a bedroom with a man! If she had been in
trouble before, it was nothing to the disgrace she would
be in if this got out; the gossips would have even more

to keep their tongues wagging. It would condemn her to social purgatory forever.

Before she could do anything to remedy the situation, there was a knock at the door and he got up to open it to a servant who held a bottle of brandy and a glass. Adam took them from him and returned to Maryanne. He poured a generous measure of the spirit into the glass. 'Here, drink this.'

She sipped it and pulled a wry face.

'All of it—it is good French cognac.' He smiled; did she know what the sight of her like that did to his insides? She looked like one of the hundreds of little urchins who ran about the streets of Paris, barefoot and in rags, scurrying about that beautiful city made ugly by the atrocities committed there, and making a living in any way they could. They were alone in the world, except for the companionship of each other and that ceased when richer pickings were offered. They had no scruples; it was everyone for himself. It was where he had learned to keep his wits about him, where he had discovered you could trust no one, where he had been turned from a well brought-up twelve-year-old to a cynical, unloved and unloving adult, and all in the space of four years. By the time he was sixteen he was a full-grown man.

Not that Maryanne was cynical and unloving—he did not believe that—but she *was* alone. And she needed her wits about her to survive, because none of the Danbury family cared a jot for her. Could he, in all conscience, leave her to their tender mercies? But he had to, not only now when he should be out with the crowd, doing his duty, but later when he had to keep his promise to the Count. If only he could be in two places at once!

'That's better,' he said, as she drained the glass. 'Would you like something to eat?'

'No, thank you.' She paused to look up at him. 'I am sorry to be so much trouble to you.'

'It is my pleasure and privilege to serve you.' Better

speak formally because he wanted to kiss her again and that ought to be resisted. 'I have to leave you, but I want you to stay here until I come back.'

'But I can't! I must find Mark; he will be out of his mind with worry.'

He gave a wry smile. 'It will do him no harm, might even teach him to take more care of you in future.'

'You are being unfair! I said it was not his fault, it was mine. He would never knowingly lead me into danger; he loves me.'

'Does he, now?' The sardonic smile lifted the scar on his eye. 'And what about you? Do you love him?'

'I. . . I don't know.'

He chuckled. 'Then you do not, for if you did you would surely know it.'

'You think so?' She sounded eager and wistful at the same time and he longed to throw caution to the winds and take her in his arms, to tell her that he would teach her about love. But he couldn't; he had no time and no right to; and what did he know about the subject anyway? He was saved from making a fool of himself by a light tap at the door, and a girl, slightly older than Maryanne, bustled in carrying a bowl of warm water and towels.

'We shall soon have the young lady looking herself again, Captain.'

'Good.' He turned to Maryanne. 'Madame Clavier will look after you.' He smiled and stood up to leave. 'I know how anxious you are to rejoin your escort, but I must counsel patience until I return. Now I have to deal with more pressing matters.'

Anxious to leave him and return to Mark? If he only knew the truth! 'How long will you be?' she asked.

'Rest assured, no longer than I can help. Stay here until I come back, then I will make arrangements to have you taken home.' He went to the door, but turned back as he reached it, opened his mouth to say something, then changed his mind, turned on his heel and left.

'Now, miss,' said the servant, standing the bowl on
the table beside Maryanne. 'Let's have you out of those
torn clothes. I'll find some of mine for you.' She looked
Maryanne up and down. 'Not that they will be up to
what you are used to. . .'

'Oh, pray do not consider that,' Maryanne said. 'I
am very grateful for your help. But I do hope Mr Saint-
Pierre will not be long.'

The girl laughed. 'Oh, you mean Cap'n Shoecar. He
will be back as soon as maybe.'

Shoecar! How many more names did the man have?
And why were they necessary? The more she found
out about him, the more he seemed to have to hide.
'Do you know the captain very well?' she asked, as she
struggled out of her gown and stripped off the ruined
stockings.'

'My husband served with him—he was very devoted
to him.'

'In the British army?'

Madame Clavier smiled. 'No, miss.' She waited until
Maryanne had washed her face and arms, then set the
bowl of water on the floor at her feet and knelt down
beside it.

'You don't have to do that,' Maryanne said. 'I can
manage.'

'If the cap'n says to look after you, then that's what
I shall do. Come, put your feet in the water.'

Maryanne obeyed. 'Was he in the French army?'

'Who?'

'The captain.'

'Yes.'

'He served Napoleon?'

'He was serving before Boney became Emperor.'
She shrugged. 'Approve of him or not, you couldn't up
and say you'd changed your mind about being a soldier
after you were sworn in, could you?'

So Mark had been right. Did that make her feel any
differently? 'But you're English.'

'Michel, my husband, was French,' she said. 'He

died of his wounds after the Battle of Orthez. 'Twas only a month before the end of the war. If only. . .' She busied herself at Maryanne's feet. 'But there, it's no good sighing for what might have been. The cap'n promised him he'd look out for me, so he brought me back to England and found me this place.' Her voice betrayed the devotion she had for the man who had helped her. 'But for him. . .'

Maryanne reached down and put a hand on her shoulder. 'I am so sorry. It must have been dreadful for you.'

'Yes, but I tell myself Michel's at peace now and he wouldn't have settled in England and he dared not stay in France, not after. . .' She stopped suddenly as if she realised she was being indiscreet. 'You were lucky you weren't trampled to death, miss.'

'Yes, I had no idea how unruly a crowd can become. It was like a great tide, unable to stop. And for one man. The Duke is greatly loved, is he not?'

'Yes, miss.' She sat back on her heels and spread the cloth over her knees, then she lifted Maryanne's foot on to it and began very carefully to pat it dry. 'You'll need a salve on your heel, miss. I'll go fetch some and a gown for you.'

She disappeared and Maryanne was left sitting on the settle in her underskirt with her bare feet stuck out in front of her. So, the Frenchman had been a captain in Napoleon's army and he was known as Shoecar in military company. Put him with the ton in an elegant drawing-room and he became Adam Saint-Pierre, the dandy. And, yet again, dress him in labouring clothes and set him down in the country and he became Jack Daw. Why, oh, why?

The brandy had made her drowsy and she was warm and comfortable; it was a pity she had to dress again and go out. If she stayed, would she learn more about Adam? But Mark must be searching for her and going mad with anxiety. And she had been compromised enough. Not that it was her rescuer's fault; it was she who had been foolish, just as she had been foolish at the ball. It seemed she was fated to find herself in the Frenchman's arms. Mark would never understand that, but suddenly she found she didn't care. She lay back and shut her eyes.

When Adam returned, he found her curled up like a kitten, fast asleep.

CHAPTER FIVE

MARYANNE stirred a little but did not open her eyes; she was too comfortable and, if truth be known, reluctant to let go of her dreams and face reality.

'What are you going to do?' The whispered words of the woman penetrated Maryanne's consciousness.

'I don't know. What can I do?'

'Go and see Danbury.'

'No.' Adam almost forgot to whisper. 'Not yet. I must have proof, and, besides, until the Count's affairs are settled. . .'

'Pooh to that. What is the Count de Challac to you? Let him take care of his own affairs. You watch out for yourself. Even in England, even after the war is ended, there is danger. . .'

'Who told you that?'

'Mr Rudge's housekeeper.'

'Jeannie should have held her tongue.'

'Don't blame her. I asked and she is worried about you. And now you have made a fool of yourself over this one.'

Maryanne kept her eyes tight shut and lay very still, knowing she ought to let them know she was now fully awake, but unwilling to do so.

'Not a fool,' he said, and his voice ground out his anger. 'A coward and that is worse.'

'Anyone who knows you knows that is nonsense. Are you going through with the race?'

'Of course.'

'Did you go to Hatchett's?'

'Yes, the new curricle will be ready by the end of the week.'

'Markham has promised to lend you his greys, but I

advise you to have some practice or that young blood will beat you.'

'I have no time for practice, I shall have to rely on luck.'

'Luck will not be enough. If you are determined to win, then you will need more help than that. What is it they say? All's fair in love and war.'

'This is not war.' He paused slightly before going on. 'Nor love, come to that.'

The dream Maryanne had been holding on to finally faded to nothing. Once again she was faced with her own foolishness; once again she was in a predicament of her own making. Why had she not stayed close to Mark? Why had she allowed herself to be carried into this house? How many people had seen it happen? How many people would learn about it in the next few days? How could she face Lord Danbury, who trusted her to behave as a lady should, and Mark, who had only that morning proposed to her? She opened her eyes and turned towards the speakers.

Adam was standing by the hearth, staring morosely into the empty grate. Beside him stood Lady Markham, wearing a blue silk burnous with the hood thrown back. She heard Maryanne stir and turned towards her.

'There, my dear, awake at last.'

'Yes. I don't know why I fell asleep like that.'

'I'm afraid we put something in your drink,' Adam said. 'Not to harm you, just to keep you here.'

'Keep me? Am I a prisoner?'

'Lord, no!' He laughed, but she did not smile. The words 'nor love' burned themselves into her brain so that everything he did and said took on a more sinister aspect and even his laughter seemed no longer genuine. 'Jeannie was afraid you would do something foolish like trying to find your erstwhile escort.'

'What is foolish about that?'

'Oh, my dear,' Lady Markham put in. 'Just think. You cannot go through the streets alone and on foot, looking for someone who might be anywhere, even discounting the scandal of arriving home looking like that.' She indicated Maryanne's borrowed clothes.

'But Mark will be very worried.'

'And feeling guilty too, I hope. He should not have taken you into the crowd and he certainly should not have let you out of his sight.'

'We were celebrating our engagement,' she said. If he had denied love, then she must let him know she did not care; she had other fish to fry.

'Engagement?'

'Yes. He proposed this morning and I accepted.'

'*Mon Dieu*!' He began poking with a hessian-booted foot at the logs which lay in the grate.

'Is there anything wrong in that?' she demanded.

He faced her. 'Nothing at all. My felicitations, ma'am. When is the ceremony to be?'

'We haven't decided yet.' Why did she feel no elation, no joy, no swifter beating of her heart at the prospect? 'You are the first to be told.'

He bowed stiffly. 'I am honoured.' He turned to Lady Markham. 'We had better do something about salvaging Miss Paynter's reputation before the Honourable Mark changes his mind and I have to marry her in his place.'

'I wouldn't agree to marry you however compromised I had been,' Maryanne retorted. 'So you may relieve yourself of that worry.'

'Come, my dear, you are a little distraught,' Lady Markham said, taking Maryanne's arm. 'And small wonder. Let's leave this grumpy man to his own devices. I've come to take you home with me.'

'It's very kind of you, but I must go back to Danbury House—everyone will be worried.'

Beth Markham gave a little sniff as if she didn't believe it. 'No, they won't, for I sent a message that you are with me and won't be returning until tomorrow. I asked them to send your maid with some fresh clothes. You can't return to Danbury House looking like that.'

'Tomorrow, but why?' She was acutely aware of Adam standing with his back to the fireplace, watching her, but she dared not look at him in case he saw the bleakness in her eyes.

'You need to get over your ordeal, my dear, and, besides, it would be better for you to be seen returning home with me than with. . .'

Maryanne began to laugh shakily. 'How kind of you to worry about my reputation, but I think it might well be too late.'

'Of course it isn't, my dear. It was unwise of Mr Danbury to take you into the common crowd, but there was nothing disreputable about it, though, if my husband had not been among the group welcoming Wellington and seen you lost and hurt, who knows what might have happened?'

'Your husband?' Maryanne queried, looking from Lady Markham to Adam, whose face betrayed nothing of what he was thinking. 'He saw me?'

'No, but that is what we shall say. It was Markham who rescued you and sent for me, and you were in no state to continue home to Danbury House; in fact you had collapsed and can remember nothing of how you came to be with me.' She laughed suddenly. 'Remember that and all will be well.'

'And Mr Saint-Pierre's part in it?'

'We will leave him out of it, shall we? He is in enough trouble with Mark Danbury as it is.' She turned to Adam. 'Remember what I said about that race.'

'I wish it didn't have to happen,' Maryanne said miserably. 'I'm sure someone will be hurt.'

'Would you rather we fought a duel?' Adam asked.

'No, of course not, but I don't see why you have to do either.'

Lady Markham smiled. 'Oh, the men must test each other's mettle now and again, and racing a pair of horses in harness is rather less dangerous than some of the antics they get up to. And, in any case, I rather think that the real contest is between Mark and the

Duke of Wiltshire. Mr Saint-Pierre was only asked to
join them afterwards, so do not let your conscience
trouble you. Am I not right, Adam?'

'Yes. Miss Paynter need not flatter herself that it has
anything to do with her.' He spoke flatly, his voice cool
and controlled.

Beth laughed and tapped his arm with her parasol.
'Now that was a very ungallant remark, sir, even if it is
true.' She turned to Maryanne. 'I have a closed carriage
outside, so come, let us smuggle you to Bedford Row,
before your family come calling to see how you are. I
want you tucked up in bed by then.' She began hustling
Maryanne towards the door.

Maryanne turned to Adam, her coolness matching
his. 'I must thank you for your help.' He bowed in
acknowledgement and she went on, 'I would also like
to thank Mr Rudge for allowing such a disreputable
character into his house, and Madame Clavier for
looking after me.'

'Robert has gone out,' Adam said. 'And Jeannie is
in the hall with your clothes done up in a parcel.'

'Come along, my dear.' Lady Markham was all
efficient bustle again. 'Doubtless you will be seeing Mr
Rudge again, and Adam too, at the race.'

Maryanne allowed herself a glance at him. He was
looking grim as if that idea displeased him. She desperately wanted to make him smile, to return to the easy
relationship they had had before, but the man who
stood by the hearth and bowed stiffly to her was a
proud stranger. 'I preferred Jack Daw,' she said. 'He
was an altogether more cheerful character.' Then,
without waiting for a reply, she followed Lady
Markham out to her carriage.

She stayed two days at Bedford Row, cosseted like an
invalid. James came to see her, bringing Rose and a
basket of clothes. He told her how worried they had all
been and that Mark had spent hours searching for her.
They were all so relieved to hear she had been found

and very grateful to her ladyship for looking after her.
He made Maryanne feel guilty; she was not ill and
although she had been very distressed at the time she
had soon recovered. 'I feel a fraud,' she told Beth
Markham when he had left. 'He has done so much for
me.'

Lady Markham laughed. 'You must be a little selfish
now and again, my dear, or they will walk all over you.
Mark must be taught a lesson, because he doesn't value
you as a prospective husband should.'

'Oh, I had forgotten I told you that. You won't
repeat it, will you?'

'Why not? The world already knows—the announcement is in the "Thunderer" today.'

The teacup in Maryanne's hand shook as she set it
carefully down on its saucer. So Mark had taken her
prevarication for consent and published their engagement, and Adam would think that was what she had
wanted. Now what was she to do?

'What is the matter, child? You have gone white as
a sheet.'

'Nothing.' She made a sound that was meant to be a
laugh but was almost a sob. Was there no end to her
foolishness? 'I thought that after I went missing he
might change his mind.'

Lady Markham searched her face and Maryanne
knew she had not deceived that astute lady. 'You mean
you hoped he would.'

'No. . . Yes. . . I don't know. Mr Saint-Pierre said I
could not be in love with Mark if I couldn't make up
my mind. Was he right, do you think?'

Beth Markham smiled. 'You must follow your heart,
not your head, in these matters.'

Follow her heart. How could she do that when her
heart was plainly misleading her?

'It's Adam, isn't it?' Beth asked softly. 'I grant he is
a handsome beast, but he has no time for women, you
know.'

Maryanne's spirit returned. 'You do surprise me.'

She stopped when she realised she was about to blurt out that Adam had kissed her, and more than once. Lady Markham, kind as she was, was not averse to gossip, and for the family's sake she must say nothing of that.

'He has other things on his mind just now.'

'Curricle races?'

Lady Markham laughed. 'Not only that.' She paused. 'He is very concerned for the plight of the French aristocrats who want to return to their estates now Louis has been restored to the throne. They want to pick up their lives again, but their homes are in ruins, their lands confiscated and many of them are heavily in debt, dependent on their English hosts. Adam is trying to help them. There are others, of course, who would stop him; they do not want to see a return to the old regime of rich and poor.' She smiled suddenly. 'After all the years of war, they are all poor, peasants and aristocrats alike. The country is in a mess.'

'Is that why he is in England?'

'Partly, though I believe he intends to return to France soon.'

'When will he go?' Her heart felt like lead. It was no good deceiving herself; she wanted him to stay, she wanted him to stay for her sake. But she was engaged to marry Mark and there was no way out of that without a scandal. Perhaps it would have been better if everyone knew where she had been those few hours when she was 'lost'; Mark would have called off the engagement, there would have been no announcement and Adam would have felt duty bound to marry her. Duty bound! Was that what she wanted? No! No! If he did not love her, then she must put him from her mind and try to pretend she had never met him.

'I don't know. Not until after the race. But I hear the Dowager Duchess is not well again and the Duke has returned to Castle Cedars, so the race has been postponed yet again.'

'Perhaps it will never happen.'

'Oh, it will take place, I'll lay odds on it; there is too much money at stake to abandon it.'

'How foolish men are!'

'Indeed, yes.' She smiled cheerfully at Maryanne. 'But what would we do without them?'

Maryanne did not consider that question required an answer, and turned to gaze out of the window. 'I think I should return home.'

'Tomorrow,' her ladyship said firmly. 'I have said you need at least two days to recover, and I want everyone to see you; there must not be the least doubt in anyone's mind where you have been staying. I mean to take you back in style.'

Lady Markham was as good as her word. The carriage that took them both to Danbury House was painted in a pale pink, with elegant lines of a deeper shade of the same colour. The rims of its wheels were black, but the spokes were of a deep pink, and even the horses had pink plumes. On the high box sat a negro boy in pink satin livery with a huge black turban. Lady Markham, followed by a bemused Maryanne, sailed from the house to get into it, a vision in pink satin and net. 'I had it done especially for the celebrations,' she said, patting the seat beside her and nodding her head so that the long feather in her hat bounced up and down. 'What do you think of it?'

'It is very—er—striking,' Maryanne said, as they moved off up the street at a pace slow enough to ensure that everyone saw them.

Her ladyship laughed. 'I'll lay odds that this time next week there will be any number of pink carriages in the park.'

'Then yours will no longer stand out.'

'Oh, then I shall change it for another. I like to set the fashion, not follow it.'

If her ladyship's plan had been to make sure that they were stared at, she certainly succeeded. Everyone turned to look as the barouche went by, and some laughed while others called out a ribald comment, to which Beth Markham had a ready reply. Maryanne felt like a goldfish in a bowl. 'If you have something worth seeing, then flaunt it,' her ladyship said. 'It doesn't matter if it is ugly or beautiful; there is nothing worse than being ignored.' She laughed. 'I, too, have a reputation to preserve.'

'How did you meet Mr Saint-Pierre?' Maryanne asked. She could not imagine Adam being attracted to such flamboyance.

'Robert Rudge introduced us. Adam came to England looking for his father's lawyer, but old Joseph was dead and Robert had taken on the practice. He realised Adam needed an entrée into society and he thought of me.' She laughed. 'He has been an apt pupil, but then, with his breeding, it is hardly surprising.'

'His breeding?'

Her ladyship, caught out in an indiscretion, laughed in an embarrassed way. 'I believe his father was a wine grower, a landowner of some importance.'

'What else do you know of him?'

'I gather everything was lost during the Reign of Terror except a little money that Monsieur Saint-Pierre had smuggled to London. More than that I cannot tell you.'

'What has Mr Saint-Pierre got against the Danbury family?'

'Nothing that I know of.' Her ladyship reached up and tapped the young negro with her fan. 'You may whip the cattle up a bit, Dandy, we have dawdled enough.'

Maryanne was almost jolted from her seat as the horses seemed to take to the air, and they fairly flew over the ground, weaving in and out of the traffic like a flashing pink comet. They slowed to a walk again as they entered Piccadilly and drew up outside Danbury House.

'Now, don't forget your story,' her ladyship admonished as the front door was opened by a footman. 'And please, for my sake, do not look too robustly healthy.'

Caroline and Mrs Ryfield were alone in the house and Lady Markham stayed only long enough to pay her respects. Maryanne dreaded her going, knowing she would be subjected to a cross-examination as soon as the extraordinary carriage had rolled away. She tried to forestall it by asking, 'Where is Mark?'

'He is out,' Caroline told her. 'Did you expect him to wait in, kicking his heels, until you decided to come home?'

'Lady Markham's physician recommended two days in bed for me and she would not hear of me leaving.'

'How cosy for you!' the younger woman said. 'Comfortably in bed while Mark scoured the city, imagining all sorts of fate for you, each worse than the last, though why he bothers with you I do not know. If you got yourself trampled underfoot, you have no one but yourself to blame.'

'I fainted in the crush,' Maryanne said, refusing to rise to the bait. 'Fortunately Lord Markham saw me being carried from the crowd and had me taken to the home of a friend while he sent for his wife.' It was as near the truth as she could make it without denying the story that Lady Markham had told. 'His housekeeper lent me some clothes, my own were badly torn. I shall have to return them.' At least taking the gown back would give her an opportunity to talk to Jeannie again and she might learn more about Captain Shoecar from her.

'Tell me this friend's name. We must thank him properly.'

'I don't know it. I was not there very long and, besides, I had fainted. . .'

'Then how will you return the clothes?'

Maryanne was nonplussed; she was not used to telling untruths and it was easy for Caroline to see that she was hiding something. Oh, why did it all have to be so complicated? Why couldn't she tell everyone that

Adam had rescued her? But no one, especially Caroline, would believe they had been in the same place at the same time quite by chance. She found herself wondering if the secrecy was more for his benefit than to protect her reputation and, if that was so, was she helping to cover up something evil or illegal?

'Well?' Caroline's voice broke in on her thoughts.

'I shall have to ask Lady Markham his direction, shan't I? she replied tartly. 'Now I'm going to my room. Please send for me when Mark returns.'

It was cool in her room because the window was open and a light breeze played with the curtains, throwing a pattern of shadow across the wall. A bird which had been perching on the window-sill flew up and into one of the trees in the garden. She ran to the window and saw it perching on a branch, regarding her with its head on one side. In its beak it held something shining. 'A jackdaw,' she said aloud. 'The little thief!' Jackdaw. Jack Daw. Shoecar. *Choucas*. She began to laugh. Oh, what a joke, and all at her expense, she was sure. *Choucas* was the French word for jackdaw. She stopped laughing suddenly. Jackdaws were known for their thieving. Was that how he got his name? Was he no more than a common thief?

She sank into a chair by the window and watched the bird fly away. It was free as the air, free as he was; she was the only one in captivity, captive of her own stupidity. Now it was too late, she realised why she had been reluctant to accept Mark. She loved Jack Daw, who had stolen her heart, stolen it with nothing more substantial than a kiss. Was that grounds enough to imagine herself in love? After all, what did she know of the man? Nothing except that he had brown eyes that could be tender one minute, cold the next, that he could make her laugh, but could also make her cry, that his mother had been English, that he was involved in some way with the French *émigrés* and he didn't like the Danburys.

On the other hand, Mark's background was an open
book, his intentions clear and unequivocal; there was
no mystery about him. If she married Mark, she knew
exactly what her life would be like. Why did she persist
in trying to compare the incomparable? She leaned
forward as the jackdaw swooped on a group of spar-
rows pecking at crumbs on the grass, scattering them,
then soared away into the sky. *Le choucas*, wild, free,
a thief.

Mark returned just in time for supper. He greeted her
with a swift peck on the cheek and a, 'Hello,
Maryanne, glad to see you are no worse for your
adventure,' then turned to the subject of the curricle
race, which he had decided was to be held in the
grounds of Castle Cedars. He was so full of it, she
could not speak to him of their engagement, which he
took so much for granted.

'His Grace declines to return to London,' he said, as
they went into the dining-room. 'He maintains it is
because of his mother's illness, but I think he'd as lief
cancel the whole thing, having no stomach for anything
that requires a little exertion. . .'

'Then why don't you call it off?' Maryanne put in.
'Is it so important?'

'Of course it is.' He seated himself opposite her and
beckoned a servant. 'A man must pay his debts.'

'And suppose you lose?'

'I will not lose.' His features were set in hard lines,
his dark brows drawn together in angry determination.
'I have the best team in the land and I *can't* lose.'

'And have the others agreed to race at Castle
Cedars?'

'Others?' He watched the footman heap his plate
with food. 'Oh, you mean that rascally Frenchman. He
agreed to any time or place I cared to mention and he
cannot back out of it now without losing what little
honour he has.'

'Do you hate him so much?'

He turned sharply to search her face and she felt the colour rising in her cheeks. 'You look embarrassed, madam, but I hope it is not because you have a liking for the damned fellow's kisses.'

'No, no, how can you say that?' She felt like a Judas; she should have told him the truth. She cared for Adam's kisses more than Adam cared for hers. He had made a fool of her and denied he had any feeling for her and that must be the end of it. Mark, at least, was a gentleman, worth two of Adam Saint-Pierre.

'It was you who suggested they should race in the country,' Caroline said. 'You can hardly grumble if Mark takes your advice.'

'If we race on private land there will be no chance of injuring bystanders, will there?' Mark said.

'No, I suppose not.'

'You might show a little more enthusiasm, my dear— the outcome affects you too, you know.'

'How?' Surely he didn't mean that she was included in the wager? She shuddered and took a sip of wine to steady herself. 'I have been assured that it has nothing to do with me.'

'Oh, and who told you that? Could it have been that damned Frenchie? Have you seen him again? If you have——'

'It was Lady Markham,' she said quickly. 'She said the race was really between you and His Grace to settle a gambling debt.'

'So it is,' he said, regaining his good humour. 'But the outcome affects our future prospects. You must surely be interested in whether you are marrying a rich man or a poor man?'

'I am not marrying you for your money,' she said. 'In fact. . .' She stopped suddenly. Had she been going to say she did not want to marry him at all? If so, it was badly timed, with the whole family present, not to mention two or three servants standing silently in the background, able to hear every word. She was saved having to continue by his lordship.

'Mark, I sincerely hope the stakes are not as high as that. A modest wager is one thing, but to risk all. . .'

Mark laughed. 'A paltry few pounds and a pair of horses—what's that, if not modest? I am going to Castle Cedars tomorrow to oversee the staking out of the course and make the final arrangements. I take it everyone is coming too?'

'I wouldn't miss it for the world,' Caroline said, before anyone else could answer. 'His Grace has thrown the whole house open and half the ton will be there. He has asked me to be his hostess, so I shan't be going home to Beckford.'

'In that case,' James said firmly, 'I think we had all better stay at Castle Cedars, so that I may be on hand to help.'

Caroline had not exaggerated; the country home of the Duke of Wiltshire was crowded with guests, many of whom, Maryanne was convinced, he did not even know. And because Mark was busy supervising the laying out of the course for the race and Caroline was in a seventh heaven ordering His Grace's servants about and deciding on who should have which room, what they would all eat and how they would all be seated at the table, Maryanne was largely ignored. On the second day, after paying her respects to her grand-mother, she decided to go for a walk through the woods.

Estate workers were busy marking out the course with stakes driven into the ground and joined by white-painted rope. Maryanne followed its line where it began in a meadow behind the house, across the park and then up over a rise, where she was able to look out across the downs, almost to the sea. She stood a moment, breathing deeply, remembering the walks along the shore she had taken with her mother, who had looked wistfully out across the grey sea as if her happiness lay beyond it. Had she been thinking of her family? Had she ever wished they could be reunited?

Had she accepted the estrangement as the price she had to pay for love? If only she had been able to talk to her about it, Maryanne might have been better able to understand her own feelings now.

She remembered her own words with something akin to anguish—'a man I can love and one who loves me'. At no time had she wondered what she would do if she fell in love with someone who did not return that love; it put a whole new complexion on things.

She made herself stop thinking about it; it would be time enough to make decisions after the race, after Mark or Adam or the Duke had won, after all the excitement was over and the guests had gone. She turned and followed the white rope as it wound down the hill, round a pond, and entered the wood. Some of the trees had been hacked down to make the path wide enough for one curricle, perhaps two at a pinch, and the ground levelled. The felled trees had been stripped of their branches and the logs piled up to one side of the new track. This part of the wood had been spoiled, desecrated for the sake of one day's sport, for man's vanity which went by the name of honour. She could hear the sound of axes and men's voices as she made her way along the course.

"Elp he said he needed, and 'elp 'e shall 'ave,' said one somewhat breathlessly. 'This 'n should do it.'

'How d'yer know it'll work?'

"Cos I shall see that it do. Now do you tidy up them branches and get 'em off'n the track.' The man who had been speaking looked up as Maryanne came round the slight curve in the track which brought her into sight. 'Mornin', miss.' He was standing by a large oak which had just been felled. Its foliage had been stripped and it had been cut into logs and these were piled alongside the track. His companion was busy dragging the smaller branches along the path and piling them up to one side. 'It's a grand day for it,' he went on, as Maryanne stopped.

'Yes, indeed, but what a pity to lose so many fine trees.'

'They'll make good logs for the winter and there's plenty more; don't you fret over a few trees. Why, they felled thousands when they wanted warships, and you can't tell the difference.' He kicked the ground. 'Just look at all them acorns—they'll most on 'em make trees theirselves, one day.'

'Yes, I suppose so.'

'You going' to watch the race, miss?'

'Yes.'

'Won't see much in the woods,' he said, giving a meaningful look at his companion, who had stopped work and was staring at her with his mouth open. 'Why not go back to the park and see Lord Danbury start 'em off? Then you c'n move over to the finish and cheer the winner in.'

They stood, blocking the path, and she was reluctant to force a way past them. 'You don't want to be on the track when they come along, do you, miss? Three curricles going full tilt will take a deal of stopping, 'specially on this narrow part.'

'There is plenty of time,' she said. 'They are not starting until two o'clock.'

'Beg pardon, miss, they've changed it. It's noon the gun's bein' fired. Mr Danbury said they'd all have a better appetite for dinner once the race was over with. He came along an' told us so hisself.'

She had no idea of the time but it had gone ten when she set out and she had spent some time on the hill before coming into the wood; it could not be far off midday. She turned to retrace her steps, leaving the men to finish clearing the track.

She had not gone far when she heard the crack of a pistol and a distant cheer. They had started! How long before they reached the spot where she stood? The wood-cutter had been right about the narrowness of the track; she did not want to be caught in the middle of it. She stepped off the path and among the trees to wait until they had passed.

If was another minute to two before she heard the thunder of hoofs, the crack of whips and the shouts of the drivers, and then they came into view. Mark was in the lead, but only just. He stood in the vehicle like a Roman charioteer, cracking his whip over the backs of his horses and yelling encouragement to them. Behind him the Duke and Adam were neck and neck, their horses thundering side by side and the wheels of their carriages almost locking. Adam looked grim and determined, while His Grace's face was purple with the effort of controlling his high-spirited horses. He was staring ahead at the narrowing path and yet Maryanne had the feeling he saw nothing, that he was lost to outside influences. She clapped her hand over her mouth to stop the cry which might have distracted them as they hurtled past her with their outside wheels off the prepared track and rumbling over undergrowth. When they came to the narrow part of the course, where the logs were piled up, one of them would have to give way. She found herself running after them, without knowing why she did it. They disappeared round the curve. She heard a shout of warning, then the sound of a crash and after that the neighing of frightened horses.

She stopped abruptly when she rounded the bend and saw the carnage. The first curricle must have touched one of the piles of logs and brought the whole lot cascading down. One of the carriages had been smashed beyond recognition, the other lay on its side. A horse lay dead, another lay shrieking its terror, and the others had broken free and were careering down the path and out of sight. She could see neither driver.

She heard a stream of curses which, luckily for her, were mostly in French, and ran over to Adam's upturned curricle. He hauled himself out of it and stood beside her. His face and hands were cut and bruised and his clothing was torn, but he appeared to have no other injuries.

She realised she was sobbing as she put out a hand to help him. 'Oh, I am sorry, so sorry. . .'

'Stop talking nonsense, woman,' he said gruffly. 'I'm not hurt, at least, no more than a few bumps where there shouldn't be. Go and look to His Grace.'

She turned to look around her. The Duke's curricle was nothing more than firewood, crushed under a great tree-trunk, and there was blood all over the place. She was almost afraid to look.

Adam strode over to it ahead of her and heaved at the tree-trunk which imprisoned the curricle, hacking at the greenery with the little dagger he always wore at his belt. 'Here, give me a hand.' She lent her weight to his and they managed to shift the timber far enough to see the Duke, and then she was almost sick on the spot. His Grace was laying in a grotesque position, his legs doubled up under him, his head flung back and blood pouring from a wound in his chest where a sliver of wood, as sharp as a sword, stuck out through this torn coat. Adam reached out and touched him. There was no response; he did not groan or flinch, nor was there the slightest flicker in his eyes. 'He's dead,' he said flatly.

'What are we going to do?'

He stopped throwing broken pieces of wood to one side and looked at her, as if for the first time. 'Where did you spring from?'

'I was standing in the trees when you went past. I was going for a walk. There were two woodmen here—they must have heard what happened. Do you think they went for help?'

He shrugged. 'If they were responsible for the dangerous way those trunks were piled up, I hardly think they'd wait about to face the music.'

'But you were both trying to get through the gap at once; one of you should have given way.' Had she really meant to sound as if she was blaming him? She wanted to explain that her relief at finding him unhurt made her say things she didn't really mean. It was no more his fault than the Duke's, and really the track had been made too narrow. But, before she could frame the words, Mark, together with two or three estate workers, came hurrying through the trees and there was no chance to say anything.

Adam's curricle was righted, the horses caught and harnessed to it so that the body could be taken back to the house. Maryanne, walking beside Mark as he led the horses, moved as if in a nightmare. No one spoke until they came out of the trees into the sunlight of the park, where a crowd of people thronged about the finishing tape, many of them still holding the glasses with which they had toasted Mark's victory. Now they turned, almost in unison, and watched the approaching cavalcade, Mark, leading the horses, the estate workers, Adam and Maryanne.

It seemed to take a lifetime to reach the silent watchers and then everything exploded round them; hands reaching out, exclamations of horror, a scream from Caroline, and James, tight-lipped, sending everyone away and taking charge of the situation, issuing orders and then leaving to go and break the news to the Dowager. Above it all, Mark's voice was loud and insistent. 'He could not win by fair means; he had to resort to trickery. In my book, that is murder.'

'No! No!' Maryanne cried. 'You can't mean that, you can't. It was an accident, the path was too narrow. . .' She stopped speaking, suddenly aware that everyone else had become silent and turned towards her. 'I mean,' she added nervously, 'those two men must have misunderstood your orders about the trees.'

'What two men?' His dark eyes narrowed. 'What are you talking about?'

'The woodmen I met. They were clearing the wood.'

'That was all done yesterday; there was no one working there today.'

'But I saw them. . .'

He took her arm to lead her away from the curious onlookers. 'Maryanne, my dear, you are distraught and no wonder.' His voice was calm and affectionate, though his grip was painfully tight. 'Go and rest and leave us to do what we have to do.'

She looked past him to where Adam stood beside his curricle from which the body had been removed. He did not speak but his expression was one of fury and there was a noticeable twitch to the corner of his eye which lifted the tiny scar and gave his face a lop-sided appearance; one side was unlined and handsome, the other bore the evidence of a life she could only guess at. He had been a soldier; death was no stranger to him, but he would not kill needlessly—she had to believe that, wanted his assurance of it. She pulled herself away from Mark and took a step towards him, then stopped when she realised there was nothing she could do or say which would change anything. The Duke was dead, killed in an accident, and when Mark had time to think clearly he would realise how unjust he had been.

She turned and went into the house and up to her room. Even there, she could not escape; her window overlooked the park, where everyone had gathered in such high spirits for the start and finish of the race and where they now milled about, discussing the disaster and speculating about the reason for it. The speculation would go on for days, weeks perhaps, and it had not been helped by Mark's outburst. What had made him say it? What justification was there for it? He had been responsible for laying out the course, not Adam.

Her knees buckled and she sank on to her bed as Beth Markham's words came forcefully to her mind. 'Luck will not be enough. If you are determined to win, then you will need more help than that.' They found an echo in the woodman's words: ''Elp he said he needed, and 'elp 'e shall 'ave.'

From across the room, her reflection came back at her from the long mirror, a white-faced, wide-eyed young lady in a torn white gown, covered in mud and blood. Her hair had come down and there was a leafy twig caught in it. It was like looking at a stranger, a wild, deranged stranger. 'Meet Miss Maryanne Paynter,' she said, with a cracked laugh. 'Granddaughter of the fourth Duke of Wiltshire, intended bride of the Honourable Mark Danbury and prize fool. Oh. . .' The girl in the mirror put a hand up that shook uncontrollably, and removed the twig. 'Correct that. Not the Honourable Mark—things have changed; he is the Marquis of Beckford now that his lordship is the new Duke. The lady has made a good match.'

She flung herself back on the bed and pulled the pillow over her head, both to deny that accusing reflection and shut out the sounds from outside, but she could not shut out her thoughts. They whirled about in her head, giving her no peace, and at their centre was a tall proud figure of a man with laughing brown eyes and gentle hands. 'Oh, Adam, why? Why?' But she was not talking about the accident.

CHAPTER SIX

OUTSIDE the sun shone and the birds sang but inside the church was cold. Through the open door Maryanne could see the grave-diggers, standing by the newly opened vault, waiting to seal it again. Only the essential work of looking after the animals was being done, and even the haymaking had been halted, so that all the estate workers and servants could attend the funeral. They stood at the back, in their Sunday best, heads downcast, fumbling with prayer books, and waited while friends and relatives of the family filed into their places. The day seemed timeless, eternal, caught between the living and the dead.

As the rector began the service, Maryanne, standing beside a tight-lipped Mark, became aware that a latecomer had tiptoed in through the open door and had slipped into a pew at the back of the church. It was not until they turned to file out behind the coffin that she realised, with a gasp of astonishment, that it was Adam; as far as she knew he had left immediately after Henry's body had been carried into the house. She glanced at Mark, but he continued to acknowledge the curtsies of the village women and the nodding heads of the men, and did not appear to have noticed him. He had maintained that Adam's departure and the disappearance of the two workmen, who had not been estate workers at all and had probably been paid by the Frenchman to upset the logs, was a sure sign of the man's guilt, and he would never dare show his face again. But here he was, tall and upright as ever, his head held proudly, for all the world as if he had a right to be among the congregation. If Mark had him arrested and she was called upon to give evidence, what would she do? Could she maintain her silence?

Ought she to? She looked across the aisle at James, but he had not seen him either.

He had dismissed Mark's accusations as something said in the heat of the moment, and she could not bring herself to voice her own suspicions, even when he questioned her about what had happened. She had suggested that Mr Saint-Pierre himself was the best person to ask. 'I would do so if I knew where he was,' he had said. 'He is a most elusive gentleman. I tried to find him in London, but by the time I had tracked him down he had left town.'

There had been a note in his voice which reminded her of their earlier conversation about Adam. Something had happened in the past which made him sad, someone he had known, something he had done or not done, and Adam figured in it somewhere. It made her feel guilty that she had not told him the truth about her rescue and her visit to Robert Rudge's home. 'I spoke to him when he arrived here only minutes before the race began,' James went on. 'We arranged to talk later, but, with all the commotion, he left before we could do so.'

She risked a glance behind her, but Adam had not come out with the rest of the congregation. She waited until the interment was over and the mourners were making their way back to the house, then touched Mark's arm. 'I left my gloves in the pew; you go on.' Before he could offer to fetch them for her, she hurried back into the church.

Adam was standing looking up at the memorial tablets to generations of Danburys set in the walls, but turned towards her when he heard her step. 'Miss Paynter.' He inclined his head.

'What are you doing here?' She found herself trembling as she stopped beside him. 'Don't you think the family is upset enough without you intruding on their grief?'

'I have no wish to intrude.' His voice was cold

enough to send a chill through her heart. 'I came to pay my respects and offer my condolences.'

'You know Mark has accused you of deliberately. . .' She paused. looking for a word other than murder, though it was the one Mark had used.

'I know.'

'Then why come back?'

He smiled slowly, but the smile did not reach his brown eyes. 'I said he was a rogue, didn't I? But even I did not think he would stoop so low.'

'What do you mean?'

'The accident, if accident it was, has made him a marquis and heir to a dukedom. And I make a very good scapegoat.' His voice was bitter.

She was shocked into silence. It could not be true. Neither Mark nor Adam had wanted the Duke dead; it had been a terrible accident caused by avarice and pride, but it was not murder. 'Oh, Adam, is there to be no end to it?' It was only after she had spoken that she realised she had used his given name and felt the colour rush into her cheeks.

'There has to be an end,' he said, controlling the anguish in his voice with an effort. Did she know how beautiful she was, how difficult this was for him? 'One way or another we have to make an end of it. I am leaving, going back to France.'

'Running away?' It was out before she could stop it.

'No.' He wanted to take her by the shoulders and shake her, to make her see what she was doing to him, but if he touched her he knew he could never bring himself to leave her. 'I do not run away.'

She laughed. 'Like a good general, doing what is expedient at the time, is that it? Will you, like Napoleon, return with the violets?'

'I do not think so.' He paused, watching her face. 'The Danburys will be rid of me.'

'Why do you hate us so?'

'Us? You include yourself in that?' he asked softly. 'Do you know, I had never thought of you as one of them?' He put out a hand and lifted a stray curl from her cheek with one finger and let it fall again. 'I do not hate at all. If war has taught me one thing, it is that hate is a dangerous and destructive emotion and leads to muddled thinking and ill-considered actions.'

'Then what have you got against the family that needs a cool head and careful planning?'

He smiled. 'Nothing, my dear Miss Paynter. It is over now. I came to say goodbye.'

Goodbye. The word had such a finality about it that she wanted to cry. She had asked if there was to be no end and, although she had been referring to the accusations and enmity between him and Mark, he had answered her in his own way. She could not look into his face for fear of betraying the misery she felt. 'When do you leave?'

'Tomorrow I sail from Portsmouth.'

'Then go now,' she said sharply. 'Go before Mark finds you here. If he sees us together——'

'Mark! Mark! It's always Mark with you, isn't it? Well, so be it. I wish you happiness.'

She had meant that if Mark arrived there would be more accusations, perhaps another challenge, perhaps a constable sent for, and all she wanted was to prevent that; but he was so angry that she could not explain.

'And you? What of you?' Her voice was barely above a whisper. 'Will you go back to the army if Napoleon rises again?'

'I may have to.'

'Then let us pray he doesn't, for it will make us enemies.'

'What will you do?'

'Me? Go back to the others. . .'

'And pretend nothing has happened?'

'Nothing has happened.'

'No,' he said bitterly. 'Nothing changes.' He took a step towards her, then stopped. '*Sacre Dieu*! This is impossible.'

'What is impossible?'

'Saying goodbye.' He took her shoulders in his big hands and held her at arm's length, searching her face. 'Come with me. Now. . .'

She was so taken aback she could do nothing but stare up at him with wide violet eyes. 'You must be out of your senses,' she said at last. 'I could not leave without telling anyone, even if I wanted to, and if you think I am the sort of woman who would desert the man I am engaged to marry to run off with the first handsome rake who propositioned me, then you have made a big mistake.'

He threw back his head and laughed aloud, making the sound echo round the empty church. 'So I am a handsome rake, am I? If that is how you think of me, then so be it—I will give you something to remember.' He took her face in his hands and lowered his mouth to hers. She squirmed in his arms, but he would not let her go and his lips were sweet on hers, making her tremble with longing. She gave up the struggle and let herself go and then very slowly put her arms round his neck and clung to him, returning his kisses. Her senses reeled and her knees buckled, but she leaned into him and felt the warmth and strength of his body against hers, supporting her. It was a moment she was to remember with bitter tears and great anguish for a very long time.

'Goodbye, little duchess,' he said softly, then put her from him and strode out of the church. She sank into a pew and was still sitting there, in a daze, when Mark came to find her.

'Maryanne, what are you doing?' His voice burst stridently into her bemused brain. 'I have been waiting an age. Come along, do.' He stopped speaking when he realised she had not been listening. 'Is anything wrong? You are not ill, are you?'

'No.' She picked up her gloves and reticule and stood up slowly, testing the weakness in her limbs, and was surprised to find that she could stand without falling over. 'I felt a little faint. It's the heat and this gown is so heavy.'

He took her arm. 'When everyone has left you can change. We must keep up appearances, but it's no use pretending we are all broken-hearted, is it? Henry was a wastrel, even his own mother acknowledges that, and I for one do not intend to let it make any difference to me.' He laughed suddenly. 'Except it is gratifying to be called "my lord" by all and sundry, though I am not so sure Father likes being "Your Grace"; it doesn't seem to fit him somehow.'

'No,' she said. 'He is a man of the people.'

He looked sideways at her. 'Perhaps. But when I am the Duke of Wiltshire——'

'Mark! How can you speak so with your cousin hardly cold in his grave and your father still a comparatively young man?'

He smiled. 'No, my dear, you are right to scold me. Now, as to the wedding.'

'Whose wedding?'

He stopped walking and turned towards her. 'Why, ours of course. It will have to be postponed while we are officially in mourning, but we can still make plans for it. The ceremony and reception will naturally be held here. And afterwards we will make our home at Beckford Hall.' He began walking again and she fell into step beside him like an automaton. 'Father will live here from now on and so will Caroline until she marries. Henry was never right for her and I told her so.' He did not seem to be aware that she was only half listening. 'I am going to Beckford tomorrow. You'll come, won't you?'

'If you wish.'

'Of course I wish it. You may want to make changes to the house; you can plan those while I go round the estate. Where would you like to go for a wedding trip? Shall we go to Italy? Now the war is over, there will be no difficulties. We could go to Venice and Rome, or even Vienna. All the heads of state will be there for the Congress. . .'

Too miserable to stop him, too full of her parting from Adam, too beset by doubts and a terrible sense of doom, Maryanne could not speak and allowed him to go on, making one grandiose plan after another, until she could bear it no longer.

'Stop! Stop!' she cried out. 'Can't you see how impossible it is?'

He looked genuinely puzzled. 'Impossible? Maryanne, my dear, nothing is impossible, given the will and the money to do it. You are not worried about what it will all cost, are you? When all's said and done, I won that race, and Father, as the heir, will have to pay old Henry's debts, even if it does stretch him a bit. Father will fork out for the wedding too, being your guardian. Besides, you will have your inheritance in a couple of months.'

She stopped to stare at him, looking for any sign of the Mark who had been so kind to her when she first joined the family, the Mark who seemed to be so careful of her reputation, the Mark who had professed to have 'feelings'; but his grey eyes looked back at her and failed to stir anything inside her at all. She turned and ran back to the house, intending to go to her room, but at the head of the stairs she changed her mind and went along the corridor to the Dowager Duchess's room. She knocked and was admitted by a nurse.

'Grandmother, may I come and talk to you?'

'Of course, my child; got you down, have they? All that humbug, pretending to mourn, pretending respect, when there isn't one of them wouldn't have put a knife in Henry's back when he was alive if they'd had the courage, concocting virtues for him and forgetting the vices which made them hate him, glossing over the fact that half the ladies swathed in black down there are mothers to his bastard children. Hypocrites, the lot of 'em.' She indicated a chair by the bed.

Maryanne was shocked. 'You can't mean that, Your Grace.'

'Oh, I do. They're all alike.' She paused to get her breath after the longest speech Maryanne had ever heard her make. 'Except James. Didn't fall in the usual Danbury mould for some reason.'

'How was he different?'

She laughed. 'Stubborn. Independent. Couldn't make him conform. Goodness knows what he'll be like now he has the reins in his hand, but I hope he is astute enough to pull the irons out of the fire.' She sighed. 'Thank God I'm too old to worry about it any longer. There is an heir—he has done his duty by the family in that respect.'

'Mark.'

'Yes, and I suppose that is the reason for this unexpected visit. You don't humbug me, child. What is troubling you?'

'I don't think I can marry him. I don't love him.'

'What on earth has love to do with it?'

'Everything,' Maryanne said miserably.

'You are as foolish as your mother. You like Mark, don't you? You have no particular aversion to him?'

'Of course I like him,' she said slowly. 'He has been kind to me, but. . .'

'Kind! Don't you know, child, the Danburys are never kind? They are selfish and arrogant and insular, and Mark is no exception, but that doesn't mean he won't make a good husband, provided you keep him on a tight rein.'

'But I don't want to be like that. I want a man I can look up to, not one I must continually try to master.' Why did she keep thinking of a pair of laughing brown eyes? No woman would ever master the owner of those.

'Bit late to say so now, don't you think? You accepted Mark and the announcement's been made. If you back out now you'll cause a scandal, and this family has had enough of those to last for generations.'

'If you mean my mother. . .'

'Not only Helena; James too, though he had the sense to see the error of his ways and come home.'

Maryanne gasped, suddenly remembering Caroline's accusation that she was one of James's by-blows. 'You mean they ran away together?'

'No, foolish child. James was back before Helena left, though it might have been better if he hadn't been, then there'd have been no one to help her make a fool of herself.' She paused, peering into Maryanne's face in a short-sighted way. 'I can't make you marry Mark, but I advise you to think very carefully before you set the cat among the pigeons. Your inheritance, like your mother's before you, is conditional on your making a marriage approved of by your guardian.'

'In other words, the inheritance is not meant for me, but my husband?' Maryanne asked.

'Yes, but there's nothing out of the ordinary in that. And it would be best kept in the family.'

'It can't be that much, surely?'

'I have no idea how much it is, except that it has been wisely invested ever since your mother left home and it has grown into a sizeable sum. It is the only bit of the family fortunes Henry couldn't get his hands on and squander.'

'My mother gave it up for love. I could give it up for lack of love.'

'And do you think she was happy?' The old lady snorted her derision. 'Living in that hovel in the slums of Portsmouth with that terrible old man. The husband she had sacrificed everything for was never at home and there was barely enough money to feed you both. Do you think she was content? I tell you now, she was miserable.'

Maryanne sat and stared at the old lady as if she were a witch who had put a spell on her; she felt numb. Her mother had loved her father, she had never doubted that, but, when she sat staring into the fire or out across the grey sea, had she been regretting leaving a comfortable home?

'That's made you think, ain't it, girl?' And when Maryanne declined to answer she added, 'What's the matter? In the dismals because I failed to say the comforting words you wanted to hear? You get only home truths in this room, as anyone who knows me will tell you. Now go and find Mark and tell him I want to see him.'

'Will you tell him I can't marry him?' Maryanne pleaded.

'Certainly not. And you won't tell him either, do you hear?' The old lady's voice softened suddenly. 'Believe me, child, I know what I am talking about. Give yourself time to think about it. There is no hurry with the family in mourning.'

Maryanne stood up, dropped a curtsy and left her to look for Mark. The mourners had left, the house guests had gone to their rooms to change for dinner and the servants were clearing away the glasses and crumb-laden plates in the empty drawing-room. She was about to return to her own room when she heard Mark's voice coming from the library. 'I want to enclose the Downend pasture.'

'You will do nothing of the sort,' she heard James answer him. 'It is the villagers' common land.'

'Father, it is no longer considered sensible to have vast tracts of land which are almost unmanageable. The latest thinking is to enclose. You can ask higher rents that way.'

'I refuse to discuss it, Mark. I have always been looked on as a fair landlord, not a greedy one.'

'Are you saying I am greedy, Father? How can I take over the estate if I am not allowed to make decisions?'

'You may decide anything to do with the running of the estate, not the disposing of it. You will rouse the fury of the villagers if you take away their grazing.' He looked up as Maryanne came into the room.

'Maryanne, my dear, were you looking for us?' He sounded relieved by her interruption.

'Grandmother would like to speak to Mark. I came to fetch him.'

Mark drove them to Beckford in his curricle next day. It was an unfortunate choice of vehicle because it reminded Maryanne so forcefully of that tragic race. She found herself musing on the fact that the compensations of being the Marquis of Beckford had overcome his sorrow remarkably well, and then scolded herself for her uncharitable thought.

Once at Beckford, he had a horse saddled and set off to tour the estate, leaving Maryanne to amuse herself. She wandered about the lower rooms and then went upstairs and gazed out of the long window at the end of the corridor across the neatly tended gardens to the park and beyond that to the fields. The villagers were cutting hay, taking advantage of the warm dry weather. There were children working with them and she smiled to herself; attendance at the rectory school would be poor until the work was done and then it would be good until the harvest, when the children would be needed again. She sighed and turned away. As Lady Beckford, she would have money and influence to help the inhabitants of Beckford. She could also do something for all those helpless children orphaned by the war. Mark had asked her to marry him, Adam had not; he had simply suggested going away with him and that was not the action of a gentleman—then why was it so difficult to make what seemed, on the surface, to be an easy decision? Trying to think calmly and objectively only produced a mental image of someone with laughing brown eyes and gentle hands, and made matters worse.

She was very quiet on the return journey, answering Mark's enthusiastic chatter about the changes he meant to make with little more than monosyllables, until, in the end, he demanded to know what was wrong.

'Nothing.'

'It doesn't seem like nothing to me. Her Grace said you were nervous, said I was to be especially careful of you.' He held the reins in one hand so that he could put his free hand over hers. 'There's nothing to be nervous of. You will make a capital Marchioness. . .'

'Mark, why are you upsetting the villagers?'

'Who said I was?'

'I heard what you said to your father.'

'That was simply a discussion about what is best for everyone. You need not concern yourself with it. Your province will be the house and running it efficiently. Surely that is enough?'

She tried arguing with him but that only made him angry, and in the end she gave up and they travelled the rest of the way home in uncomfortable silence.

It was dusk when they arrived, and there was a hired chaise standing at the door. Assuming it had brought more callers offering condolences, they went straight to the drawing-room, but Caroline was there alone, picking at a piece of embroidery.

'Mark, thank goodness you are back,' she said, jumping up and scattering canvas and wools on the floor. 'That Frenchman is with Papa—they have been closeted in the library for *hours*.'

Maryanne gasped, making Mark look sharply at her, but she managed to bite off the exclamation she was about to utter.

'I thought Papa meant to have him arrested,' Caroline went on. 'But he told me, as calm as you please, that he had seen him in church and asked him to call. Something's going on and I don't like it.'

'Neither do I,' he said grimly. 'If he thinks he can humbug Father, he will find he has to deal with me.' He strode out of the room and across the hall to the library. Light flooded out for a moment and then was cut off as the door was slammed shut. There was a smirk of satisfaction on Caroline's face which made Maryanne want to slap her.

'Now the man will hang for sure,' she said, sitting down and gathering up her embroidery.

Maryanne was too restless to sit; she went and stood by the window with her back to her tormentor. It was dark now, but there was a moon which threw long shadows across the garden and made a silhouette of the waiting chaise. Adam obviously intended to leave for France as soon as his interview with James was over. If only. . . She turned to Caroline. 'I am tired; I think I'll go to bed.'

'Don't you want to hear what happened? Aren't you curious?'

'No,' she lied. 'It is no concern of mine.'

In the privacy of her room, she sat in the window seat and continued her contemplation of the empty chaise; the driver was probably being entertained in the coach-house. She imagined Adam coming out and getting into it, being carried out of her life forever, leaving her behind to face a future that, in spite of a title and all the comforts money could provide, looked bleak indeed. Whether she married Mark, knowing there was no real love on either side, or remained a spinster, there was nothing to look forward to. But with Adam. . . Supposing he was right and Mark had caused the accident? Supposing Mark was right? Did it make any difference to how she felt? Did it make her love Mark the more or Adam the less? Could she let him go out of her life? Could she stop him? No, she decided, he was his own master; he would follow his destiny. And she must follow hers.

She stood up suddenly, went to the wardrobe and began feverishly throwing garments about the room. She changed out of full mourning into a grey jaconet dress with a high waistline and narrow tight-fitting sleeves, then she pulled out a travelling bag and stuffed it with a change of underwear, a wool gown for cooler weather and the barest minimum of toiletries. She had arrived with next to nothing; she would leave with nothing. She sat down and scribbled a hurried note to

Mark to tell him she could not marry him and another to James apologising for the distress her disappearance would cause, though in her mind she substituted 'scandal' for 'distress', which was all they really cared about.

Then from the top drawer of her dressing-table she took two guineas—all she had; it had never occurred to James to provide her with money—put them into her reticule and, throwing a cloak over her shoulders, crept out on to the landing. A single lamp burning in the hall and a sliver of light beneath the library door told her that the men were still talking. She made her way slowly down the stairs and out of the front door. With a quick glance about to make sure she was not being watched, she darted across to the carriage and clambered into it.

Adam's travelling cloak lay untidily on the seat. She sat on the floor and pulled it over her, trying to make it look as if it had fallen there, hoping he would not pick it up until they were on their way. It was a poor hiding place but it was better than nothing.

She was only just settled to her satisfaction when she heard the sound of footsteps on the gravel and then Adam's voice. 'I am in great haste, so drive as fast as you can, but I don't want dead horses at the end of it.' The door opened and she felt the carriage lurch as he put his weight on the step. The next moment he had settled in his seat and they moved off. Maryanne held her breath, expecting him to stoop to retrieve his cloak, but he let it lie. She was almost sorry because it was stifling her and she needed to come up for air. The driver waited until they had gone out through the gates, then he cracked his whip and set the horses into a gallop. The carriage swayed and lurched in sickening fashion as they picked up speed and Maryanne was wondering how soon she dared reveal herself when he said, 'Don't you think you would be a little more comfortable on the seat?'

Startled, she threw off the cloak and scrambled up beside him. 'You knew I was there all along.'

'I knew *someone* was there.'

'Why didn't you say something straight away?'

He chuckled. 'It occurred to me that whoever had taken the trouble to hide themselves in my coach must have wanted to leave Castle Cedars very badly.'

'Oh.'

'Do you?'

'What?'

'Want to leave very badly?'

'Yes. Yesterday you asked me to come away with you.'

'That was yesterday,' he said laconically. 'Said in the heat of the moment, and, if my memory serves me, you were adamant that you would not consider it.'

'I. . .' She paused; this was going to be very difficult. 'I changed my mind.'

'And if I have changed mine?'

'You haven't, have you?' she said slowly, noting with a certain amount of satisfaction that he had given no order to stop the carriage. 'And I don't want to go back.'

'You are being very foolish,' he said quietly. 'Everyone will be distraught about your disappearance and your bridegroom will conclude that he has another crime to lay at my door. *Mon Dieu*! How do you think that makes me feel? It is an accusation I find particularly galling.'

'Because, unlike the others, it isn't true?'

He looked sideways at her, but could not see her face. 'I wonder you are prepared to trust yourself to me, if your opinion of me is so low.'

'There is no one else,' she said, unaware of how much her words wounded him. 'Besides, I can't go back, even if I wanted to, you must see that. The family will disown me. The scandal. . .'

'You should have thought of that before you set out on this adventure.'

She felt miserable and humiliated. What had made her think he would welcome her with open arms? A couple of kisses and a few light-hearted words which had obviously meant nothing to him. 'Stop the coach, then,' she said angrily. 'Stop it this instant and let me off. I'll walk.'

'Back to Castle Cedars? It's a fair step.'

'No! Didn't you listen to a word I said? I will not go back. I am going to stay with my uncle in Portsmouth. I had hoped you would take me there.'

He sighed and leaned back in his seat, the better to see her against the moonlight, which caught in her hair and made it look like gossamer. Her eyes were large and bright with unshed tears. He wanted to take her in his arms and tell her he would never let her go, but how could he? He cursed the impulse which had made him suggest she could come with him; it had been foolhardy, if not downright criminal. But if he insisted on taking her back, what would happen to her? His imagination painted horrendous pictures of the torment she would be subjected to and he knew he could not do it. 'I mean to travel all night,' he told her.

'I don't care.'

'You don't even know where I am going, do you?'

'France. You told me so. And from Portsmouth too.'

He sighed. 'Very well, that is where I shall leave you.'

'Thank you.' Her voice, even in her own ears, sounded small and muffled, as if someone were trying to choke her.

'I suggest you try and sleep.' He rolled his cloak into a pillow for her and put it behind her head. 'I can't slow down, I'm afraid; I was much later leaving than I intended.' She leaned back and shut her eyes and before long her head was lolling off the makeshift pillow. He shifted himself to put his arm round her and make her more comfortable. Her head found his shoulder and nestled there. He smiled and brushed his lips against her soft hair. 'Sleep, little one,' he murmured. 'Sleep while you can.'

It was dawn when the coach slowed to enter the

town. Maryanne stirred and sat up, shaking her tousled head, and then looked out at the half-remembered streets. On both sides, ancient ramshackle buildings stretched down to the arch of St James's gate; shops, taverns, chandlers, cookshops and pawnbrokers huddled together. The combined smell of seaweed, tarred rope and strange spices gave the place its own particular odour. It was strange how a smell could be so evocative of the past; that more than any other sense brought back a place, a scene, something half forgotten. The road ran into the beach where lightermen ran their boats on to the shingle to unload and where the ticket porters in their strange hats and leather shoulder-cushions waited to carry the chests of naval men and the luggage of travellers to and from the boats that plied between the shore and the ships anchored in the bay.

Maryanne looked out towards Portsea dockyard where merchant ships and men o' war lay at their moorings. Beyond them a line of dark hulls, without their masts, lay low in the water, strung out in line, bow to stern, rising and falling on the swell. These, she knew, were the hulks which, during the war, had housed French prisoners of war. 'Were you ever on one of those?' she asked, pointing.

'Not as a prisoner, thank God, but I have been aboard.' He stopped speaking and tapped the front of the coach and the horses drew to a stop. 'Give me your uncle's direction. I have little time to spare.' Why had he sounded so brusque? He didn't fool himself and he did not think that he fooled her either; she must know how the prospect of leaving her was affecting him.

'It is only a step from here,' she said. 'I need detain you no longer.' Before he could stop her, she had picked up her bag and jumped down. 'Thank you for your help.'

'But I must see you safely there.'

She turned and waved. 'No need. I am home, among my own people. *Bon voyage!*' Then she turned and ran in among the crowds that thronged the street. He watched until he saw her turn into the doorway of a small cottage set back a little way from the road, and then paid off the coachman and set off along the shingle.

The cottage where Maryanne had been born was tucked right at the end of Broad Street, as near as Ben could be to the sea without actually living on it. She felt a pang of guilt that she had not visited him before, but the Reverend Mr Cudlipp had always refused to bring her and she had not considered making the journey alone. She would make it up to him, she promised herself.

She knocked and waited, but when no one answered she stepped back to look up at the house, and saw for the first time that it was empty and deserted; some of the windows were broken and the tiles slipping from the roof. She tried the door, but could not open it and when she peered through the window she found the rooms bare, and covered in dust and cobwebs. Of Uncle Ben there was no sign. 'He's dead,' she said, with sudden conviction, looking back to where she had left Adam, but there was no sign of man or coach. 'And now I'm in a pickle.'

Slowly she slid down to sit on the step and lean her head against the doorpost with its peeling paint. Her brain refused to function. She was too exhausted to think clearly, she told herself, and if she could only have a few hours' sleep she would wake refreshed and be able to decide what to do. She rose and went round to the back of the house, where she climbed in through one of the broken windows. She stood in the empty cottage, ignoring her bleeding hand, and looked about her, trying to imagine it as it had been, trying to put life and laughter back into a place which had long since surrendered both. Finding an old blanket in one of the rooms, she lay down in the corner and curled herself up in it, putting her bag under her head. Outside she could hear the noise of the streets and the sea breaking on the shingle. Nearer at hand, the wind sighed through the broken windows. It was like a lullaby and, too exhausted to notice how hard the floor was, she fell into a troubled sleep.

She was woken by a sound outside and sat up with a jerk. Someone was approaching. She crept across the room to look out of the window, but whoever it was had gone round the side of the house. With her heart pounding, she moved silently to stand behind the door, picking up a poker from the hearth as she went. The door had been bolted from the inside and did not give at the first push, but a heave with a strong shoulder sent it crashing back, just as she stepped out from behind it and brought the poker down on the man's head with all her strength.

He fell like a log, face down on the floor at her feet, and did not move. There was blood on the back of his dark head, running in a little pool on to the floor. She pushed her fist into her mouth to stop herself from screaming and forced herself to bend over him and touch his temple. There was still a strong pulse there; he was not dead. She turned his face towards her and cried aloud, because the man she had felled was Adam. She knelt beside him, wondering how to staunch the bleeding and bring him round. She dashed out into the yard, found a tub of rainwater and dipped her towel into it, then ran back and knelt beside him to dab at the cut. It was a messy wound, but not very deep, and she breathed a sigh of relief. When he regained consciousness, he would have a headache and perhaps a nasty bump, but—please, God—nothing worse. She wished he would open his eyes, but they remained firmly closed, although his breathing was easy.

She stroked his forehead and murmured his name, wondering if the damage was worse than she thought. 'I'll fetch a doctor,' she said aloud. 'Please don't die, please don't.'

The next minute she was lying on the floor beside him and he was holding her in his arms, and there was no weakness there, but an animal strength that held her against all her struggles.

'You! You. . .brute!' she cried, kicking out at him. 'How could you frighten me so? I hate you!'

He let her go. 'Good, that saves a deal of trouble.'

She scrambled to her feet. 'What do you mean? And what are you doing here, anyway? And why did you pretend to be knocked out cold?'

'I didn't pretend,' he said, sitting up and rubbing the back of his head. 'That blow was enough to fell an ox.'

'Well, you are an ox, and you deserved it, creeping in like that.'

'I didn't creep.' He looked around at the bare room. 'Your uncle's dead, isn't he?'

'I think he must be, but you haven't answered my question. What are you doing here? I thought you had sailed. . .'

He smiled, thankful that she had stayed and not run off when she found the place empty or he'd never have found her. 'Who said anything about sailing? I went to see someone off and mentioned Ben Paynter to the man who carried his chest on board. I was told the old fellow was dead. Died two months ago.'

'So you came back to find me?' She could not understand why her heart was suddenly singing.

'I couldn't leave you, could I?' he retorted.

'Why not? What does it matter to you what I do? Why are you so angry with me? Is it because I hit you with the poker?'

He smiled ruefully, getting to his feet. 'Is that what it was?'

'I'm sorry. Does it hurt very much?'

'Abominably.'

'Are you sure you don't want a doctor?'

'Certain.' He took her arm. 'Come on, we must get some way along the road before the day is out.'

'Road, what road?' she demanded. 'If you think you can take me back. . .'

'No,' he said, picking up her bag and leading her out

to where a second coach stood waiting. 'What's done is done and there is no going back now, though what I am going to do with you I have no idea.'

It was hardly a proposal, but she didn't care. She would rather be with him, who did not love her, than with anyone else who did, and, as long as it lasted, she would rejoice in that.

CHAPTER SEVEN

THE crush outside the Lord Markham's London home in Bedford Row was worse than it had been on the night of the ball and it was obvious Lady Markham was having one of her renowned assemblies. The driver stopped the chaise just short of the patient line of carriages waiting to discharge their passengers and called down, 'Do you want me to go on, guv? It'll be an hour or more afore you get to the door.'

Adam looked at Maryanne, huddled in the corner of the carriage. 'Well?'

'No, no, I cannot be seen in public like this; it would be too mortifying.'

He understood her reluctance. Three days on the road staying in rudimentary accommodation and with only one change of clothes had left her looking exhausted and bedraggled and she was in no state to pass off her predicament with any degree of confidence. And it would need more than confidence, it would need defiance to explain away leaving home so suddenly and travelling for three days alone with a man who was not her husband. He had pretended to be her guardian when they had stopped for the night, but that had fooled no one and she had been only too aware of the smirks of the inn servants when they thought she wasn't looking.

It would not have been so bad, she thought, if he had made some effort to be entertaining, but he had said very little, sitting in brooding silence in the opposite corner of the carriage for mile after mile, not even finding the energy to quarrel with her, for that would have been better than nothing and, at least, let her know he was aware that she was there. But it was no good complaining; she had brought it on herself and must put up with it.

She had been more than relieved when, on the second day, he broke the silence to tell her he intended to take her to Beth Markham and seek her advice. 'She helped once before and I think she understands,' he had said. 'She might agree to put it about that you had planned to go back to visit her all along.'

'With you as my escort?' There had been a quirk to Maryanne's mouth that was almost a smile.

He had grinned and the brown eyes had softened. 'How you arrived will have to remain a mystery.'

'And do you intend to leave me with her?'

'What else do you suggest?'

What else, indeed, short of marrying her? But he apparently had not even considered that and she was not even sure that was what she wanted, if marrying him meant taking a husband who spoke in monosyllables and gave every appearance of being irritated by her presence. 'Nothing,' she had said. 'I don't know why I did not think of her ladyship myself.'

Adam put his head out of the coach door and called up to the driver, 'Drive on to Adelphi Terrace.' He turned to Maryanne as the vehicle manoeuvred its way between the waiting carriages and set off again. He wanted to take her in his arms and offer another suggestion, but she seemed absorbed in looking out of the window at the long line of carriages and their glittering occupants and even managed a little laugh as she caught sight of a bright pink landaulet. The words stuck in his throat and all he could say was, 'I'll send a message to Beth Markham to come as soon as she is free.'

'Yes,' she said, in a very small voice, wondering what mischievous devil had made her get into his carriage in the first place. He had not wanted her; his kisses had meant nothing. Her pride had been badly dented but she still had enough spirit to know that she could never have married Mark and her reasons for

Take 4 Medical Romances

FILL IN THE FREE BOOKS COUPON OVERLEAF

Mills & Boon Medical Romances capture all the excitement and emotion of a busy medical world... A world, however, where love and romance are never far away.

We will send you 4 MEDICAL ROMANCES absolutely FREE plus a cuddly teddy bear and a mystery gift, as your introduction to this superb series.

At the same time we'll reserve a subscription for you to our Reader Service.

FREE

Every month you could receive the 4 latest Medical Romances delivered direct to your door postage and packing FREE, plus a free Newsletter filled with competitions, author news and much more.

And remember there's no obligation, you may cancel or suspend your subscription at any time. So you've nothing to lose and a world of romance to gain!

Your Free Gifts!

Return this card, and we'll send you a lovely little soft brown bear together with a mystery gift... So don't delay!

FREE BOOKS COUPON

YES Please send me 4 FREE Medical Romances together with my teddy bear and mystery gift. Please also reserve a special Reader Service subscription for me. If I decide to subscribe, I will receive 4 brand new books for just £6.40 each month, postage and packing free. If, however, I decide not to subscribe, I shall write to you within 10 days. The free books and gifts will be mine to keep in anycase. I understand that I am under no obligation - I may cancel or suspend my subscription at any time simply by writing to you. I am over 18 years of age.

EXTRA BONUS

We all love mysteries, so as well as the FREE books and Teddy, here's an intriguing gift especially for you. No clues - send off today!

12A2D

Ms/Mrs/Miss/Mr

Address

Postcode _____ Signature

One per household. Offer expires 31st January 1993. The right is reserved to refuse an application and change the terms of this offer. Readers in Southern Africa write to Book Services International Ltd., P.O. Box 41654, Craighall, Transvaal 2024. Other Overseas and Eire, send for details. You may be mailed with other offers from other reputable companies as a result of this application. If

Reader Service
FREEPOST
P.O. Box 236
Croydon
CR9 9EL

NO STAMP NEEDED

SEND NO MONEY NOW

leaving were as valid as ever; it was only the way she had left that she regretted.

'I will go and make sure he's alone,' Adam said when the vehicle drew up at Robert's house. 'If he is entertaining too, then we will have to think again.'

Passing the drawing-room window on the way to the door, he could see Robert sitting in an armchair with a glass of brandy on the table at his elbow, studying some papers. Relieved that his friend was alone, Adam tapped lightly on the glass.

It was a moment or two before the man inside heard him, but when he did he moved quickly to the window and opened it. 'Adam! What in heaven's name are you doing here?'

'If you let me in, I'll tell you.'

Robert Rudge flung the window open wider. 'Better come in this way, don't you think?'

Adam scrambled over the sill and shut the window behind him, while the lawyer poured another glass of brandy, which he handed to his visitor. 'You know there is a warrant out for your arrest?'

'It doesn't surprise me.'

'On a charge of murder?'

'Not that old chestnut. . .'

'No, not that. The new Duke of Wiltshire was stabbed to death in his library three nights ago.'

Adam sank into a chair, drained his glass and held it out to be refilled. He did not speak.

'You are the prime suspect and. . .' Robert paused. 'The girl.'

'Maryanne, you mean?'

'Yes, Miss Paynter. How did you come to involve her? Haven't you got enough to contend with?'

'I didn't exactly involve her; it was the other way around.'

'Where is she?'

'Outside in the chaise.' He sounded exhausted.

'Get rid of her. She will hamper you no end.'

Adam took a mouthful of brandy, savouring its

warmth on his tongue. 'She already has, but, as for getting rid of her, I can't.'

'Why not? You haven't gone and fallen in love with her, or anything as foolish as that, have you?'

'Now there's an interesting question,' Adam said, tipping back his head to empty his glass. 'It's one I shall have to give some serious attention to.'

'Send her away—you are best alone, at least until this matter is settled.'

'I cannot. Robert, she is very tired and has nowhere to go.'

'What does she know?'

'Nothing that I am aware of, but I haven't questioned her on the subject.'

'Don't you think you should?'

Adam shrugged. 'It would make no difference and it has nothing to do with falling in love, fascinating as that prospect might be.'

'Tell me about it.'

'I'll do that, but first may I fetch her in?'

'Very well. I can hardly refuse a lady in distress, but I can't help feeling I am going to regret it.'

As soon as Maryanne was fetched, she was bustled up to a guest room and Jeannie Clavier sent to help her undress and bath. The girl made very little effort to hide her disapproval. 'A lady shouldn't travel without her maid,' she said, pulling the hairbrush through Maryanne's hair with more vigour than finesse. 'I wonder the captain agreed.'

'He didn't,' Maryanne said. 'I made him.'

Jeannie laughed. 'The captain can't be *made* to do anything.' She paused. 'Though he's changed since he met you. Gone soft, he has.'

'There, Madame Clavier, you are wrong. There is nothing soft about the Jackdaw.'

'How did you come to know that name?' Jeannie asked sharply.

'He told me it himself and, besides, you called him Captain Choucas.'

''Tain't the same thing.' She paused. 'He don't need your problems on top of his own, so why don't you leave him alone? You'll get him killed.'

'I never heard such nonsense,' Maryanne said angrily. 'I wish him no harm and tomorrow, as soon as Lady Markham arrives, I shall leave. Will that satisfy you?'

'How do you know she will have you?'

'She is a friend, she helped before. . .'

'That was before. . .' Jeannie stopped suddenly.

'Before what?'

'Before the Duke's death, before they started blaming the captain for it. Friends!' she said contemptuously. 'They don't know what the word means.'

'And you do?' Maryanne asked.

'Indeed I do. It's all about trusting someone, knowing them inside out, being sure, deep inside you, that, however black they're painted, inside they are good and true. Do you feel like that about the captain, Miss Paynter? Can you put your hand on your heart and say you never doubted him? If you loved him, you could.'

Realising she had said more than she ought to have done, she picked up Maryanne's discarded clothes and left the room, saying she would send someone up to take away the bath water and bring her clothes back after they had been pressed.

Half an hour later, feeling a little more refreshed and dressed in the best of her two gowns, Maryanne returned to the drawing-room, where Adam and Robert were deep in conversation, brandy glasses in their hands.

'I have only been partly successful,' Robert was saying. 'The difficulty is trying to tie up events that took place in two different countries, and, what with the war and records being lost. . . You must be patient.'

'It's not a question of patience, Robert, it's one of keeping out of gaol long enough to prove it.'

'And having Miss Paynter with you doesn't improve your chances.'

'Agreed, but it cannot be helped.'

'I will soon be gone,' she said, coming into the room. 'The minute we hear from Lady Markham.'

Adam turned and took a step towards hers. 'Things have changed, Maryanne. Come and sit down; I have something to tell you.' He took her hand and led her to a sofa where he sat beside her. The gesture was so unexpectedly gentle that she was taken aback. She looked up into his face; his expression was sombre and his eyes darker than usual; they seemed to have lost their gold flecks, as if they were only there when he was laughing, and he was certainly not laughing now.

'Lady Markham will not have me,' she said. 'It is not altogether unexpected. You need not concern yourself; I can find a position as a companion or a governess.' She turned to Robert. 'If I might presume upon your hospitality just for tonight?'

'Maryanne,' Adam began, cutting off Robert's answer, 'Beth Markham was here earlier today and she brought news. . .' He paused to put a glass of cognac into her hands. 'Bad news. The Duke of Wiltshire has been murdered.'

'But that was an accident,' she cried. 'And why bring that up now?'

'I mean James,' he said. 'The new Duke.'

It was a full minute before she could reply, then all she could say was, 'I don't believe it,' over and over again.

'I am afraid it is true,' Robert said. 'The news reached London ahead of you, I imagine, because you went first to Portsmouth.'

'But when? How? Why? Who would want to murder him?'

'He was stabbed to death in the library the night you left and papers and money stolen,' Robert said, because Adam was too busy watching her face to speak. 'Beth had it from Mark Danbury himself, when he came hotfoot to London to see his lawyer.'

'We must go back,' Maryanne said, putting down the half-finished brandy and jumping to her feet. 'Now, At once. . .'

'No!' Adam grabbed her wrist, making her sit again. 'You have not heard all of it. You left on the very night His Grace was murdered and——'

'So did you!' In her agitation, she shouted the words. 'You did it!' Everything came rushing back: the way he turned up on Danbury land, his dislike of the Danbury family, Henry's death in the curricle race, his haste to leave that last night, his dark mood ever since. What an impediment to his flight to freedom she must have been! But why hadn't he just left her in the empty cottage and sailed away, why come back for her? Did he think she knew more than she did? Enough to condemn him?

'Rubbish!' Robert said, because Adam seemed incapable of speech; he was staring at Maryanne as if she had struck him. 'You are distraught.' He smiled slowly but it did not lighten the atmosphere. 'And you are not above suspicion. The story going about is that you did it together and then fled.'

'No one would believe that,' she said, trying to smile at the idiocy of it. Inconsequentially she wondered if James had seen the note she left her him on the hall table, but then realised that if he had never come out of the library alive he could not have done. 'We must go back and tell them the truth.'

'And if all they want is a scapegoat?' Adam asked. 'What if we cannot prove our innocence; what then?'

'In English law the onus is on our accusers to prove us guilty.' She glanced at his belt and wondered when he had stopped wearing his little dagger. Its absence confirmed her worst fears. 'Can't you see, it's the only way?'

'But you do not believe in my innocence, so what chance have I of convincing anyone else?' He was

deliberately forcing her to think about the conflicting
emotions which beset her.

'What I believe does not matter.' Unable to face his
searching eyes, she turned away. 'You are not answer-
able to me, but to the law and, in the end, to your
Maker.'

'My Maker I can trust; the law I do not, especially
when it is manipulated by Mark Danbury. If you will
not listen to me, please listen to Robert.'

She did not answer and Robert said, 'In any other
circumstances I, as a lawyer, would advise you to stand
trial and let them prove your guilt, but I am afraid
justice would not be done. Beth Markham says Mark
is angry enough to kill you both on sight.'

'I don't believe that,' she said. 'He would never do
such a thing.'

'I wish I had your faith,' he said. 'Now, if you will
excuse me, I have things to attend to.'

The silence he left behind was unbearable. Maryanne
hardly dared look at Adam for fear of weakening. He
uttered a sound that was very nearly a groan and began
pacing the room, head down, deep in thought. He
could not understand why, knowing Maryanne and
professing to love her, Danbury had already condemned her publicly, unless it was because he thought
she knew more of the truth than she really did and
wanted to silence her. It was the first time the idea had
occurred to him and it put him in a cleft stick. Filled
with helpless anger for the first time since he had been
forced to witness his father's execution, he was unable
to decide what to do.

He turned when he reached the window for the
second time and came back to where she sat, searching
her face as if etching it on his memory. 'Do you think
you could convince everyone of your innocence?' he
asked. 'Do you think they would believe you?'

'It's not just my innocence, but yours too.'

'Forget me, we are talking of you,' he said sharply.
'You must lay the blame on me, tell them you wit-

nessed the killing and I forced you to come with me, to save myself. You will be the little heroine and your reputation will be intact.'

'I couldn't do that,' she said quickly. 'It is not true. You didn't force me and I saw nothing.'

'It is the only way you will get them to believe you,' he insisted.

'No,' she said flatly. 'I must tell the truth.'

'And if the truth will not serve, what then? Mark Danbury has set his heart on seeing me hang.'

'One man alone cannot condemn you,' she asserted. 'It takes a jury.'

'But one woman can,' he said softly. 'You are in this with me, my sweet Maryanne, right up to your pretty little neck.'

'You know I had nothing to do with it.'

'Then save yourself.'

'With perjury?' She turned from him because she could not look into his face without wanting to cry. He had not murdered James, not deliberately in cold blood, she was sure of that, but had he killed him in the heat of passion? Had his hate and anger got the better of him? His military training would have done the rest. She remembered how he had reached for his weapon when she had surprised him in the vestry. 'We go back together or not at all.'

'Then it is not at all,' he said, suddenly making up his mind. 'If you will do nothing to save yourself, why should I sacrifice myself trying to help you? You forget that before all this happened I was on my way back to France.' His voice was clipped as if the words themselves were painful to him. 'We will leave as soon as the arrangements have been made.'

'We? You mean you and I?'

'That is exactly what I mean.'

'But I can't come with you.'

'Why not? Was that not what you had in mind when you hid in my coach?'

'That was before. . .'

'Before you learned I was a murderer?' His laughter was harsh.

'No, I wasn't going to say that.'

'There is no alternative,' he said flatly. 'And you need not worry about your reputation; we will be married just as soon as it can be arranged.' The words were out before he had considered how they might sound to her. It was certainly not the way he had wanted to propose. He watched the look of horror cross her face and knew he would never be able to mend that particular piece of clumsiness. But, if it made her see the precariousness of her own position, so much the better.

'I told you before I would not marry you however compromised I had been,' she retorted, angry for the first time. 'And I would have to be desperate indeed to accept such a proposal.'

'Then you will come with me unwed, for I am determined to take you.'

'Against my will?'

'If necessary.'

She blinked away tears of self-pity; they were out of place. She had brought this on herself and had only herself to blame. 'Then I am in your hands.' The words were wrung from the depths of her despair. To want someone so badly and then to find, when what you most desired was yours, that it was completely joyless was the height of irony. 'Do what you will.'

His grim expression did not change; he seemed neither relieved nor sorry. 'I'll go and fetch Jeannie,' he said. 'We will need her.'

Maryanne was persuaded to go to the bedroom she had used earlier and try to rest, while the men and Jeannie made what preparations were necessary. She could find no peace and instead sat numbly on a chair by the window, staring out at the dark water of the Thames. There were ships moored near by, frigates with sails furled, merchantmen, laden and unladen, rocking on the swell. Two coal barges made their way slowly upstream, and, away to her left, a ferryman was rowing his passengers across to the other side where a sprawl of urban buildings covered what had once been green fields. But wherever she looked, whatever her eyes saw, she was confronted with an image of James.

He had not been quite a second father, but certainly like a favourite uncle, and she mourned for him and condemned his murderer. Could it have been Adam? She remembered how gentle Adam could be, how easy she was in his company, how he made her laugh, how his soft brown eyes looked at her, how his kisses felt on her lips. He had kindled in her a feeling of her own worth, when everyone else diminished it. She desperately wanted to believe in his innocence, when all the evidence pointed to his guilt. She found herself murmuring, 'Why? Oh, why?' and, finding no answers, flung herself across the bed and sobbed herself into an uneasy sleep. She did not hear the door open, nor the quiet footsteps crossing the room to her bed.

Adam's grim expression softened at the sight of her. Her hair was spread about her face and her cheeks were streaked with weeping. She held the pillow in her arms as if, like a child, she derived comfort from it. He stooped and brushed her lips with his, tasting their sweetness. 'My love, I never wanted this for you,' he whispered. 'I am sorry, more sorry than you will ever know.'

Half in sleep, she became aware of his breath on her cheek as he stooped over her and felt the back of his hand stroking her forehead very gently. 'Time to wake up,' he said, turning to light a candle. 'It wants only an hour to dawn.' There was nothing for it; she opened her eyes.

He had bathed and changed into brown kerseymere pantaloons topped by a fawn-coloured frockcoat, over an embroidered waistcoat buttoned high to a yellow silk cravat flamboyantly tied and held by a diamond pin. A thigh-length pelisse was fastened across one shoulder, military fashion. He smiled at her expression of surprise. 'Behold Sir Peter Adams!'

'Another name?' She wished she did not have to wake up and face the day. 'Do you change your name as frequently as your clothes?'

'Very nearly,' he said cheerfully, determined that their last few hours together would not be miserable. He wanted to remember her with a smile on her face and laughter in her eyes.

She looked at her own crumpled dress; why had she not had the sense to take it off before falling asleep? Beside him, she looked a dish-clout. 'What about me? Have you decided to leave me behind after all?'

'No. Nothing has changed. We are going for another little coach ride.'

'Why won't you give yourself up? If you are innocent. . .'

'*If*?' He turned to face her and the aggrieved look in his dark eyes turned her heart over; she felt it thumping so hard that she was almost breathless.

'Are you innocent?' she asked him.

'Don't you know?'

'Of course I don't know. How could I? You were in the library with James when I left the house.'

'I thought a woman always trusted her intuition; what does your intuition tell you?'

'You are deliberately trying to confuse me.'

'Because I ask you to come to terms with your own feelings, to be honest with yourself? If you trusted me, it would not matter what I had been accused of, nor what the evidence was.'

'Couldn't we stay here for a day or two just to see what happens?' She was grasping at straws.

'That would make Robert an accessory,' Adam said. 'He is too good a friend to implicate in that way.'

'You can't go on running away the rest of your life.'

'I don't intend to.' His tone was grim. 'I will be back.'

'Where are we going?'

He laughed. 'Wait and see.'

'You don't trust me, do you?'

'I trust you with my life,' he said seriously, 'every day we are together.'

'Oh,' she said in a small voice.

He picked up her hand to put the palm to his lips, making her shiver. 'Now I want you to dress as quickly as you can. Make yourself into Lady Adams.'

'Lady Adams?' Had he really meant it when he said he would marry her? But he would not try to force her into making marriage vows, would he? What could he possibly gain by that? The answer came to her with sudden clarity; as his wife she could not give evidence against him. Did he feel that unsure of her?

He stood up, smiling. 'It would be best, don't you think? A husband and wife will attract less attention than a man-about-town with a woman who, beautiful as she is, looks like a wanton.'

'I look like a wanton?'

'Look like one and are one,' he said.

'That's not true!'

'No? Is it the normal behaviour of a well-brought-up young lady to throw herself into the arms of a strange man and then jump into a carriage in order to be carried off by him?'

'No, but nothing is normal in this affair, is it?'

'Affair? My dear Maryanne, who said anything about an affair? Nothing is further from my thoughts.'

'No, I suppose not, when it is your intention to force me into marriage so that I cannot give evidence against you.'

'Good God, woman, what do you take me for?' His bantering tone changed abruptly to one of anger. He flung a heap of clothes on to the bed. 'Put those on and come downstairs. I'll give you five minutes; if you are not down by then I'll come and dress you myself.'

The clothes consisted of a flannel petticoat, a fine lawn underskirt and a high-waisted blue taffeta gown with a frilled neck and tight sleeves. Afraid that he would carry out his threat, Maryanne dressed hurriedly and, inside the allotted five minutes, had joined him in the hall, where he threw a full-length burnous around her shoulders and hurried her out to a waiting coach.

Beside it stood Jeannie, dressed for travelling. 'Is Madame Clavier coming too?' Maryanne asked.

'You cannot travel without a chaperon.' He spoke flatly as he lifted her bodily and put her on to the seat, then turned to help Jeannie in beside her. 'Watch her,' he told her. 'She has a habit of running away.' Then he shut the door and climbed up on the driving seat beside the driver. As the wheels began to turn, a cock in a nearby yard crowed in the dawn.

By the time it was fully light, they were out in open countryside, but instead of whipping the horses up Adam allowed them to go at little more than walking pace.

'Why are we going so slowly?' Maryanne asked.

Jeannie smiled. 'Getting anxious, are you?'

'No.'

They fell into silence again, until Maryanne could stand it no more. 'How long have you known the captain?'

'Five years or thereabouts.'

'Before you met your husband?'

'No, later. I met Michel after the Battle of Busaco.' She paused to look at Maryanne, as if wondering whether to tell her any more. 'I'd been married before. It wasn't much of a marriage; we were both too young. We were poor and my parents' farm wasn't big enough to support us all, so when the war started Joe enlisted.' She smiled ruefully. 'Did it without telling me and then put my name in the ballot to go overseas. I was lucky.' She laughed. 'Or unlucky, depending on how you looked at it.'

'You became a camp follower?'

'Yes. We went to the Peninsula. The women stayed in the camp when the troops went off to fight, and we got on with our work and prayed; there was nothing else we could do. After the battles the men came back on their own two feet, if they could, or in carts if they'd been lucky enough to be picked up.'

'And he didn't come back?' Maryanne could easily feel for the other woman.

'Not after Busaco. I did what all the others in the same plight did—I went out to the battleground to look for him. It was terrible, dead and dying everywhere, French and Spanish and British all mixed up together.' She shivered. 'The smell and the cries of the wounded made me feel sick, but I was determined to find him.'

'And did you?'

'In the end, all of a heap with three dead Frenchmen. I knelt beside his body, not knowing what to do, just sat there wishing that I would wake up from that terrible nightmare and find myself at home. It was growing dark and I had just roused myself to make my way back to our own lines when I was captured by half a dozen French soldiers. They decided to have some sport with me. . .'

'Oh, no!'

'Michel came along and stopped them. He was a sergeant. He took me to the French women's camp.' She smiled. 'It was no different from the English, except I couldn't understand the lingo.'

'He married you?'

'Not straight away, but he gave me money and came every day to see how I fared, and later he brought the captain to translate for him.'

'You spent the rest of the war with them?' Maryanne asked.

'With Michel. Captain Choucas was not always there; he had other duties. Next to Michel, he is the finest man who ever breathed, and what he wants he shall have, if I have anything to do with it.'

'Even to giving him up?'

'To the law? No, I'll never do that.'

'No, I didn't mean that. If you love him. . .'

'If you mean why haven't I married him, then why not say so? Because he hasn't asked me, for one thing, but even if he had it wouldn't do. He's a gentleman and, besides, he does not love me.'

'Does that signify?'

'Certainly it does. It's only you aristocrats who marry with such calculated coldness. 'Twouldn't do for me.'

'Then why are you so against me? I thought. . .'

Jeannie looked sideways at her and laughed aloud. 'You thought I was jealous. No, it is what you are doing to him I'm against. The risks he is taking. . .'

'I know,' Maryanne said miserably. 'But he won't give himself up——'

'I should think not! But what he's doing now will put a rope round his neck just as surely.' She reached across and seized Maryanne's arm. 'Tell me this, and tell me true. Do you love him?'

Maryanne did not answer immediately and the girl shook her roughly. 'Don't you know?'

'Yes.' The word was a whisper. 'I love him, but. . .'

'There can be no buts. I'm going to tell you something now, though he'll half kill me for it.' She paused, then lowered her voice. 'You don't think he means to drag you across the Channel whether you will it or not, do you? He's let that devil know he's got you. He's going to stage a little play for the benefit of Society, to stop the gossip and save your reputation.'

'I don't understand.'

'He'll make it look as though he is forcing you to go with him and then he's going to allow Mark Danbury to free you.' She laughed suddenly, but it was an empty sound. 'After a suitable struggle, of course. And then he's going to rely on his friends to get him away safely.'

'Without me?' Maryanne whispered.

'Yes. That way honour is satisfied. The new Duke—the devil rot him—will be able to marry you and your fortune, and, if God is on our side, the captain will get clean away.'

Maryanne could picture the scene quite clearly. It was Adam's answer to her refusal to perjure herself. Did he care that much about her? Or was it his way of ridding himself of the encumbrance she had become? Did the foolish man not realise that she would not go back to Mark whatever happened? She was so deep in thought that she did not hear Jeannie speak to her until she shook her again.

'I said, is that what you want?'

'No, but how will Mark know where to find us?'

'I told him.'

'You?' She didn't try to hide her astonishment.

'Yes, the captain sent me to inform on him while you were resting.' Jeannie gave a cracked laugh. 'The bugger paid me well too. I gave it to a beggar on my way home.' She paused. 'Well, are you going to let the captain put his head in the noose for you?'

'No,' said Maryanne.

'What, then?'

'I'll leave on my own when we stop for a change of horses. You'll help me, won't you?'

'He'll come looking for you and put himself in even more danger.'

'What else can I do?'

Jeannie laughed. 'You are a muttonhead, aren't you? You admit you love him. Don't you want to go with him—of your own free will, I mean?'

Maryanne smiled wryly. 'Would he have me, after all this? I practically accused him of the murder myself and. . .' she paused '. . .of wanting to marry me to stop me giving evidence against him.'

'You said that? No wonder he prefers to ride on the box with the driver.'

'I was confused, I still am. . . Oh, I don't know what to think!'

'Stop thinking and obey your heart.' Jeannie gave her another little shake. 'You must make him abandon that lunatic plan before Mark Danbury kills him, for

he surely will. What you do with your life after that is
your affair.'

Maryanne attempted a smile; it was as if she were
just seeing the light at the end of a long, dark tunnel.
'I'll think of something.' She saw the expression of
doubt on Jeannie's face, and smiled. 'Don't worry, I
will do it somehow.'

They stopped twice to change the horses and take
some refreshment, but Maryanne found every attempt
to speak to Adam alone was balked. Either he had to
see to the horses, or pay the innkeeper, or the luggage,
which was no more than a half-empty trunk put there
for appearances' sake, had slipped loose and he must
tighten the straps which held it to the roof. It was
almost as if he knew what she wanted and was avoiding
talking to her.

They arrived in Dover the following morning just as
dawn lightened the sky and lit the cliffs with a pink
glow, and Maryanne had still not spoken to Adam. She
sat with her hands clenched and her heart in her mouth
as they made their way down the hill towards the
harbour. If Jeannie was right and Adam had planned a
confrontation with Mark, it would come soon, and her
nerves were as tight as drum skins, the hairs on her
neck tingling with apprehension. She found herself
fervently praying that Jeannie had been wrong, that
Adam had no plan, that he really did intend to take
her to France. But the more she thought about it, the
more she knew he did not intend that, and the nearer
the time came, the more she realised she did not want
to be left behind.

Workers were coming out of their doors as they
turned along the coast road, and women began hanging
bedding out of upper windows to air. Children and
dogs and the smell of cooking breakfasts brought the
town to life. On the water, fishing boats were bringing
in their catches and, nearer at hand, swinging on its
moorings at the end of the jetty, was a cross-Channel
packet. They stopped just short of it and Adam jumped

down and opened the door for Maryanne, holding out his hand to help her down. She pressed herself further back into the cushions and dug her feet into the floor, ready to resist.

'Come, madam, there isn't much time.'

'I refuse to budge until we have settled something between us.' Maryanne was aware that Jeannie had slipped out of the coach on the other side, but she did not think she had gone far away.

'I haven't time for any more of your foolishness,' he said. 'Do you want me to pick you up bodily and carry you on board?'

She tried to laugh but the sound that came out was more like sob. 'That would suit you, wouldn't it? It would make your little charade more convincing.'

He looked swiftly up and down the street and climbed in beside her. 'Maryanne, what are you plotting now?'

'I am not the one who plots, I leave that to you. You have no intention of taking me with you, have you?'

He sighed. 'Sometimes Jeannie exceeds her duty.'

'Don't blame her. She loves you. She is afraid for you. . .' Maryanne paused, watching his face. 'As I am.'

He opened his mouth to make some cutting retort but decided against it when he realised she was serious. Her face was deadly pale, but there was a sparkle in the depths of her violet eyes which made him catch his breath. If only he could trust her! 'It's too late.' The words were wrung from him.

'You would return me to a man I cannot love?' Her lovely eyes brimmed with tears. 'You want that for me? Can you imagine what my life will be like?' She lifted her face to his, searching it for reassurance, for a sign that what she was doing was right.

He groaned and lowered his face to hers, finding her mouth in a kiss whose sweetness filled her with unbearable yearning. As the pressure of his lips deepened,

she was swamped by an emotion so powerful that it
swept away all notion of time and place, all fear, all
guilt, and because, at that moment, time stood still,
there were no yesterdays, no hate, no intrigue, no
murder, and because there were no tomorrows there
could be no revenge, no retribution, no decisions to be
made. While his arms were about her, his mouth on
hers, there was only the present, and she felt secure,
untouched by evil.

He released her at last. 'Maryanne, in God's name,
what would you have me do?'

She did not answer, remembering Jeannie's words—
that if she truly loved him she would have no doubts—
and just now, when he had kissed her, there had been
none, only the longing to stay with him forever, for
without him she was incomplete. She did not hear him
repeat his question, she heard only a small voice inside
her telling her that her living and dying were inexorably
linked with his. 'Take me with you,' she said.

'Where?'

'Wherever you go. I don't care.'

He laughed and shook his head. 'I'm blessed if I
understand you, Maryanne. Why, when you tried so
hard to persuade me to trust in the law, are you
swinging to the opposite view?'

'I don't know. Maybe Mr Rudge was right and Mark
is not interested in justice.'

'I know he is not,' he said grimly.

'Then we have no time to lose, have we?'

'No, by God!' He called to Jeannie, who returned to
the carriage. 'Change cloaks with Maryanne.' While
the girls did as he asked, he took off his pelisse and
threw it up to the coachman. 'A guinea if you wear this
for the next half-hour. And you can keep it afterwards.'
The man took it eagerly and Adam turned back to
Jeannie. 'Take the coach right up to the loading-point
and go on board as quickly as you can. Get the driver
to carry the trunk; it might fool Danbury long enough

for us to escape attention. Come off just before she sails.'

Jeannie smiled. 'That I will, and God be with you, Captain.' She turned to Maryanne. 'If you do anything to make him unhappy, I'll haunt you forever, do you hear? You will never know a moment's peace.'

Adam smiled and bent to kiss her cheek. 'Michel would be proud of you.' He turned to Maryanne. 'I had other plans for my own departure. Come.' He held out his hand and she put hers into it and stepped down beside him. The die had been cast; whatever happened from now on, they were in it together, puppets of fortune, and he prayed that fortune would favour them.

He hurried her through the crowds gathering to board the packet, towards a spot on the beach where two men were busy lauching a small fishing boat. They had covered half the ground when they heard a shout behind them. 'Halt!'

Maryanne glanced over her shoulder, though she did not need to look to know that Mark had found them. He was standing with two burly men higher up the beach. The men held sporting guns and Mark had a pistol which he was levelling at Adam. 'Stop or I fire!'

'Run!' Adam commanded, pushing her away.

She hesitated, then flung herself between Mark and his quarry. 'Stay where you are, harlot!' Mark shouted. 'You need not think I will desist for fear of hitting you. Stand aside or you will die too.'

She hesitated only a second, but it was enough for Mark. She heard the crack of the pistol, saw Adam fall and, in that brief moment, knew with terrible certainty that Mark did not intend to take him alive.

CHAPTER EIGHT

MARYANNE gave a huge gasp of relief when she saw Adam stumble to his feet. 'For God's sake, keep going,' he said breathlessly, seizing her by the arm and dragging her along, as another shot sounded loud in her ears. 'He has to reload.'

'Fire, damn you!' She heard Mark's voice screaming at his companions. 'Don't let them get away.'

Bullets kicked up the sand behind them as she struggled through the water towards the boat with Adam behind her. She felt herself being dragged across the side with her petticoats up round her waist, as the men in the boat reached out to haul her inboard. There were more shots as they turned from her to grab Adam by his coat and pull him in beside her, where he landed in a heap at her feet. The crew left their passengers to fend for themselves while they set about pushing the boat off the sand and floating it. Only when she felt the jar as the craft lifted on the surge of the outgoing tide and saw the sails begin to fill did she allow herself a peep over the side.

It was broad day now and she could see Mark and the two men standing on the beach, up to their knees in water, trying to reload their weapons before their quarry sailed out of range. She turned to Adam with a cry of triumph which became a cry of horror when she saw his coat was covered in blood. His face was deathly pale and his eyes were dark pools of pain.

She fell on her knees beside him, opening his waistcoat to see the extent of the wound. The bullet had entered his shoulder, but there was no exit-point. 'We'll have to go back, you need a surgeon,' she said.

'I have no intention of letting a little scratch turn me

148

back,' he muttered. 'Bind me up. I'll be as good as new
in a day or two.'

She tore up her petticoat to make a bandage and tied
it round him, making him wince, though he did not
complain. 'I'm no good at this sort of thing,' she said
'You must have a doctor.'

'Later,' he muttered. 'Later, if necessary.'

She finished her task and made a pillow for him with
Jeannie's cloak. 'Can't we put in somewhere else along
the coast?'

'Not on this side of the Channel. There is no safe
harbour for us in England now.' He struggled to sit up,
then hauled himself over to the man in the stern.
'Enough of playing the invalid; give me the tiller.' The
man relinquished his place and went forward to help
trim the sails, while Adam settled down to steering the
small craft. 'Don't look so glum, my dear,' he said,
smiling at Maryanne, though even that was more a
grimace of pain. 'All will be well.'

She wished she could believe him. She was miserable
and unsure of herself and, now she had nothing to
occupy her, felt desperately ill because the seas were
running high and the boat was being tossed on the
waves like a piece of driftwood. And that was all they
were—driftwood, floating aimlessly on a sea without a
haven.

Beckford was not exactly a haven, but it was home
and, though she did not think she would ever have
married Mark, even if she had not met Adam, at least
she had friends there—the rector and the village
people, and James. . . Her wayward thoughts were
halted abruptly by the realisation that James was no
more. The events of the last twelve hours came flooding
back, the arguments, the indecision, Jeannie's lecture
and that kiss of Adam's which had dispelled her doubts.
But had it? While his lips were on hers, his arms
around her, yes, but they could not be forever in each
other's arms; could she have the same kind of faith
when he was distant? Every time they had a disagree-

ment or a set-back would her doubts return, as they
were doing now?

'Can we never go back to England?' she asked,
moving over to sit beside him.

'One day we will, but not now.' He paused to
concentrate on a change of tack, and then went on,
'Seasickness and homesickness are a deadly combi-
nation. Fight them, fight them for all you are worth,
because I need you to be strong.' His eyes were bright
but his skin had a pallor which frightened her; it was as
if all the blood had drained from him, leaving him an
empty grey shell. 'Take the tiller, will you? Hold it so.'

She had hardly changed places with him, when he
fell in a heap at her feet. She cried out in alarm and
one of the other men came to his aid.

'Keep her on course,' the man said brusquely, before
helping Adam to the tiny forward cabin. She dared not
leave her seat, and the agony of not knowing what was
happening made her forget her own sickness. 'Let him
not die,' she prayed, all too conscious of the fact that it
was because he was saddled with her that he was in
danger of it. Alone he could have eluded his pursuers.
'Please, God, be kind to him.'

The man came back. 'I'll take over here, miss—you
will do him more good than I can.'

She did not need a second bidding and for the next
two hours she sat beside the narrow bunk on which he
lay and watched over him as he fought to retain his
hold on a life which seemed to be ebbing away. She
had already used one of her underskirts to staunch the
loss of blood from his shoulder, and now she tore
another layer up to dip in water and bathe his brow.
That was what he meant when he had said he needed
her to be strong; she had to take over the ordering of
their lives, to make the decisions. And she was torn by
doubt and anxiety.

'Where are we?' she called to the men. 'Can we turn
back?'

One of them put his head in the door. 'No sense in

doing that, miss; we're over halfway and the wind and tide would be against us if we tried to turn.'

'Can we go any faster?'

He smiled. 'We are in the Lord's hands; He sends the weather.'

She turned back to Adam, who was thrashing about on the narrow bunk and in danger of falling off it. She pinned his arms down and soothed him and he seemed to fall into a peaceful sleep. 'You knew what you were about, didn't you?' she whispered. 'You knew if you could hold on until we had passed the halfway mark there would be no going back. But how am I to get you ashore? And, when I do, what happens next?'

Three hours later, the elder of the two fishermen called, 'Land ahoy! We'll beach in half an hour.'

She left Adam to allow herself a brief glimpse of a distant shore, then returned to try and rouse him. 'Adam, wake up, we'll be there soon; please, please try and stay conscious.'

He moved and groaned and uttered something unintelligible, then first one eye and then the other opened, and they were clear and bright.

'Praise be!' she said. 'How do you feel?'

'Sore.'

'Try sitting up.'

He had a strength and resilience which amazed her, and, although he moved slowly, a few minutes later, with her help, he was standing upright with his arm round the mast, scanning the coastline. 'Can you take her along the coast and into a river mouth?' he asked the men. 'I know a spot where you can tie up.'

Under his direction, they sailed slowly and silently up a quiet estuary and into the mouth of a river. There were a few people on the towpath, going about their lawful business, and they looked up in curiosity as the English boat crept forward on the minimum of sail. When the wind failed, the two men jumped ashore and towed the craft, pulling it along like a couple of barge horses, aided by half a dozen short-skirted fishwives who were thrown a few sous for their trouble.

They were about a mile up river when they came upon a tumbledown little inn with a tiny quay. Here they tied up and the men helped Adam to disembark, supporting him between them.

Adam was looking very ill again and Maryanne, following them into the inn, realised that the effort of remaining in command of his senses and directing operations had taken their toll. She decided it was time she took charge.

'A bed for the gentleman,' she ordered the innkeeper in her best French. 'And please send for a doctor—he has been wounded. And the other two need food and drink.'

'*Oui, madame.*'

The few people who were about were already pointing at the boat and chattering among themselves, and before long they would begin asking direct questions. The sooner they moved on, the better.

'Bed for you,' she said to Adam.

He managed a wry grin. 'I've never succumbed to petticoat government yet and I don't intend to start now.'

'As you please. Bleed to death if that is what you want,' she retorted.

'The lady is right, Captain,' said the elder of the two fishermen. 'We will help you to your room.'

'Very well, if I must, but I shall go alone.' He rose awkwardly and made his way over to the stairs, moving from one piece of furniture to the next. Maryanne went to help him, but he shrugged her off. 'Leave me be. Don't fuss.'

'Fine wife I'd look if I allowed you to struggle on your own,' she retorted, following him up to the room which had been prepared for him.

He grinned lop-sidedly and allowed her to help him off with his coat and boots. 'I can do the rest myself.'

'Why so coy?' She undid his cravat as she spoke and

then looked about her for something sharp to cut away his shirt. 'You would allow a nurse to help you, wouldn't you?'

'That's different.'

She found a small pair of scissors on a table by the window and set to work removing the blood-stained shirt. The sight of the ugly wound in his shoulder made her feel faint and the only way she could continue was to take a deep breath and make herself forget that this was Adam Saint-Pierre, whom she loved, and pretend it was a stranger who needed her help. 'Why is it different? You think I am too squeamish, is that it?' she asked.

She heard a discreet cough behind her and whirled round to face the plump little man who had come unannounced into the room. Flustered, she smoothed her skirts, and stepped away from the bed. 'Are you the doctor?'

'*Oui*. Now stand aside, *madame*, and let me see the extent of the injuries. A gunshot wound, I 'ave been told.'

'Damned excisemen,' Adam said in the sort of terrible French an Englishman might use. 'Took a pot-shot at me, didn't seem to realise the war had ended. . .'

The doctor smiled. 'If you will indulge in these dangerous pastimes, you must expect a leetle trouble.'

He began poking about in the wound with an instrument he had taken from his bag, making Adam grunt with pain. 'How long ago did it 'appen?'

'Ten hours, around dawn this morning.'

'Ten hours! It is a miracle your whole system 'as not been poisoned. I shall 'ave to do—what do you say?— a leetle excavating.' He turned to Maryanne. 'Go and order 'ot water and a bottle of brandy to be brought 'ere, then find somet'ing to do for the next 'alf-hour.'

She passed on his request to the innkeeper but she had no intention of leaving Adam and quickly returned

to his side. She poured a generous measure of brandy
into a glass and took it to the bedside.

'Take 'im the bottle, *madame*, the bottle,' the doctor
said impatiently, then added. ''Ave you ever seen your
'usband dead drunk, *madame*?'

'No.'

'Then you are going to now. Give 'im all of it.'

'Send her away,' Adam said, taking the bottle and
tipping it up to his mouth. 'Send her away.' He was
gulping at the fiery liquid, as if he could not find
oblivion quickly enough.

She made no move to leave, but stood and watched
as the contents of the bottle diminished and the doctor
prepared his instruments. Adam began to sing, but that
soon fell away into a mumble and then the bottle
dropped from his hand.

The surgeon set to work, probing gently at first, but
when it became apparent that Adam had lost consciousness completely he worked more swiftly, delving
deeper into the shoulder. Maryanne handed him his
instruments when he asked for them, gulping to stop
herself from feeling sick or faint, and watched Adam's
face for signs of returning consciousness.

''Ere it is.' The doctor's calm voice made her turn,
as he extracted a hard metal object from the pool of
blood in which he was working, and dropped it into the
empty brandy glass. 'Now, let us bind 'im up before 'e
comes to 'is senses.'

She helped him to do that, while Adam remained
unconscious, his face whiter than the rather grubby
sheet that covered him. The doctor, satisfied with his
handiwork, reached for his coat. '*Madame*, your 'usband 'as lost much blood, but 'e will soon make it up.
'E must have rest and have good food and no more
sailing, nothing energetic. . .'

'When can he travel?' she asked, looking down at
the invalid and praying for his complete recovery.

'Not for a week and then only if you go very
doucement. Where were you going, *madame*?'

She did not know. 'Paris,' she said.

'It is too far. You must wait until that wound 'as properly 'ealed.'

She wondered if Adam would obey that instruction when he regained his senses, but she smiled and said, 'I will make sure he rests, Doctor, and thank you.' He had to be paid and she had no money, so there was nothing for it but to go to Adam's coat, which had been thrown across the back of a chair. 'Your fee, *monsieur*?'

'An English guinea will do very well, *madame*.'

Feeling more like a thief than a wife, she put her hand inside the pocket and was surprised to find it was unusually roomy, almost like a poacher's pocket. From it she withdrew a sheaf of papers and ruffled through them looking for a purse or paper money, but what she saw brought her up with a start. In her hand she was holding what were obviously legal documents and they bore the Danbury crest!

For a moment she was unable to move because she had realised with a dreadful certainty that these were the papers which had been stolen from James's desk on the night of the murder.

'What are you doing?' Adam's voice seemed to come from a long way off. She whipped round guiltily to find him watching her with eyes which were bright with fever, but there was no doubt he was fully conscious. For a moment she did not speak and they looked at each other with a great chasm of suspicion between them.

'I'm sorry, my dear,' she said, and astonished herself with the calm way she spoke. 'I was looking for something to pay *monsieur*.'

'Give it to me.'

She bundled everything together again and handed it to him. Then she said, 'Excuse me,' and fled downstairs and out of the door.

She ran along the towpath, her mind in such a whirl that she did not know where she was going. That was why he had refused to give himself up, that was why he made such elaborate plans to escape and why it was so important to him to remain conscious and in control until they had gone too far to turn back. He was not an innocent man, unfairly accused, but a guilty one fleeing from justice. And she had thrown herself at him and told him she would go with him anywhere! How stupid she had been and how he must be laughing at her! And Jeannie Clavier too. She stopped suddenly and sat down on the bank beneath a weeping willow to gather her wits and decide what to do.

The water was clear and she could see her own reflection. It looked the same as it always had, except for the lines of fatigue around the eyes, but it belonged to a different woman from the one who had owned it twenty-four hours earlier, and that woman had been different from the girl of six months before. She should have no compunction about handing him over, but to whom and how? She was in a foreign land, with no money and no friends and her French was too inadequate to explain her predicament to anyone. She put her face in her hands and groaned in anguish.

'Oh, Adam, Adam,' she whispered. 'How can I love you after this?'

'Miss.' It was the elder of the two fishermen, who had come to find her. 'The tide is on the turn and the wind is with us. We must set sail now, if we are to get back to England tonight.'

England! Should she ask to go with them? Should she leave Adam to his fate, whatever that was, and return home? Once the fishermen had left, her last links with her homeland would be broken and she would be entirely alone. . .except for Adam. Did she really want to turn her back on the man who lay so ill in the inn behind her, and who, until a moment ago, she had trusted with her life and her future? Because she had doubts, did that mean she did not love him enough? She had to get to the bottom of the whole affair if she was ever going to know peace of mind again, and there was only one way to do that.

'Have you been paid?' she asked, dreading the thought of having to go back to Adam for more money.

'Yes, most generously. If you ever want to return, you have only to send for us.'

'Thank you, I'll remember that.' She watched the men manoeuvre the boat out into the river, where the sails picked up the breeze and sent it slowly downstream, then she took a deep breath to calm the swift beating of her heart and returned to Adam.

The doctor had left and the patient was sleeping peacefully. Some of the money lay on the table by the bed, but there was no sign of the documents. His coat had been hung on a hook behind the door and she wondered if he had left his bed to do it, or asked someone else to hang it up. Silently, she went to it and felt in the pocket. It was empty, which could only mean that Adam knew she had recognised the papers for what they were and had hidden them away. She needed to know what they contained for her own peace of mind and began a systematic search of the room, looking for them. She had to give up when Adam became restless, moving his head from side to side and flinging out his arms.

She hurried over to the bed and sat on the side of it, taking his hand. 'Lie still,' she whispered. 'Lie still or you will bleed again.'

Her voice roused him and he opened his eyes. 'Maryanne, my faithful Maryanne, still with me, I see.'

'Where else would I be?' she asked with some asperity, then, regretting her sharpness, added, 'How do you feel?'

'Better. You know, Maryanne, we cannot linger here; our arrival was too conspicuous. I wonder how often they see an English fishing boat as far inland as this, and how often a gentleman and his lady disembark, not to mention the gentleman being wounded. News of that will travel fast, you can be sure.'

'Surely no one will follow us to France.'

'I wish I could be sure.' He paused to study her face. 'Is anything wrong?'

'Wrong?' How difficult it was to behave naturally. 'What do you mean?'

'I don't know, but you seem tense and afraid, and that's something you have never shown before, not even when you were alone in your uncle's cottage, nor when we were being shot at; nor, according to the doctor, did you flinch when he dug that bullet out of me.'

She made an effort to sound light-hearted. 'There's nothing wrong with me that won't be put right as soon as you are well again.'

'Oh, my poor Maryanne. I'm so sorry, my little one, but you coped well, very well.'

'I did nothing, and it was my fault you had so much trouble. You could have escaped unscathed without me.'

He smiled and lifted her hand to his lips. 'I could not have left you behind, my love; you know too much.'

She jerked her hand away, as if his touch had burned it, and began straightening the bedcovers, anything to cover her dismay. 'I promised the doctor I would see that you rested, so no more talking. Tomorrow we'll decide what is to be done.'

'Very well, but please rest yourself. I don't need a nurse and you are not looking at all like my high-spirited Maryanne.'

It was easy to convince the innkeeper that she was afraid she might disturb her husband and that what she needed was a room to herself, and one was soon found for her along the corridor. She ordered a light meal to be taken there and retired for the night, hoping that her fatigue would make sure she slept. But again and again her thoughts echoed his words—'you know too much'—as if repetition would make them go away or mean something different. The trouble was, she knew nothing, nothing at all, and she would not rest until she

found out what was in those papers The knowledge
might be dangerous, but she had to risk that.

When she went to him next morning, he seemed
much stronger and although he occasionally grimaced
with pain he did not seem to be suffering too much and
he was inordinately cheerful. 'Ah, Maryanne, my love,
I do believe I feel well enough to travel. . .'

'The doctor said. . .'

'Be blowed to the doctor. I mean to take you home.'

'Home? Back to England?'

He smiled and reached for her hand. 'You must stop
thinking of England as home or you will never become
a real Frenchwoman. *Maman*, you know, forgot she
was English when she married *Papa*. For her, Challac
was home and she never wanted anything else.'

She smiled wanly. 'She had married the man she
loved.'

'Yes.' He spoke abruptly and pulled himself into a
sitting position. 'I think the time has come to. . .' he
smiled wryly '. . .to put that little matter right. We can
be married before the day is out.'

'No!' She spoke so sharply that he looked up at her
in surprise. 'I mean,' she added, before he could
comment, 'let's wait until you are fully recovered.
There is no hurry.'

He grinned. 'No, I suppose the damage has already
been done as far as the world is concerned. I wonder
what they are saying about us in the drawing-rooms of
London.'

He had not said he loved her; he had not said he
wanted to marry her for herself; he had not said
anything at all to put her mind at rest, and yet he must
know that she was troubled by more than what people
might be saying about her. She smiled to herself,
remembering the Dowager Duchess; enough scandal
for generations, she had said, and that was before
Maryanne had added to it. And for what? For a man
who had held her in his arms once or twice and kissed
her, a man who might be a murderer. It was nothing to

smile about. 'It will be a nine-day wonder,' she said, 'soon forgotten.'

'By all except Mark Danbury. He will not forget. And I do not wish him to. He will live to regret the inconvenience he has put me to.'

'Inconvenience!' She threw back her head and laughed. 'Is that what you call me?'

He grinned and swung his legs over the side of the bed. 'I am glad you can laugh about it, my dear. Now I must dress. Be so good as to see if the coach is coming.'

'What coach?'

'The one I ordered yesterday. If you had not taken it into your head to make a little excursion on your own, you would have known what the arrangements were. Where did you go, by the way?'

'Just for a walk. I wanted to be by myself for a while.'

'You were alone?'

She looked at him sharply. 'Of course I was alone. Why do you ask?'

'I don't know. I wondered if you might perhaps have wanted to return with the boat. . .'

'Why should I want to do that?'

'A change of mind perhaps.' He paused. 'Or a change of heart.' He sat on the edge of the bed looking up at her, searching her face. 'I was right, you are tense. Do you think I cannot tell when something is wrong with you?'

'Nothing is wrong.'

'Is it because I subjected you to a rough crossing and being shot at and having to nurse me? I thought you were made of sterner stuff than that, Maryanne Paynter,' he said.

'None of that would have made the slightest difference if. . .' She could not go on.

'If what? Come along, tell me. We can't go on with this between us; it will be unbearable. Do you want to leave me and go back? I'll make what arrangements I can, but I can't guarantee your safety.'

'Is that what you want me to do?'

'What I want is of no consequence. I am asking you, once and for all, are you going back or coming with me?'

'You are determined to go, then?'

'Yes. Are you coming?'

'I have no choice, have I?'

'My dear Maryanne, you have always had a choice. You chose to come with me in the first place, remember?' He smiled but there was evidence of pain in his dark eyes. 'Come along, we are wasting time.'

They were saved further argument by the sound of horses' hoofs and carriage wheels on the road below the window. She went to help him dress but he shrugged her off, insisting she wait for him downstairs.

He followed soon afterwards, moving slowly and painfully, but he disdained the offer of her arm and made his own way out to the coach which waited for them at the door. It had certainly seen better days; its paintwork was scratched, its hood torn and, what was worse, its springs looked decidedly lop-sided.

'How far are we going in that?' she asked, knowing it would be uncomfortable for someone fit and well, but for a wounded man it would be excruciatingly painful.

'To Challac.' He opened the door and motioned her inside. 'Five days, a week perhaps more, who knows?'

'A week! No, Adam, you will never survive. Couldn't you find something a little better sprung?'

'Nothing is new in France these days,' he said, climbing in beside her and giving the order to move off. 'Unless it belongs to a wealthy Englishman. There are plenty of those lording it about. They are not exactly loved by the French, you know, and we need to avoid making ourselves conspicuous.'

'You didn't think of that when you dressed in that finery.' The coach lurched as the wheels began to turn and she looked at him to see if he was in pain, but if he was he concealed it well.

'I had your support then, or at least your compliance. Sir Peter and Lady Adams, on a sightseeing tour.' He sighed and looked down at his clothes. He had discarded the embroidered waistcoat, which had been too blood-stained to clean, and put the diamond pin in his pocket, and, although his coat had been cleaned, it was not what it was when they left Dover. 'Now it will have to be Adam Saint-Pierre returning home from the wars and unsure of the welcome he will receive.'

'Why are you unsure?'

He smiled. 'The people are not always pleased to see the landowners returning to their estates; too much has happened in the years since the Revolution. They have found a kind of independence and going back to a life that was little more than serfdom is something they will resist.'

'But wise landowners will not try to turn the clock back, will they?'

He laughed. 'Tell that to the Bourbons. Louis thinks he can pick up where his brother left off and ignore the fact that the Republic and Napoleon's Empire ever existed. I fear he will learn the hard way.'

'You don't think the bad times will return, do you? Surely everyone is sick of war and anxious to make peace.'

He laughed. 'You wouldn't think so with all the bickering that is going on. They are trying to carve up the Continent as if it were a slab of cake, and the French people wait and watch.'

'For the Emperor's return?'

'I don't know. Perhaps for a sign that their lives will improve.'

'Surely that is up to those who govern them?'

'Precisely. That is one of the reasons for going home; I must do what I can for my own people,' Adam asserted.

'How long is it since you went home?'

'Not since. . .' He paused, trying to remember. 'I believe it was six years or more ago. I was quartered near by and decided to go and see what the old place was like. It was a mistake.'

'Why?'

'Memories, Maryanne, memories of times which could never return, some happy memories of childhood but others too painful to dwell on. I did not stay.'

'Then why are you going back there now?'

'It is time to try again. The place cannot be left to fall apart and we need somewhere to lick our wounds, do we not?'

'If you get there alive,' she said sharply. 'This journey is madness.'

'Have you a better idea?'

She did not answer, because answer there was none. She could not leave him, even if she wanted to; she was committed to staying with him at least until he was well and she had unravelled the mystery of James's death. And, in any case, for all his saying he would arrange to send her back, she doubted he would do it, not after telling her she knew too much. She wished she did know; most of all she wished she knew what went on in that head of his. Innocent or guilty? Why would he not tell her? 'Only the guilty flee,' she said. 'So what are we guilty of?'

He smiled. 'Flying in the face of Society. We are outcasts, you must know that.' He sighed. 'You are travelling alone with me, not only unmarried, but disinclined to remedy it, so would you have us travel openly?'

'I did not mean that and you know it. I was talking about the night we left Castle Cedars.'

'What do you want to know? That I did not kill the Dukes of Wiltshire?' He gave a cracked laugh. 'Either of them.'

'Yes.'

'Very well. I did not cause the death of either man.'

It wasn't exactly a straight answer, but it had to suffice. 'But you know who did?'

'Yes.'

'Who was it? Why did you not denounce him?'

'I have yet to prove it and until I do no one will believe me.'

'I might.'

He smiled. 'I doubt that.'

'Tell me anyway. I want to know.'

'The man you were betrothed to marry. . .'

'Mark?' She was shocked. 'I don't believe it. The idea is preposterous. He would not kill his own father.'

'I notice how quick you are to defend him,' he said with a twisted smile; her words were almost as painful as his shoulder, which was causing him agony with each turn of the wheel. 'You have never been that sure of my innocence. I wonder why?'

She did not answer and they journeyed on in silence, each thoughtful, each aware of the presence of the other, sitting so close that they could touch hands and where every jolt threw them against each other. And every time it happened he grunted with pain and she felt guilty, terribly, terribly guilty. She found her eyes filling with tears and wished they could start again, trusting each other.

'What have I done?' he asked softly, seeing her misery. 'You were right. I was mad to contemplate such a journey.'

'We can always stop until you have rested.'

'I was not talking of my state of health. It is you. . .'

'Me? What have I to do with it? I am no more than baggage and not to be trusted.'

If it were not so painful and if she had not been so serious he would have laughed aloud at her choice of words; as it was, he confined himself to a wry twist of his lips. 'Trust is a mutual thing, Maryanne; it has to work both ways.'

'So it does,' she said angrily. 'If I had not trusted you I would not have come.'

'But not enough, my love,' he said. 'Not enough.'

'Why do you call me your love, even when we are quarrelling?'

'Because you are my love, and nothing you say or do will alter that. You are my one and only love, now and for always, and if I live a few days or many, many years, nothing will change it; it is unchanging and unchangeable.'

His tenderness made Maryanne burst into tears and for several minutes her sobs were uncontrollable. He moved awkwardly to try and comfort her. 'I never knew such a woman.' He pulled a handkerchief from his pocket and attempted to dry her eyes. 'I didn't realise a declaration of love could reduce someone to such tears. Come, dry your eyes and we will talk.'

'T. . .talk about w. . .what?'

'Whatever you like—the weather, the scenery. France was beautiful once, but look at it now.' He nodded at the countryside through which they were passing. 'Devastated by war, all the men gone, nothing but women who work like cart horses, old men and children. How long do you think it will take to recover from that?'

'It is not only France,' she said.

'No, the whole of Europe.' She was not sure if he wanted to cheer her up, or to avoid answering questions. He need not have worried; she was incapable of thinking clearly. 'I pray we are given the time to put things to rights. Take that château over there; it looks beautiful with the sun shining on its roof, but if we were to go closer I'll wager we would find it in ruins. My old home is like that, but we will do what we can to bring it back to life, you and I.' When she did not reply, he went on, 'It is especially beautiful in the autumn when the trees around it are changing colour and the vines have withered and all that's left on them are the big purple grapes of the late harvest, so full of juice, it makes you feel thirsty to look at them. They make the best wine of all, did you know that?'

She shook her head. Her sobs had subsided but she could not bring herself to look up into his eyes for fear of another outburst. Why was he so kind and gentle with her? Why, if he were a murderer and knew that she knew it, did he carry on as if conducting her on an afternoon's ride through the park?

'I'll teach you about wine,' he said. 'I'll show you how they tread the grapes, how they store the vats underground in huge vaults. I'll take you to the cellars where the monks make a local liqueur, which is smooth as silk and tastes of heaven.' He bent to kiss her without passion. 'Just as your lips give me a taste of heaven.'

'Oh, Adam, I don't know what to think any more. . .' Maryanne sighed.

'Then don't think. Trust me now and time will do the rest.'

If only they could be sure of being allowed that time. Would they both end on the gallows, unable to prove their innocence? Dared she allow herself to hope? He had said he loved her; she had to believe that, or what was the point of going on?

'You need to rest,' he said firmly. 'Looking after an invalid can be very tiring, especially when he is as contrary as I am, but I am on the mend and feeling stronger by the minute, so close your eyes, my lovely Maryanne, and I will watch over you.'

Exhausted, she lay back against the cushioned seat and shut her eyes. What was the good of fighting? She was lost before she had even started. His voice continued to murmur endearments in her ear, like a softly sung lullaby, and, in spite of the jolting, she was soon asleep.

She awoke briefly when they stopped to change the horses, but soon drifted off again, unaware that his shoulder was giving him so much pain that he was having to fight to remain conscious. How long he could keep going he did not know, but they were still too near Calais to relax. When darkness came and with it the need to stop for the night, he forced himself to walk into the inn they had chosen, as if his wound were no more than a minor irritation. The place was, like everything else, run-down and dirty, but his request for separate rooms was accepted without question when he explained that he was likely to be very restive and would disturb his wife.

Maryanne had stopped thinking for herself, because to do so was painful, and even knowing that she was living in a fool's paradise and sooner or later she would have to face reality did not rouse her from her lethargy. It was almost as if she had been drugged, drugged with soft words and a soothing voice. Tomorrow would be soon enough to have it all out with him—the possession of the documents, the implication that she knew too much to be left behind, all the doubts and suspicions, once and for all. Tomorrow, she would insist on being told exactly what had happened at Castle Cedars on the night James died and why he had accused Mark. Tomorrow, not tonight.

But the next day she could not speak to him on the subject because he was so obviously worse. When he appeared at the breakfast table, his face was grey with pain and there was fresh blood on his shirt. She was allowed to renew the dressing on his shoulder, but that was all; her arguments that they should stay at the inn and rest until he recovered were swept aside with bad-tempered intransigence. 'We go on,' he said. 'Don't fuss, woman.'

She followed him out to the coach, convinced she would have a corpse on her hands before the day was through and unable to do a thing about it. Pain or no pain, he was still strong enough to clamber in the vehicle and order the driver to go on. There was nothing for it but to climb in beside him and hope that her prayers for him would be answered. She told the

driver that *monsieur* was very ill and ordered him to
drive very slowly and carefully.

In spite of that, Adam could not leave the coach
when they stopped for a midday meal and a change of
horses; he remained ashen-faced, spread out on the
seat, too ill to move, almost too ill to argue. Food was
brought out to him, but he could not eat and Maryanne
knew she would have to defy him and take him to a
doctor. When she enquired for one, she was told the
nearest and best would be in Paris, and as that was
now only a few kilometres further along the road she
decided, whatever he said, that they would stop there
and find help.

As it happened he did not protest because he was no
longer conscious. So much for avoiding the main roads,
she thought, as they rumbled up to a rough wooden
palisade and through tall gates guarded by indolent
soldiers into a city which was a labyrinth of narrow, ill-
paved streets and crumbling old houses. Lanterns,
strung across the streets, swayed in the wind and cast
pools of sickly yellow light in which could be glimpsed
throngs of noisy, ill-clad people who made Maryanne
shiver with fear. She ordered the coachman to hurry
through without stopping and to find a small hotel in a
more salubrious area. 'Clean,' she said. 'And respectable, but not luxurious. And not in the fashionable
area.'

He grinned and took them to a small lodging house
at the lower end of Rue Lepic within sight of the
Moulin Rouge. Adam became conscious as the concierge's husband and the coachman lifted him down
and carried him indoors. They took him up to a
bedroom, where Maryanne made him comfortable
while she waited for the doctor to arrive. Here they
were and here they would have to stay until he was
completely recovered. Challac and the vineyards would
have to wait. And the confrontation she had planned
would likewise have to wait. So would proving his
innocence—or guilt—and so would a wedding

ceremony. She smiled, as she bathed his feverish forehead with cold water; what price her reputation now? Thank the good Lord there was no one who knew them in Paris.

CHAPTER NINE

IT WAS a month before Adam improved enough to take notice of his surroundings, a month during which Maryanne watched over him and nursed him with devotion and care, but it was also a month in which she found time to search every particle of his meagre belongings looking for the tell-tale documents. But they were not to be found and she reluctantly came to the conclusion that he had disposed of them. It proved one thing above all else—he trusted her no more than she trusted him. How could love, either his or hers, be based on such suspicion? How could they come together with such a chasm between them?

While he lay so ill she did not often move far from their tiny room but it was necessary to shop for good food to help his recovery, for ointments to put on his shoulder, for fuel for a fire and mops and brushes to clean their quarters. At such times the concierge would sit with him and Maryanne would escape from the noisome air of Montmartre for the city, where at least some effort had been made to clean up the evidence of the last days of fighting in which so many young soldiers had died.

At such times, on her way to and from the markets of Les Halles, she would step aside to explore. She found the other face of Paris—the wide tree-lined boulevards, the Palais Royal, the Ile de la Cité, Notre Dame, the restaurants and pavement cafés, the Royal parks with their statuary and fountains, the Louvre crammed with Napoleon's stolen art treasures, the Arc de Triomphe, begun after Napoleon's victory at Austerlitz but yet to be completed. Here Paris played host to visitors of all nationalities—British, Russian, Prussian; they seemed to have a wild determination to enjoy themselves, to make the most of what the city had to offer, as if it would all blow away, like dandelion seed, at the first puff of wind.

And it seemed there might be some justification for that belief because, beneath the outward enthusiasm, beneath the cries of *'Vive le Roi!'* whenever Louis passed in a well-sprung carriage there were others of *'Vive l'Empereur!'*

The Duke of Wellington arrived at the end of August to take up his appointment as British Ambassador, and moved into the beautiful mansion in the Rue du Faubourg St Honoré, which he had bought from Napoleon's sister. Gone was the popular acclaim of the early heady days of peace, gone were the cries of *'Libérateur!'*; he was looked upon as the conqueror of a nation too proud to own defeat. Maryanne, moving unnoticed through the crowds and with her French improving daily, was aware of the undercurrents and felt a certain apprehension. Could the Emperor, confined to his tiny kingdom of Elba, really return? In the autumn of 1814 it seemed impossible and yet she could not help recalling Adam's words about generalship. Surely Napoleon was watched, surely the national leaders, soon to convene in Vienna, would succeed in making a lasting peace?

But in truth she was more concerned with caring for Adam, now slowly recovering, than with state boundaries, more worried about how to eke out Adam's dwindling store of money than with whether the Louvre should keep its treasures. She knew Adam would soon be well enough to take control of his own life and, with it, hers. What, she asked herself again and again, did she intend to do when he was fully recovered and no longer needed her? Would she, could she, leave him? Was she his prisoner? But how could a strong, healthy woman be the prisoner of a helpless man too ill to fend for himself? If she really wanted to, she could throw herself on the mercy of the new Ambassador, who would surely arrange for her safe return to England.

But she could not leave. Well or ill made no difference; the thought of spending the rest of her life still in
doubt about his guilt or innocence was intolerable. She
found herself going over and over in her mind the
events which had brought her to this seething city; it
was as if it had been written in the stars, immutable
from the day she had been born. That being so, what
was the use of questioning it?

When the leaves on the trees along the Grands
Boulevards began to turn to yellow and russet and drift
to the ground beneath her feet as she walked, Adam
began to move about, restlessly pacing the room,
cursing his weakness and the time they had wasted,
and at such times she was glad to escape and leave him
to his grumpiness.

It was a grumpiness caused by frustration. Did she
not realise how difficult it was for him to hold back
from her, to refrain from taking her in his arms and
kissing her until she understood his need? His coolness
towards her was an act he found more and more
difficult to sustain, but until she softened towards him,
until she confessed she had searched his belongings and
truthfully told him why, until all suspicion had melted
away, he could not make love to her, he could not even
re-affirm the love he had so rashly declared in the
coach. He did not want to persuade her with words or
passion, he wanted her to realise, in her heart, in the
depths of her soul, in whatever intuitive place women
knew these things, that he was not only innocent, but
wronged.

He had hoped they could put the past behind them,
to forget why they left England and make a new life
together, united in trust and love, but now he realised
that had been a fool's paradise. Until he cleared his
name there would always be this chasm between them.
It was time to rouse himself.

She came back one day to find him dressed and
shaved and sitting at the table writing a letter.

'What are you doing?' she asked pleasantly, taking

off her cloak and hanging it behind the door. It was the one Jeannie had given her, very grubby and much darned. He didn't recognise the dress she wore under it, but it was of some cheap woollen material with no pretension to style. She had probably bought it in the market for a few sous. How she had managed these last few weeks was nothing short of miraculous and he marvelled and, at the same time, was angry with himself for failing to provide for her. She removed her bonnet and shook her head so that her hair swirled about her shoulders, and turned to smile at him; it was enough to make an angel weep, and he was no angel.

'Writing to Robert. He has no idea where we are and he might have news for us. Besides, I need funds. It is time Sir Peter and Lady Adams re-emerged.'

'Why?'

'You have nursed me unstintingly and it is time we moved from here to more comfortable quarters,' he said. 'You need a maid and a wardrobe and I want to show you the best of Paris before we go to Challac.'

'You still mean to go, then?' she asked.

'Of course—nothing has changed.'

No, she thought, nothing has changed. Although, on the surface, he spoke affectionately to her, there was a part of him he held back. She could not imagine him repeating the words of love he had uttered in the coach when they were travelling. It was almost as if she had dreamed them. Perhaps she had, perhaps the whole thing was a dream. . .or a nightmare.

When money arrived from Robert, Adam lavished it on her, taking her to all the beautiful shops and buying her clothes and jewellery as if his purse were bottomless. He rented a house in the Faubourg St Germain, which belonged to a returning émigré who had no money to return it to its former splendour. It had a faded gentility and, above all, it was quiet. Adam hired servants and a carriage and horses and generally set out to impress. She had no idea whether he could really afford it all, but her greatest concern was their unmarried state. He had not mentioned marriage again since she had so adamantly turned him down, and now she did not think he ever would. He had, on his own admission, brought her with him because she knew too much; it was his reason for wanting to marry her, and hers for refusing. But, married or unmarried, she could never give evidence against him; surely he should have realised that by now? And what did she know? Nothing.

When she could put that from her mind, she enjoyed herself, and sometimes, for an hour or two, she could forget she was anything else but Lady Adams, could put from her mind the fact that she was the hostage of an unkind fate, that her future happiness was in the hands of a man wanted for murder. They sauntered along the boulevards and sat at the pavement cafés; they went to the packed theatres and dined at famous restaurants like Quadron Blue, Jardin Turque and Frascati's. They wandered along the Seine, visited the Louvre and Notre Dame and admired the public buildings, which far surpassed anything that could be seen in London.

'I've heard it said,' Adam remarked, 'that if Napoleon had reigned another ten years there would not have been a city to match its splendour.'

'But do you think that making a city beautiful justified all those deaths, all that devastation, all the plunder?'

'No. I was merely making an observation,' he told her.

'I sometimes forget you are a Frenchman,' she said. 'It is bound to give you a different view.'

He did not answer and she fell to wondering once again what would happen to them if conflict broke out again between their two countries. 'Do you think that the war will start up again?'

'I pray to God it does not,' he said grimly.

'If it does, will you serve again?'

'I may have to.' He smiled. 'But we should not be

thinking such sombre thoughts. Nothing will happen. The French are just as tired of war as the rest of Europe. What would you like to do for your birthday?'

'Birthday?'

'Surely you had not forgotten that tomorrow you will be twenty-one?'

'No, but I thought you had.'

'I could not forget the day you throw off your shackles and become an independent woman.'

'Except for my dependence on you.' She laughed, making a joke of it. 'You know I will never be able to claim my inheritance? It was conditional on my guardian approving my marriage.'

He smiled. 'What a good thing I am a wealthy man. What about the opera? Shall we dress up and show ourselves to the world?'

On the evening of her birthday Maryanne dressed in a gown of Brussels lace over silk, with burgundy satin ribbons slotted round the high waist and hem and along the length of the long sleeves; it set off her figure, now regaining its former curves, and made her look almost ethereal. Around her throat she wore the ruby pendant he had bought her as a birthday present. Seeing her coming down the stairs towards him, Adam found himself with a lump in his throat. 'You look like an angel,' he said.

She laughed. 'But you and I know I am no angel, don't we? The wicked Lady Adams is pretending to be what she is not.'

'If anyone but you said that, I would run them through.' He took her arm. 'Come, let us go; I want to show my lady off. I shall be the envy of Paris.'

'You look very handsome yourself,' she said. He had eschewed the cossack trousers which were the latest fad for black pantaloons which were moulded to his long thighs and shapely calves. His well-tailored evening coat was undone to reveal a fine embroidered waistcoat and a lavishly tied cravat. 'Quite the dandy.'

After the performance, which was all she had hoped
it would be, he took her to Tortoni's for supper. She
was in a happy and relaxed mood as she allowed the
waiter to push in her chair for her, knowing they made
as handsome a couple as any who were there. While
Adam ordered their meal, her attention was drawn to
a noisy party of English people on the other side of the
room.

'You should have seen him!' a woman's voice said.
'Taking off old Boney to perfection. The old fellow
couldn't be sure if it was his Emperor or not and he
didn't know whether to fall to his knees, kiss him or
arrest him. I don't know how I kept a straight face.'

Maryanne froze in her seat, because the voice was
unmistakably Caroline's. She tugged at Adam's coat
skirts. 'Adam, Caroline is over there.' She jerked her
head backwards.

He smiled. 'So she is, but we will not let that spoil
our meal.'

'Adam, please, let's go. For all you know, Mark is
with her.'

He craned his neck to see over her head. 'I do
believe he is. And Caroline's friends—the Halesworth
girls and Lord Brandon. I heard he had been appointed
to the embassy staff.'

'What are we going to do?'

'We are going to have our meal, Maryanne. Mark
does not frighten me and, in any case, there is nothing
he can do to us here.'

'It will always be the same, won't it?' she said, as the
waiters came and set pâté and fish and English beef on
the table, together with a bottle of champagne. 'We
will never be able to stop running.'

'You could stop now,' he said. 'Go back to him, if
that is what you want.'

'You know it is not. I was referring to the fact that
we have to skulk in corners for fear of being seen.
What I want more than anything is to be able to look
the world in the eye.'

'Do you feel guilty?'

'No, why should I?' She looked up at him, trying to guess what was going on behind that scarred brow. 'Do you?'

'No.' The word was said quietly but he was angry. What right had he to be angry with her? She was innocent of any crime—except doubt, but was that a crime?

'I could almost believe you wanted him to see you,' she said angrily. 'What will you do if he does?'

'What will *you* do? Will you rush into his arms and beg forgiveness? Do you think he will take you back?'

'I know he will not.' At any other time she would have enjoyed the luxury of the fruit-flavoured ices which the waiter set before them, but now she pushed hers away.

'Not even for your fortune?' He smiled, but it was a twisted smile which lifted the scar above his eye and made him look sinister. 'Do you regret forgoing that? Would you like to turn the clock back?'

'It is not in our power to do that. If it were, you would, perhaps, have done it yourself.'

'You are right,' he said, thinking of what he had brought her to—a life which obviously made her miserable. 'We must make the best of what is here and now. You and I, my dear Maryanne, are indivisible. Are you ready to leave?'

She nodded and he beckoned the waiter to fetch her cloak. It seemed to take an age to help her into it and then for her to cross the room, with Adam's hand under her elbow.

'Evening, Saint-Pierre, I see you are enjoying the delights of Paris.' Mark's words sounded more like a threat than a pleasant enquiry and Maryanne turned towards Adam, hardly daring to breathe. His face was white, the scar over his eye stood out and a muscle in his throat twitched. He remained frozen like that for several seconds while Mark's smile died on his face and was replaced by a look of animal fear.

Caroline seized his coat tail and made him sit again. 'Leave it, Mark, please.'

'You are right,' he said with a twisted smile, directed at Adam. 'He is not worth the effort and neither is she. My lawyers have found a way to release the inheritance back to the family. As a criminal, she has forfeited it.' His laugh was an ugly sound and made diners from other tables turn to look at them. 'He is welcome to the whore for I no longer need her.'

'I say, Mark, that's a bit strong,' Lord Brandon said. 'He could call you out for it.'

'No,' Mark said. 'He dare not fight me.' He turned to Adam, his confidence returned. 'You won't, will you, no matter what I say?'

Maryanne tugged at Adam's sleeve. 'Please, Adam, let us go. He is only trying to goad you into something foolish. Please, please, let's go.'

He shrugged her off, still looking at Mark. 'May I suggest you go armed in future?' he said evenly. 'Paris is a dangerous place for Englishmen at present. But then I have no doubt you have brought your body-guards.' He affected to look round the room. 'Where are they, by the way? I hope their aim has improved; when we last met they could not hit a barn door at twenty paces.' With that he took Maryanne's arm and walked out to their waiting carriage, with Mark's harsh laugh echoing behind them. He bundled her inside and got in beside her.

'Why did you have to speak to them?' she demanded. 'Why? We could have ignored them.'

'It was you who said you wanted to look the world in the eye. . .'

'I did not need a demonstration that we could not do it—I know that already.'

He turned and seized her arms. 'You would have me ignore his insinuations? For two pins. . .'

'It was me he insulted, not you, and I do not care what he says. We often say things when we are hurt that we would not otherwise dream of uttering.'

'Hurt? *He is hurt*? *Mon Dieu*, why do you always have to find excuses for him? After what he called you. . .'

'He is like a spoiled child who can't have what he wants. I don't understand why you attach so much importance to it. If we are to appear in Society at all, we shall have to become used to being reviled.'

'I will make him eat those words,' he said. 'As heaven is my witness.'

'And I wish you would release my arms; you are hurting me,' Maryanne said.

He dropped his hands and mumbled an apology, and they arrived at the house without either of them saying another word. He escorted her to the door, where he lifted her fingers to his lips and turned to leave her.

'Where are you going?' she asked.

'I have business to attend to.'

'Adam, you won't do anything foolish, will you?'

'Foolish, my dear Maryanne?' He gave a cracked laugh. 'It seems that these days I do little else. Go to bed; I will not wake you when I come in.'

No, he would not wake her, she thought, and how she wished he would! They lived openly as Sir Peter and Lady Adams and yet, in private, they were no more than companions, not even friends. And now there was Mark to contend with. Why had he come to Paris? She had been terrified they would come to blows. As it was, she was not at all sure the incident was over. If she had any idea where Adam had gone, she would have followed him. Instead, she climbed the stairs to a bedroom that was nothing short of luxurious and stripped off her finery, wishing they could go back to the humble lodgings in Montmartre where, because he was dependent on her, they had been so close. Now they were as far apart as ever.

Adam, pacing the streets, could not have wished it any more fervently than she did. He fumed with frustrated fury at a fate which seemed to be determined to deny him the one thing he wanted above all other. Maryanne had been right—he should have walked right out of that restaurant without speaking, but his pride would not let him; he had wanted to show her that they had nothing to fear while they remained in France, that he was master of the situation. But was he? One way or another, he had to resolve his dilemma, even if it meant going back to the man who was the cause of all the trouble. But he could no more indulge in a duel now than he could in London, as Mark very well knew, though with a right arm which was still not functioning properly the odds had certainly turned in the other's favour.

And Maryanne. What in heaven's name was he going to do about her? Send her back to England?

'Choucas!' The voice came to him from out of the darkness, and he realised he had wandered far from the genteel, civilised side of Paris and was in the Stygian gloom of the narrow alleys of the Quartier de St Antoine. It was here, as a twelve-year-old, he had found himself after the death of Louis Saint-Pierre. Here, he had become known as *Le Choucas*; here he had fought, eaten, slept and thieved to stay alive, until one day, when he was sixteen, nearly seventeen, his closest companion had died and he had realised that before long he would go the same way, just one more death in the thousands that went unknown and unmourned in a city that did not care.

He had enlisted. But some of his links with that past had survived the years; they were often a source of information no amount of bureaucracy could match, though if any of them realised the use he made of what he had been told his life would not be worth a sou.

He turned to face the speaker who, at first glance, appeared to be a wizened old man, but on closer inspection was found to be no older than Adam himself. 'Lerue, *mon cher ami*!' Adam grinned and held out both hands, which were immediately clasped. 'How are you, *mon vieux*?'

'The same as ever.' The little man laughed. 'But you have come up in the world, I can see. Not in the army now?'

'Discharged.'

'Come home with me, share a bottle of wine and we will talk,' said Lerue.

'I am not sure I can,' Adam began, thinking of Maryanne. 'I am not alone in Paris. . .'

'The English *mam'selle* can wait. I have something to tell you. . .that is if you want to hear it?'

'Yes, but how did you know about the lady?' Adam asked.

Lerue tapped his nose and laughed. 'I know. Lady Adams! That is a good joke, *n'est-ce-pas*? You, who swore no woman could hold you, are enslaved.'

'It is no jest, *mon ami*, and I wish you would drop the subject.' They made an incongruous pair, as they made their way along the dingy street, the one tall, broad-shouldered and elegantly dressed, the other bent and grey-haired and indescribably dirty.

'Then tell me this, are you turned *anglais*?'

'I have never made a secret of the fact that my mother was English,' Adam said, carefully controlling his voice so as to sound relaxed and easy, but he was acutely aware of the shadows in the darkness. What had they found out? Was he to die in this filthy slum after all?

'And *bourgeois*, I know, but you have been forgiven for what you cannot help, and that is not what I meant. There is going to be trouble.' They had reached a tumbledown hovel tucked into a dark courtyard. Lerue opened the door, ushered Adam inside and groped around for a taper to light a candle.

'Trouble?' Adam looked round the filthy, barely furnished room. It seemed incredible that he had once lived like this and it was only by the grace of God that he had escaped. 'For whom?'

'Monsieur Villainton,' he said, using the derogatory name the French Press had given the British Ambassa-

dor. 'He is a great soldier but. . .' He paused to fetch
a bottle of wine and two cracked cups from a cupboard.

'But no diplomat?' Adam guessed.

'On the contrary, he is proving to be a very good
one. He manages to calm the fears of the *législatif*
while he consorts with the Bourbons and makes an ally
of Talleyrand.'

Adam laughed. 'That is not difficult; the Prince de
Talleyrand has turned his coat so often, he no longer
knows which side is outside. But if it brings peace,
surely that is what you want?'

'With *Louis le Gros* on the throne? He is no more
than a puppet of *les anglais*. He would take us back a
quarter of a century to the France we shed a river of
blood to destroy. *Non, mon ami*, the people want the
return of the eagle.'

'Ahh.' Adam let out his breath in a long sigh. So this
was what the preamble was leading to. 'I thought as
much. But why are you telling me this, when you
clearly have doubts about my allegiance?'

'I did not say I doubted it, though there are those
who do. . .' Lerue paused, peering up into Adam's
face. 'And there is a way to demonstrate your loyalty.
You have the ear of the Ambassador. . .'

'No.' It was not something Adam could admit to. 'I
would not be accepted in the rarefied atmosphere of
the Ambassador's court.' He grinned. 'It is a matter of
the lady. . .'

'Pah to that,' Lerue retorted. 'The Duke is not
innocent in that respect; he understands about *l'amour*.
You must go to him, tell him to leave Paris, or there
will be a new bloodbath, beginning with him.'

'You do not care a fig about the blood of one
Englishman, so why do you want him out of Paris?'
Adam asked.

'If the eagle flies again, Wellington is the only man
on earth who can stop him. He is the only man the
prisoner on Elba fears.'

'I can't go to His Grace with a tale so flimsy—he will

laugh in my face. If there is a plot, who is behind it? Bonapartists? The army? The people?'

Lerue smiled. 'A plot? Perhaps. But be sure of this—for every shako with a white cockade there is a red cap, for every fleur-de-lis there is an eagle. Tucked into many an otherwise empty cupboard is a treasured *tricolore*. We are all Frenchmen, Choucas, we believe in the Resurrection.' He nodded at the cup Adam held. 'Will you drink to France?'

'Willingly. To France.' Adam emptied his cup and it was immediately refilled.

'And to the eagle.'

'To the eagle.'

'Death to our enemies, wherever they are.'

'That too.'

'And to peace.'

'To peace.'

'To love.'

'And love.' This was said softly, with thoughts of Maryanne uppermost in Adam's mind.

With each toast there was a fresh cup of wine and although they became slightly tipsy they could both hold their drink and were by no means drunk. They moved from making toasts to reminiscing and from remembering things past to thinking of the future, and that brought them round to their starting-point. It was nearly dawn when Adam finally left and made his erratic way home. He was aware that he was being watched and that if he did not persuade Wellington to leave he could expect retribution, but the wine and comradeship of his old friend had dulled his senses; he was in a cheerful mood. He had almost forgotten Mark Danbury.

It was dawn when he let himself into the house and crept upstairs. Outside Maryanne's door, he paused, putting his hand on the handle, but then changed his mind and went on to his own room. There was no point in waking her; he had nothing to say to her. He changed quickly into riding clothes and then went out again.

He cursed Lerue and his wine and he cursed the headache he had now. How he was going to persuade the Duke to see him he did not know, but speak to him he must. He rode to the Bois du Boulogne where His Grace liked to ride of a morning, only to discover that the Duke had cut short his exercise to return to the Embassy. Adam had no choice but to go there himself.

He was told to wait in an ante-room and then cursed his fate when the aide who came to enquire his business turned out to be Lord Brandon. 'I don't know how you have the temerity to come here,' he said.

'Why not?' Adam grinned at the other's discomfiture. 'Be so good as to ask His Grace if he can spare me a few minutes of his time.'

'You surely do not expect him to receive you?'

'If you tell him I am here, I think I can safely guarantee he will see me.'

'What can you possibly have to say which will interest His Grace?'

'I will tell him that.'

'Then write to him. His Grace is dressing and has no time to see you.'

'What I have to tell him cannot be entrusted to paper. And he is not the only one short of time. I am in a devilish hurry myself.' Adam's sword was out and pointing at his lordship's throat before the astonished man could do anything about it. 'You already believe I would not hesitate to kill in cold blood, so conduct me to His Grace, if you please.'

Lord Brandon spread his hands. 'As you can see, I am unarmed.'

'Good, then we should have no trouble.'

His lordship, remembering the bloodthirsty tales Mark had told him about the Frenchman, decided not to argue. He led the way from the room and up the stairs where he knocked on one of the many doors.

It was opened by the Duke himself, a habit which

frequently astonished his visitors. He was in grey breeches and shirt-sleeves. His uniform jacket hung over a chair and his highly polished boots stood beside it. Adam returned his sword to its scabbard and pushed past Lord Brandon. 'Your Grace, I am sorry for this unconventional arrival, but his lordship was not inclined to announce me.'

The Duke smiled. 'He is paid, among other things, to protect me from vagabonds like you.' He turned to Brandon. 'You may leave us and make sure we are not disturbed for at least five minutes.'

Lord Brandon scowled and Adam could not refrain from grinning; it was not the first time he had bested a junior official over whether the Duke of Wellington would see him, but this time he had been less sure of himself. If the events at Castle Cedars had reached the ducal ears, he might very well have been refused.

Knowing that when the Duke said five minutes he meant exactly that, he lost no time in explaining his errand as soon as they were alone. The Duke listened gravely, but refused to be intimidated by threats.

'I am aware of the situation,' he said. 'And, although I have nothing against making a strategic withdrawal, it would look decidedly odd if I were to pick up my tails and run now, don't you think? If it is found necessary to withdraw me, then I hope it can be done with dignity, but until then I stay at my post.' He paused before going on. 'Rest assured, we will be watchful, Captain.' He smiled. 'If you want to be of service, do as you have always done—watch and listen and keep me informed.'

'Yes, Your Grace.'

'Preferably in the south.'

'I had planned to go to Challac, Your Grace. It is near Grenoble,' Adam explained.

'Good. Good. That suits me very well.'

Adam took his leave; it was no more than he had expected but he didn't think his old friends would be satisfied with that and was half glad of the excuse to

leave Paris. He had been commissioned to look and
listen and report what he saw and heard, and he knew
that the Duke's mild way of putting it was an instruction to act positively. He was not expected to sit on his
estate and wait for news to come to him. If there was
going to be trouble, he ought to send Maryanne back
to Robert where she would be safe, but the very
thought of parting from her was almost more than he
could bear.

Maryanne spent the morning supervising household
tasks but returned every now and again to the letter. It
had come from England and it was addressed in a
flourishing hand she guessed belonged to Robert
Rudge. Robert had already sent money, so why had he
written again so quickly unless he had something
important to tell Adam? About the murder? Or to
warn him that Mark was coming to Paris? If so, he was
too late and the damage had been done. She felt like
going up to Adam's room and shaking him into wake-
fulness so that he would come down and satisfy her
curiosity.

   When he did appear, it was not from his bedroom,
but from the street. 'Where have you been?' she
demanded, her anxiety making her speak sharply. 'You
haven't met Mark again, have you?'

   'No, my dear, if I had intended duelling with him, I
would have done it in London. 'Tis a pity I didn't—it
might have saved a deal of heartache.'

   'Then where have you been?'

   'I went for a ride in the Bois du Boulogne to clear
my head. I am afraid I imbibed a little too much after
I left you last night.'

   She smiled her relief; it was easier to forgive him for
getting drunk than going after Mark. 'It's too late for
breakfast,' she said.

   'I am not hungry. I'll have coffee.' He picked up the
letter and ripped it open while she rang for a servant.

When she turned back to him, she was astonished by the expression on his face. It was alight with joy.

'She's alive, Maryanne. Alive. Can it be true?' He read the letter again while she stood staring at him. 'All these years. . .'

'Adam, who is alive?'

'*Maman. Maman.* The Comte de Challac has written to me—I played a small part in getting him out of the hulks at Portsmouth and reuniting him with his wife— did I tell you? Robert has forwarded the letter.' He handed it to Maryanne. 'Here, read it yourself.'

Maryanne took the sheet of paper to the window to read what the Count had written.

When I heard a rumour that there was an English-woman in the Convent of St Margaret, I went to enquire after her, thinking that I might perhaps, in gratitude for my own good fortune, be able to do for her what you did for me and restore her to her home. It is many years since I saw *madame*, but I am almost sure the lady was your mother, though pathetically thin and stooped. The nuns say they rescued her from the prison where she had been kept ever since the Terror, and though they have cared for her devotedly she is very confused. She can remember brief glimpses of the past which fly away as soon as you try to probe more deeply. I beg you make all haste to come and see for yourself. Your old home is hardly habitable, so please come and stay at the château with us. Hortense calls you her saviour and wants, above all, to give you her thanks personally.

She looked up at Adam when she had finished reading. He looked as though he did not know whether to laugh or cry. 'If only I had known!' he cried. 'I truly believed she had been executed just before her husband. I saw him die, you know. Just before they. . . just before that, I spoke to him and he said he hoped they had been merciful and I took that to mean. . . Oh, Maryanne!'

He grabbed her round the waist and swung her off her feet to kiss her. Slowly he set her down, but his mouth did not leave hers; the kiss lingered on and she felt swamped by her love for him. It came over her in waves like the sea pounding on a shore, relentless, undeniable, sweeping away all doubts. It was just as it had been in Dover—so sure, so rock-solid.

'We must go to her at once,' she said when he released her.

'We? You include yourself?'

'Of course,' she said. 'What else would I do but come with you? Wasn't that always your intention?'

'Yes, but after last night I thought you might have changed your mind.'

'What has last night to do with it? You still do not think I want to go back to England, even if I could? There is nowhere for me to go, you know that.'

'You were the one who did not want to be always running away. You could go back to the Duke of Wiltshire. . .'

She stared at him, unable to believe that their disagreement of the night before still rankled. 'That is out of the question and you know it.'

'I cannot take you to Challac unmarried. It is not like Paris, you know. . .' He stopped. Eleanor Saint-Pierre would be able to prove who he was and he prayed she was not as confused as the Count seemed to think. '*Maman*——'

'Would be horrified,' she interrupted him. 'Is that all you can think of?' She blinked back the tears which sprang to her eyes. How could he be so blind? It was almost as if he was trying to turn her against him.

'It is a little late to go down on my knees and propose in the conventional manner, Maryanne. I remember you telling me you would not marry me however compromised you had been, but we cannot go on like this. God, woman, don't you know what it's been like for me these last weeks? I won't be held at arm's length and played with like a cat plays with a mouse.'

'I haven't done any such thing!'

'Oh, yes, you have. Now, you must make up your mind, once and for all. If you come, it will be as my wife or. . .' He did not want to say it again, knowing he was tempting fate. But he had to know.

She was in tears. 'Adam, I have said I will come with you, I have always said it. . .'

'As my wife?'

'As your wife.' The words were whispered.

He let out his breath in a long sigh of relief. 'You will not regret it,' he said. 'And one day, as God is my witness, you will be able to hold up your head anywhere in the world.' He kissed her then, but she felt wooden and unresponsive, the exuberance of a few minutes before gone. If only he had wanted to marry her because he loved her, if only. . .

They were married the same day, in a quiet ceremony witnessed only by Lerue and another old acquaintance of Adam's, neither of whom Maryanne had met before. They came, she realised, from Adam's past, from his jackdaw days, and she found them rather frightening.

'They are good men,' Adam assured her. 'And who else could we ask?'

He was right, of course; all their Parisian friends believed them to be already married. It did not help her to feel any less nervous about the step she was taking. She wanted, more than anything in the world, to be his wife; she wanted to be done with pretence, to share his life and to know that, whatever happened, they were united in their love for each other. But how could that be achieved when it was all so one-sided, when his prime consideration was the silencing of gossip?

She forced herself to put her doubts behind her as he took his place beside her in the church and the parson began the service. It was done now and she must make the best of it. Perhaps, in time, it would all

come right; perhaps, when the past had been put
behind them, they could build a future for themselves.

As soon as the ceremony was over, they left Paris in
a hired chaise. Adam was relaxed and cheerful and
talked of his home and his parents and how eagerly he
awaited his reunion with his mother, so that by the
time they stopped at an inn for the night she had caught
his mood. Perhaps it was only in Paris he was so
morose, and now that he was going home she would
come to know the real Adam Saint-Pierre.

He ordered a meal to be brought to their room, but,
unable to think of anything but the big four-poster bed,
she had no appetite.

'Is it not to your taste, my dear?' he asked, after
watching her push her food round her plate.

'I find I am not hungry,' she told him.

He smiled and stood up. 'Neither am I.' He took her
hand and drew her to her feet. 'My hunger is of a
different kind.'

She stood, almost impassively, as he kissed her, but
when his tongue found hers and his hands began the
gentle task of rousing her she found herself responding,
shyly at first, then, as he removed her clothes, taking
his time, kissing her and caressing her with great
tenderness, she became more and more inflamed. Her
love, her desire, her need found expression in a passion
that not even he could have guessed at. Delighted, he
picked her up and carried her to the bed.

Not until the following morning did she realise that,
whatever happened, nothing would ever be the same
again, that irrevocably she was his wife and if he could
not find it in his heart to love her as a husband should
at least he knew how to be kind and gentle. She would
try to be content.

CHAPTER TEN

THEY reached Challac two days later, two days in which Maryanne was blissfully happy. She was almost afraid to arrive, in case it should all come to an end.

The village nestled in a valley enfolded by hills. There was a church with a very tall steeple and quaint little cottages grouped around a tree-lined square where a fountain played. There was a plinth beside it, but no statue. 'They took it down,' Adam said, smiling. 'It was one of Bonaparte. I imagine they are in no hurry to replace it with another of Louis.'

His home was called Les Cascades, he told her, because of the many little waterfalls which tumbled down the steep slopes that surrounded it. From a distance it looked a beautiful house, not quite a château, nor an English mansion, but when their coach made its way up the drive and they drew nearer they could see it was almost derelict. Windows were broken, slates missing from the roof and the oak door looked as though it had been battered down with a tree-trunk. The garden was a wilderness of weeds, except large areas where the grass had been trampled flat.

'They must have had heavy guns here,' Adam said. 'It is a wonder the place is still standing at all.'

Next to the house, they saw a tiny patch of cultivated ground where potatoes and onions grew, and here a bent old man was hoeing. He stopped what he was doing as the coach came to a stop and stood watching them. Suddenly his face broke into a grin, revealing a single broken tooth. '*Monsieur Adam*!' He turned to scuttle back into the house, crying, 'Anna! Anna! *Monsieur*, our master, is back. Come and see!'

A little round tub of a woman came to the kitchen door, wiping her hands on her apron. 'Oh, *monsieur*,

191

can it be you?' She peered short-sightedly at Adam.
'All the long years we prayed for you and now our
prayers have been answered.'

'Thank you, Anna. It is good to see you again. And
you, Henri. Maryanne, these two good people, Henri
and Anna Caronne, were here in the old days.' He
turned back to the old servants. 'This is my wife. She
is English but she can understand your French if you
speak slowly.'

The woman bobbed a curtsy. 'Come into the kitchen,
the rest of the house. . .' She paused to wipe a tear
from her eye with the corner of her apron. 'It is not fit
to see.'

They followed the old couple into the house and
were conducted round the empty rooms. They
inspected the broken plaster, the scuffed paintwork,
the scorched fireplaces, the staircases with their missing
banisters and the chipped tiles on what had once been
an outstanding mosaic floor in the main hall.

'What could we do?' Henri asked plaintively. 'We
are old.'

'You did well,' Adam said. 'And we shall soon set it
to rights, ready for *madame*, my mother's return.'

'She is alive?' Two pairs of eyes lit up with sudden
joy. 'She is really alive?'

Adam nodded. 'I believe so.'

The old woman fell to her knees, to clasp his hand.
'Praise be to God. Where is she? When shall we see
her?'

'Soon,' Adam said. 'Now we must go, but we will be
back tomorrow. I want you to make a list of all the
repairs that need doing. I mean to lose no time.'

'Yes, *monsieur*, of course. God bless you.'

'They were overjoyed to see you,' Maryanne said
when they had returned to the carriage.

'Yes.' He seemed preoccupied, as if he was not really
listening, as if he could hear other sounds, echoes of a
past she could not share.

At the convent, she waited in the coach while he

jumped down to ring the bell. A nun came to the grille and Adam spoke briefly to her, then the door was opened and he turned and beckoned to Maryanne.

'*Maman* is in the garden,' he said. 'We are to go and find her.'

'Be gentle with her,' the nun said. 'It will be a shock.' She folded her arms into her wide sleeves, smiled at them both and turned away.

They followed the path she had indicated into a secluded garden where several women sat or walked in the sunshine. They were all dressed in similar shapeless gowns and Adam could not, at first, pick his mother out. 'They are all so old and bent,' he said. '*Maman* was—— There she is!'

Maryanne restrained him as he started forward. 'Adam don't rush, go slowly. I will wait here.' She sat down on a bench against the wall and watched as he approached the woman he had singled out, took her arm and led her to a seat, talking and smiling. He was rewarded with a blank stare of incomprehension; his mother did not recognise him. He looked up at Maryanne in despair, his need for her support obvious in his face. She stood up and went over to him.

'*Maman*,' he said, reaching out his hand to draw Maryanne forward. 'This is Maryanne, my wife. We are going to take you home.'

The blank eyes looked up at him. 'Home?'

Maryanne smiled and sat beside her, taking her hand. 'Yes, but not until you are ready. This is your son. This is Adam. Don't you know him?'

'My Adam is a child. The Committee of Public Safety took him. They killed him. They killed Louis too.' She spoke flatly. 'You are one of them. . .'

'No, I——'

'Murderer!' she screamed suddenly. 'Killer of little children!'

Adam groaned and covered his face with his hands. Maryanne put out a hand to him as tears squeezed themselves between his fingers. She became aware that

his mother was staring at him with her eyes wide and
mouth open, as if something had touched a chord in
her memory.

'You are James,' the older woman said slowly.
'James Danbury. What are you doing here? Go away!
Go back where you came from!'

Maryanne turned from her to Adam and then she
saw plainly what had always been there to see—his
likeness to James. Adam was James's son! Everything
that had happened in the last year flashed across her
mind—the way they had met, his odd references to the
Danbury family, his refusal to fight Mark, the curricle
race and James's strange reaction to the mention of
Adam's name. She remembered how she had felt when
Caroline had said she was James's by-blow: shame and
anger, but most of all a vulnerability. He looked like
that now and her heart went out to him. No wonder he
was bitter, no wonder he could not talk of it. Miraculously it did not seem to have turned him against his
mother, even if she did not want to be reminded of it.
He was staring at her now, as if unable to believe his
ears.

Maryanne put a hand on his arm. 'Adam, we can't
take her away from here today—the upheaval would
confuse her more than ever. We must come again
tomorrow and every day until she gets used to us.'

He seemed incapable of speech and simply nodded
his acquiescence. It was not until they were in the
coach and travelling to the Count of Challac's château
that he spoke, and then it was in tones of despair.
'What am I to do, Maryanne? She thinks I am. . .'

'I know, but don't you see, it is a good sign? It means
the past is not entirely forgotten,' she told him. 'We
can have no idea what horrors she lived through during
her years of imprisonment, but if she was incarcerated
with revolutionaries, criminals and ruffians and shut
away from what has been going on in the world it is
hardly surprising that she is confused. Once your
mother accepts us, whoever she thinks we are, and we

take her home, things will improve. We must have patience.'

They stayed with the Comte and Comtesse de Challac while Les Cascades was made habitable. The Countess was a lively, bubbling person and Maryanne could easily see why the Count was so devoted to her. It made her all the more aware of what was lacking in her own marriage: a togetherness, an understanding that needed no words, a devotion that all could see.

They could not have been kinder, but Maryanne could not stop herself feeling depressed and homesick. It would be decidedly cool in England now and the leaves of the trees in Beckford woods would be a glory of gold and red, spreading a soft carpet under the boughs. In the rectory the fires would be lit and there would be roasted nuts and wrinkled apples and the window-panes of a morning would be misted. Soon there would be frosts. Did they have frosts in the south of France? They were in a mountainous region, so she supposed they must, but now, in October, the air was still warm and dry.

Did those at home—she persisted in thinking of it as home—still think of her as a party to murder? Or had they ceased to think of her at all? Did it matter? She had to admit it mattered a great deal and she wished she could go back and show them how wrong they were. But Adam never spoke of the possibility; all he seemed to think of was Les Cascades, the state of the country and whether war would come again.

He would not bring his mother home until the repairs had been done, believing that the sight of her home in ruins would make her worse, but by the middle of December they had finished restoring the main rooms, and as she had shown signs of considerable improvement and sometimes talked quite rationally they had moved out of the château and into Les Cascades and fetched her home.

There were occasions when she seemed much better and others when she was as confused as ever, and

Adam was frequently in despair. Apart from the fact that he loved her dearly, he had been counting on her to help resolve his dilemma in England, and that looked as unlikely as ever. Her behaviour varied from that of an imperious aristocrat, demanding instant obedience, to that of a mischievous child. Sometimes she spoke like a lady, sometimes like a gutter urchin.

The last of the old year had gone by and they were two months into 1815 before Maryanne began to catch glimpses of the woman Eleanor had once been and she could understand Adam's love for her. But by then Adam was not there to see it. She had once asked him what he did when he was away, but he had turned the question aside with some teasing comment which told her nothing except that her company was not enough to keep him at home. He had been gone much longer than usual this time and she was becoming concerned, though she said nothing of that to her mother-in-law.

The sun was warm and the wind had lost its keen edge for the first time since Christmas and, walking in the garden with Madame Saint-Pierre in the first week of March, Maryanne felt the first faint stirring of spring.

'He said he would come back,' Eleanor said, startling Maryanne, because they had been walking side by side in silence for so long. 'But I told him not to. "It's not fair on the child," I said.' She appealed to Maryanne. 'Was I right? Should I have stopped him from coming back?'

'Who are you talking about, *Maman*?' Maryanne asked gently.

'James. I told him to stay away from Adam. Adam was mine, he gave him to me. I didn't want him changing his mind and taking him back. Was I wrong?'

'No, dear, you were not wrong,' Maryanne assured her. How could anyone censure this poor muddled woman?

'He has grown into a fine man, has he not?'

'Who?'

'Adam, your husband,' she said sharply. 'Who did

you think I was talking about? He is just like James was. Do you know, sometimes when I look at him I think he is James? Foolish of me, isn't it?'

'Not at all.' She paused; was this the long-awaited recovery? 'Do you remember what happened?'

'No.' The older woman turned away abruptly. 'I do not want to remember.'

Maryanne took her arm. 'You don't have to if you don't want to, *Maman*. Come, let us finish our walk.'

'James shan't have him back, I won't let him go,' she said vehemently. 'And if anyone asks me I shall deny everything.' She gave a laugh that was almost a cackle; it reminded Maryanne very forcefully that there were periods of the older woman's life it was better not to delve into.

She was almost glad of Henri's interruption. '*Madame*, I must speak to you,' he said.

'Of course. Is something wrong?'

'There is a report. . .'

'Report of what?'

'The second coming, *madame*.'

She had been so immersed in her work in the house and looking after Eleanor that she had paid little attention to what was going on in the outside world. Adam did. He wrote and received letters and he sometimes spoke of his impatience with the Congress of Vienna, which seemed more concerned with parties and balls than completing its business, but he had expressed the hope that now the Duke of Wellington had replaced Castlereagh as the British plenipotentiary things might begin to move a little faster. He had also been extremely relieved to hear the Duke had left Paris, where trouble between Bonapartists and Bourbonists made it a dangerous place for him to be. The day he and Maryanne had left Paris a shot had whistled uncomfortably close to his head.

She smiled. 'Oh, that old rumour about Napoleon escaping from Elba. You don't believe it, do you?'

'It is not a rumour, *madame*. It has already happened.

I was told by a courier who stopped on his way to Paris to change his horse.'

'Surely the Emperor would not dare to land on French soil,' Maryanne asserted.

'He landed at Fréjus with a thousand men a week ago,' he said. 'Since then he has marched, unopposed, up behind Cannes, through Digne and Sisteron towards Grenoble, and will soon be at Challac.'

Her heart began to beat uncomfortably fast at the thought of Les Cascades being, once more, in the path of an army. Ought she to do something to defend it? But how could she with only a handful of servants? 'What should we do?' she asked.

'Nothing, *madame*. He will be heading for Paris and will not step aside from that unless he is opposed,' Henri replied.

'Isn't anyone going to try and stop him?'

He smiled his toothless smile. 'I doubt it, *madame*. The army is on his side, even if some of the officers are not, and the people have had enough of fighting; it matters little who rules us as long as we can be left to live our lives in peace.'

She hoped he was right. Until Adam returned, she had to pretend everything was normal for Madame Saint-Pierre's sake. She turned to seek her out, all too aware of the heavy burden of responsibility she carried. If Adam did not come home soon, the house, the servants and a confused, prematurely old woman would all have to be taken care of. There was Eleanor now, kneeling on the damp grass with no thought for the aches and pains which might result. Maryanne hurried to help her up. '*Maman*, the ground is too wet to kneel.'

The older woman turned to her with an expression of childish delight. In her hand she held a small bunch of violets. 'Look, Maryanne, look! Spring has come at last.'

Napoleon Bonaparte had been the ogre of Europe nearly all Maryanne's life; like all English children she had been brought up to dread his coming. 'Behave

yourself or old Boney will get you', was as familiar a
saying as, 'If you are naughty, you won't go to heaven'.
And now he was only a few miles away. Telling herself
he was only a man like any other did nothing to calm
her fears. She longed for Adam. Why could he not be
content to stay with her? Why was he not fulfilled
unless he was chasing round the countryside on some
secret errand? It almost made her angry. Perhaps it
was better to be angry; anger was easier to bear than
hurt.

The day's news was still large in her mind when she
went to bed, and she could not sleep. After tossing
about for more than an hour, she rose, put a shawl
round her shoulders and went to sit by the window.
Down in the valley she could see the church spire and
the uneven rooftops of the village. Beyond it, the lower
slopes of the mountain had been terraced to make the
vineyards, and above those the dark mass of pine trees
stretched up to a boulder-strewn peak. A light here
and there denoted a cottage or a farmhouse. From a
distant kennel she could hear the bark of a dog and
somewhere an owl hooted. Immediately below her she
could see the roof of the stables and hear the soft
whinny of a horse.

A light flickered in the distance. She stood up to see
the better. There was another and then another. She
ran down to the library and fetched an old telescope
from one of the shelves. She followed the line of the
road through the valley with the glass and then
stopped. The way was full of vehicles, carts and gun
carriages, and on both sides were horses and men,
hundreds of them. It was their camp fires she had seen.
She swept the glass round in an arc to left and right.
The whole hillside was covered with soldiers and Les
Cascades was right in the middle of them.

A movement caught her eye. A single horseman had
detached himself from the main force and was riding
along the road towards the house. She watched him for
some minutes, now shrouded in darkness as he passed

beneath trees, now plainly to be seen as he came out into the moonlight. She craned forward. It couldn't be. . . He turned one of the many sharp bends which the road took on its way to the house and disappeared from view. She held her breath, hardly daring to hope, and then there he was, entering the gates, a tall, upright figure on a big horse. She ran across the room and tore downstairs, flinging open the front door as he dismounted.

'Adam!' She threw herself into his arms.

He kissed her hungrily, then picked her up and carried her back into the house and along the hall to the drawing-room, kicking the door shut behind them with his foot. Setting her down, he held her close to his chest and bent his head to find her lips with his own. She felt the familiar tightening in her stomach and limbs, which made her forget everything in the pleasure of kissing and being kissed.

'You don't know how glad I am you are back,' she said at last. 'I've been frightened, didn't know what to do for the best. . .' She stepped back to look at him properly for the first time. He was wearing a uniform of white breeches and a dark blue coat whose braid denoted the rank of captain. 'Why are you dressed like that?' she asked.

He grinned. 'Don't you like it? I thought it rather dashing. . .'

'How can you joke about such a thing, Adam? You have enlisted again, haven't you?'

'I have no choice, Maryanne,' he said gently. 'I am needed.'

'Don't you think I need you? And *Maman*. What about us, your mother and me, and the servants? Have you no thought for your own people?'

'Do you think I wanted the regiment to come here? *Mon Dieu*, what kind of man do you think I am?' he replied.

'Then make them go away again. Do you know that while you have been gone *Maman* has been so much better? Would you throw her back into the pit of despair again?'

'That is the last thing I want.' His jaw was set.

'Then change out of those clothes before she sees you.'

'I cannot.' He took her shoulders in his hands and looked down into her troubled face. 'Maryanne, my love, you must take *Maman* and leave. I will give you funds to take you as far as Paris. Go to my bankers when you reach there and they will help you to go to England. I will come and find you.' He paused and added softly, 'Wherever you are, I will find you.'

'I won't go! I am not afraid of Napoleon Bonaparte.'

He smiled crookedly, put his finger under her chin and tipped it up so that he could kiss her lips. It was pleasure and pain in an overwhelming wave of emotion which left her breathless and crying. 'Maryanne, think of *Maman*. Think of me. If you are here when the fighting starts, do you think I could do what I have to do with an easy mind? I need to know you are safe.'

'And while I travel the length of France,' she sobbed, 'you will be fighting and killing, perhaps being killed yourself. . .'

'Maryanne, you do not understand. . .'

'Oh, I understand all right,' she retorted. 'You love war. You love the thrill of battle. You have been brought up to fight and never mind who is killed and hurt by it.'

'That is neither fair nor accurate. Don't you see, I have my duty. . .?'

'You also have a duty to me, and to your mother,' she told him. 'You leave us for weeks on end without a word and when you come back it is not to stay with us and protect us, but to send us away. We have taken months to restore this house and the garden. Is it all to be trampled by men in boots, not to mention horses and gun carriages. . .?'

He had to be angry with her; it was the only way he

could make her obey him. 'A beautiful speech, *madame*. But perhaps you should say it to the Emperor, not to me, for I have no time to listen. I have been sent to requisition this house for the regiment's headquarters.' He attempted a smile to cover his own bitterness, but all he managed was a quirk to his lips and a lifting of the scar over his eye. 'The colonel has noticed that it has excellent views all round. He will be here soon to take over himself.'

She stared at him open-mouthed. 'You can't mean that?'

'I am afraid I do.' He wanted to take her in his arms again, but dared not. 'I volunteered to come and see there was no trouble over it.'

'No trouble?' Her voice was a squeak. 'I will give you trouble. I shall refuse to budge.'

'Maryanne, if you do not do as I say, others will come and it will be out of my hands. Go and pack, please.'

'Now?'

'Yes, now.'

'But it is the middle of the night. How will we travel? Who will go with us?'

'You can go in the landaulet; it is light enough for you to drive. The Count has decided not to serve again; he is taking the Countess to England and has agreed to escort you. They will be waiting for you at the church. If all goes well and Bonaparte is stopped before he reaches Paris, I will join you very soon. But do not wait; go to Robert and wait for me.'

'That is all I ever do, wait,' she cried. 'And what happens when we arrive in England? Had you forgotten Mark and the fact that he has accused us both of murder?'

'Had *you* forgotten,' he retorted, 'that you are my wife now? I have made you into a respectable woman. That's what you wanted, wasn't it, to be able to face the world?'

'My reluctance to leave has nothing to do with the

scandal,' she said, fighting back tears. 'And you are cruel to bring that up again.'

He went to the window as the sound of horses could be heard approaching the house. 'The colonel is coming and that means I must revert to being the soldier. And Maryanne. . .' He paused. 'I am not Adam Saint-Pierre. I am not your husband. Do you understand? We have never met before today.'

'Oh,' she said angrily, as she went to the door. 'Who are you, then? Sir Peter Adams or Captain Choucas? What would they say if they knew. . .?'

'Maryanne!' He strode over to her and grabbed her arm. 'If you value my life at all, you will say nothing of that, do you hear? Nothing.'

'And what about *Maman*? How will you silence her? With a fist in her mouth? Would you like me to bind and gag her?'

'Keep her out of the way until it is time to go,' he said. 'When you are ready, go to the stables. I will see you both there.' He stood back from her as Henri admitted the colonel. '*Madame* understands the situation,' Adam told him. 'She is going to pack now.' He gave Maryanne a meaningful look, and she ran from the room, up the stairs to her bedroom, where she flung herself face down on the bed and wept. She wished she didn't love him quite so much; there were times when it was almost like a physical ache which could only be eased by quarrelling with him. And, having argued and shouted and almost come to blows, she was left with the heartache. And that was worse.

Why was their love so turbulent? Two or three months of peace, that was all they had had, and now this. How was she going to endure the parting, not knowing where he was or even if he was alive? And what devious game was he playing, pretending to be a stranger in his own house?

She could hear men's voices now, as they moved about the house, deciding which rooms would best serve their purpose, and she supposed they would soon

come to her bedroom because it had the best views.
Her pride forced her to rise from the bed and make
her reluctant preparations to leave.

When she summoned the servants to instruct them,
she discovered they had already fled, every single one
of them, except Henri and Anna, who were made of
sterner stuff and told her they intended to hide in the
cellar until it was all over. Adam had contrived to let
them know they must treat him as a stranger and they
seemed to have entered into the spirit of the charade
much more willingly than she had. She wondered if
Adam had told them more than he had told her, and
the thought annoyed her. Was she the only one to be
kept in the dark? No, there was also Madame Saint-
Pierre. Poor Eleanor! Just as she was beginning to
improve, this had to happen; better to leave her
sleeping until the very last minute.

She packed a few items of clothing for both of them,
woke *madame* and called Henri to take the baggage
out to the coach. Then she returned to the drawing-
room where the colonel had made himself comfortably
at home. He had spread a map of the area out on the
table and was discussing some points of it with Adam
and another officer.

'Colonel,' she began, 'I beg you to reconsider——'

Before he could reply, Eleanor burst into the room
behind her. Ignoring Adam, she hurled herself at the
colonel, dragging her nails down his face.

Both Adam and Maryanne ran to haul her off, but
not before the colonel had struck her across the face
with the back of his hand with such force that she fell
to the floor. He turned to Maryanne, wiping blood
from his cheek. 'Take her away,' he ordered.

Maryanne bent to help Eleanor to her feet, then
stood with her arm about her, facing him. 'You did not
need to be so brutal. Can't you see she is afraid?' She
caught a glimpse of Adam out of the corner of her eye.
He had turned away; every muscle in his face was rigid
and his hands were clenched against his sides to stop

himself moving or speaking. Whatever game he was
playing, he was in deadly earnest, if he dared not go to
the aid of his mother.

'Afraid?' the colonel queried. 'I have done nothing
to frighten her. Get her out of here, before I have her
arrested.' He turned to Adam. 'Captain, we have work
to do.'

Maryanne, in tears, put her arm round Eleanor's
shoulders and led her out to the stables, where Henri
had harnessed two horses to the landaulet and loaded
their baggage. She climbed in and took the reins from
his hand, but made no move to go.

'*Madame*, I beg you do not delay; you will make it
difficult for him,' he said.

Maryanne's misery turned to anger, anger at the
stupidity of a nation which had almost destroyed itself
by war preparing to do exactly the same again; but
most of all her anger was directed at her husband, who
had condoned the seizure of their home. She jerked on
the reins and the startled horses set off down the drive.

Adam arrived on the front step just in time to see
the carriage disappearing out of sight. He turned and
went back indoors and up the stairs three at a time to
Maryanne's bedroom, where he crossed to the window,
grabbed up the discarded telescope and watched the
vehicle until it had joined the Count's coach at the
crossroads by the church. 'Goodbye, my darling,' he
whispered. 'God go with you.'

He should have sent them away long before. He had
known what was being planned; he had sent his reports
to Vienna as he had been instructed, in the vain hope
that Bonaparte could be prevented from leaving Elba
or, failing that, stopped before he landed. Complacent
fools! Sitting on their backsides in the Congress Hall
waiting to see what would happen next. Well, he could
tell them. Without support from the great Powers, the
French alone could not, would not resist. He doubted
the colonel's capacity to stop him.

Why did it have to happen now, just when Maryanne

was beginning to put the past behind her? Why here, where they had been so happy? Why, when *Maman* had suffered so much already, should she have to suffer more? Would Maryanne be able to manage her? If only they had not quarrelled, if only he could have explained, but the colonel's arrival had stopped him. Perhaps it was just as well, for what could he have told her that it was safe for her to know?

Suddenly he was a child again, emerging from a cupboard to find all his happiness swept away and nothing left but emptiness. He sank down on the rumpled bed, still sweet with Maryanne's perfume, put his head in his hands and groaned in agony.

The Compte de Challac was almost as reluctant a traveller as Maryanne. He insisted on driving slowly, and whenever they found themselves at the top of a rise he stopped the horses and climbed on to the roof of his coach to look back through his spyglass. Sometimes they met troops marching southwards and had to pull to one side to let them pass. 'They will turn him back,' the Count said. 'Then we can go home.'

At Lyons, he called another halt, declaring his intention of staying in the town until he heard news one way or another. Maryanne was happy to agree; every mile was taking her further from Adam and if the Count was right the nearer they were to home when all was resolved, the sooner they could be back there. They found a small hotel, and while the ladies settled in for the evening the Count went out to discover what he could. He returned in great agitation.

'Colonel de la Bédoyère has turned the whole of the Seventh Regiment over to the Emperor and they are all marching north.'

'The Seventh?' queried Maryanne. 'Isn't that the regiment Adam was with?'

'Yes.'

'Have they all gone over?'

'Every last man. Your husband, *madame*, is riding with Napoleon.'

She did not want to believe it, but she was afraid he might be right; she had never been sure where Adam's allegiance lay. 'What are we going to do?' she asked.

'Go on,' the Count said. 'I do not relish the idea of being in the path of an army, especially one so hungry for victory as this one.'

They set off again at dawn. Maryanne, following the Count's coach in her own lighter vehicle, found it difficult to keep up with him. They were approaching Chalon-sur-Saône when they heard that the King's troop had changed sides at Lyons. It was all the more humiliating for the Royalists because they were being reviewed by the King's brother at the time.

'Is nothing being done?' Maryanne asked, when they stopped at an inn for the night; because they were travelling in separate vehicles, it was the only opportunity they had for discussion and making decisions. 'Surely the Allies will do something.'

'My guess is that they are waiting to see if the French can solve their own problems,' the Count said. 'And they may do so yet. Marshal Ney has undertaken to arrest the Emperor and bring him to Paris in a cage.'

'But Marshal Ney was one of the most able and loyal of the Emperor's commanders,' the Countess said. 'They would be unwise to rely on him.'

She was right. By the time they entered Paris on the fifteenth of March, the news was everywhere; Marshal Ney had been won over by one of Bonaparte's proclamations that he had come to save the French people, and now it seemed nothing could stop him. Maryanne, Madame Saint-Pierre and the Count and Countess found a small hotel and sat round the supper table discussing what they would do next.

'The Countess and I have decided to go straight on to England,' the Count said. 'I advise you to do the same.'

'I shall wait for Adam,' Maryanne insisted.

'But how can you be sure he will come?'

'He is with the Emperor, is he not?' she returned.

'What about *madame*? Is it fair to subject her to more upheaval?' the Count went on.

'It seems to me there has been no upheaval,' Maryanne said tartly. 'The advance has been entirely unopposed. And I know *Maman* would rather be near Adam.'

He could not move her and they agreed to part. She watched them leave for Calais the following morning and then set off to see Adam's bankers. He had made generous provision for her, but what was more surprising was that there was a letter for her. It was dated several weeks before and showed he had anticipated events.

If you are reading this, it means we are apart. And you must be my brave little duchess. . . If war comes, and I pray that it does not, then go to England at once. Robert Rudge will know what to do. Hold your head up, my darling wife, and know your husband, who adores you, is thinking of you and longing for you every hour of every day. If you should hear ill of me, do not judge me too harshly, and forgive me my secrets. One day, God willing, you will learn everything. Take care of *Maman* for me; next to you, she is the most precious thing I have.

She looked up from reading it with tear-blurred eyes to find the kindly man who had given it to her regarding her in some concern.

'Not bad news, I hope?'

She smiled. 'No, not at all.'

'You will be returning to England? I have instructions. . .'

'No,' she said quickly. 'I shall stay here.'

'Very well, *madame*, but please do not leave it too late.' Like everyone else, he expected the worst.

On the nineteenth, the King and his entourage fled to Belgium, and the next day Napoleon was carried shoulder-high into the Tuileries without a shot being fired to stop him. The timing of his *coup* had been immaculate.

But if Maryanne thought that was the end of it she was wrong, and if she thought the Emperor's arrival presaged the arrival of Adam, she was wrong again. She heard no word from her husband, and the political news was not good either. Before another week had passed, the European Powers had formally announced an alliance to recapture the eagle and put him back in his cage, and the Duke of Wellington had been made Commander-in-Chief in Flanders. War was inevitable and imminent.

In spite of her bravado about wanting to face the world, returning to England without Adam by her side to give her the strength to defy not only their accusers, but gossiping Society, was something she preferred not to think about. She needed no great persuasion to accede to *Maman*'s daily request to stay 'just one more day' in case Adam arrived. They had parted in anger and that preyed on her mind most of all. Would he come back to her at all, or had her shrewishness made him throw in his lot with the French army to escape her? When, at last, she woke up to the fact that Bonaparte was gathering all his forces to resist the Allies, it was almost too late. The ports had been closed; not even the smallest fishing boat could put to sea, and the only way out of France was through Belgium. But by this time there was another, very strong reason for leaving: she wanted her child to be born in England.

CHAPTER ELEVEN

THE heat was so oppressive that they could hardly breathe. The air was still as a quiet pool; not a leaf stirred, no living thing moved, except Maryanne and Madame Saint-Pierre, plodding wearily across the fields of Flanders. Even the dog, chained to the farm gate, lifted no more than an eyelid at their passing.

'There's going to be a storm,' Eleanor said, pausing to look up at the sky. 'I heard thunder.'

'It's the guns again,' Maryanne told her.

All the previous afternoon they had heard the sounds of heavy guns away to their right as they stumbled across the fields. The ground beneath their ill-shod feet had seemed to throb as if unable to bear the weight of so much concentrated machinery and so many galloping horses. What she could not see Maryanne had imagined and, terrified that the battle would come their way, she had hurried Eleanor into the shelter of a church, where they had huddled down between the pews, expecting to be blown to pieces at any moment. The noise had stopped when darkness fell and next morning they had set off again to cover the remaining twelve miles or so to Brussels and, they hoped, to safety.

Maryanne blamed herself bitterly for the predicament they were in; she should have left Paris weeks before she had, or not moved at all. Her timing, unlike the Emperor's, had been abysmal. She smiled wryly to herself as they skirted a field of shoulder-high corn. If Adam knew the trouble her delaying tactics had caused, he would be even more furious.

It had seemed a simple matter to harness their horses to the landaulet and set off for the Belgian frontier, but when they arrived at Beaumont they had found the

border closed and the only way they could pass through
was to tag on the end of the baggage train following
Napoleon's army, pretending to be camp followers.
The marching army had been an awe-inspiring and
colourful sight, setting out to war as if going on parade.
From the back, their plumed head-dresses reminded
Maryanne of a huge exotic bird stepping delicately
forward, head nodding. She had spotted the marching
columns of the Seventh and, leaving Eleanor driving
the carriage, had hurried forward on foot to ask about
her husband. 'If he's not dead, he very soon will be,'
one of them had said, drawing his forefinger across his
throat.

She dared not stop to ask him what he meant by that
threatening gesture; others were eyeing her with more
than idle curiosity. She had hurried back to Eleanor
and taken the next turning off the main road. At the
entrance to the next town she had been directed to the
commissariat, who had promptly requisitioned the
horses. Pleading with him had been a waste of breath
and they had packed what they could into bundles and
set off on foot, leaving the useless carriage at the inn
where they had stayed the night.

The ground was hard and dry and they walked
briskly, chatting cheerfully to each other. Maryanne
was continually surprised by Eleanor's resilience; she
was far more lucid and sensible than she had ever
known her; it was as if the excitement and danger had
re-awakened a lost something in her which had restored
her self-respect, her *joie de vivre*.

'We ought to find shelter,' she said now. 'We will be
soaked if we don't.'

Maryanne, who had been indulging in a daydream in
which Adam appeared from nowhere with a carriage
and horses, brought herself back to the present with an
effort and surveyed the ink-black sky, just as it was
rent with lightning, followed almost immediately by an
enormous clap of thunder. A great wind tore across
the fields and the heavens opened. In seconds they

were drenched and the hard ground was covered in miniature ponds and rivulets.

'There! What did I tell you?' Eleanor said, standing with her face tilted to the sky, laughing delightedly. 'At least it's cool.'

Maryanne smiled, tugging on her arm. 'Come, *Maman*, we must find shelter. There's a road beyond that field.'

But when they arrived at the road, their laughter stopped abruptly. The *pavé* was choked with civilian refugees, wounded soldiers still able to walk, runaway horses with stirrups swinging emptily, men who had become detached from their regiments, deserters who had thrown away their weapons, and carts loaded with wounded. 'We got good and licked,' they were told by a red-coated British soldier who limped along leaning on his musket. 'Boney stole a march on us.'

In the little village of Genappe they found an inn. 'There!' Maryanne said, pointing. 'The Roi d'Espagne awaits us.'

She was surprised that no more than a handful of those on the road were prepared to stop and chance being taken by the French, but it made it easier for them to obtain a room and refreshment and they were soon sitting before a roaring fire in their undergarments while their dresses gently steamed on the fender. The rain still poured down outside, but the exodus of refugees had slowed to a trickle and the road was almost empty again.

'How long before Bonaparte's troops march in, do you suppose?' Eleanor ventured. 'What do you think they will do with us?'

'Nothing. Why should they be interested in a couple of bedraggled women? We are French. At least, you can pass yourself off as French and my husband is marching with the French Army. . .'

'I doubt that.' Eleanor seemed so sure, but she had never really known what Adam had done in the years she was in prison. No one knew but Adam himself;

Maryanne certainly didn't. She stopped her wayward thoughts; now was not the time to renew her doubts. 'No, but we can say we are, and you speak French like a native.'

'After thirty-five years I should think so!' Eleanor exclaimed.

Maryanne could not eat the simple food that had been brought to their room. She felt sick and faint, but it was not so much her pregnancy, but despair which had suddenly swamped her. Her disappointment at not finding Adam with the Seventh, all the days of walking, all the effort to keep cheerful, the rain, those poor wounded men, all heaped themselves up in her head until she wanted to do nothing more than lie down and howl her misery. She pushed her plate away and stared into the leaping flames, her thoughts with a husband who thought so little of her that he could allow her to attempt such a journey alone. She chose to ignore the fact that if she had not delayed her departure she would have been safely in England.

'Maryanne, are you ill?' Eleanor was leaning forward, peering into her face. 'Have you caught a chill?'

'No, *Maman,* I am not ill.' She smiled; it seemed an appropriate moment to tell her mother-in-law of her pregnancy. 'I am *enceinte.*'

'Really?' Eleanor's face broke into a delighted smile. 'Oh, Maryanne, my dear, I am so pleased for you. But why did you stay in Paris so long?'

'I was hoping Adam would come. . .'

'I know, dear, but now we must make all haste to get you safely to Beckford.'

'Beckford?' Maryanne queried in surprise.

'Of course. That is your home.' Eleanor paused. 'Oh, I see, you thought I would deny Adam's birthright. Oh, my dear, I said some very foolish things, but I did not mean them. And, besides, now I am going back to England with you, it does not matter.'

'It is much more complicated than that.' Maryanne

paused, wondering whether to go on, but she had never felt more in need of someone to talk to, someone who might understand how she felt. 'His f——' She stopped and started again. 'James was murdered.'

'Murdered?' Madame Saint-Pierre put down her knife and fork. 'How? Why? Who would do such a thing?'

'They say it was. . . They accused Adam.'

'Adam!' She stared across the hearth at Maryanne in disbelief. 'But that is ridiculous. Who could possibly believe that of him?'

'There was circumstantial evidence. He had been talking to James earlier that day and there were other things. . .'

'You know it can't be true,' Eleanor protested.

'Of course I do.' How easy it was to say that now. 'I have been accused along with him.'

'Then you had better tell me all about it, hadn't you?'

'It is a long story.'

'We have time. I do not propose to move until you tell it all.'

Maryanne obeyed, beginning with the incident at the ball and the disastrous curricle race and ending with Adam's theory that Mark himself had murdered his father, making himself the Duke of Wiltshire. 'What I cannot understand is why Mark should do such a thing. He was James's heir. . .'

'No, he was not.' Eleanor spoke so quietly that Maryanne at first thought she had misheard her. 'Adam is.'

'Adam? But. . .'

'You did not know? Adam never told you?'

'No. I do not understand,' said Maryanne.

Eleanor sighed. 'It is so like Adam to keep things to himself. Even when he was little. . .'

'Please, *Maman*,' Maryanne begged, falling to her knees beside Eleanor's chair. 'Tell me about it. I am sick of mysteries and everything that comes between us.'

'You did not know that James was Adam's father?'

'I guessed that, but I thought. . .'

'Oh, I see.' She paused. 'Adam is not my son, not my flesh and blood, though I could not love him more if he were.' She stopped speaking to sip her wine, but Maryanne was too shocked to interrupt. 'James Danbury defied his family as a young man and married the daugher of one of his tenant farmers and, to escape the scandal, he brought her to Challac. I was an old friend of Anne's and, of course, Louis and I made them welcome.

'Anne died when Adam was born. James was broken-hearted, as you would expect, and he could never look at his son without remembering the wife he had lost. He was hurt and angry and guilty too, because he had taken Anne from her family. He decided to return home, leaving Adam with us. I believe he joined the navy. He only went home to Beckford when he succeeded his father as Viscount Danbury.'

'Did Adam know all this?' Maryanne asked.

'There was no need for him to know until. . .' Eleanor paused. 'When the Terror ruled France and it looked as though our lives were in danger, we told him he was the son of an English aristocrat. We thought it might keep him safe. We told him that if anything happened to us he was to go to England and see our lawyer there. I imagine that was when he learned the identity of his father.'

Maryanne sat staring into the fire for a long time, digesting this information. Why had Adam not told her? Would it have made any difference? The murder had still happened, though she thought she could see why now. 'Mark must have discovered Adam was James's true heir,' she said slowly. 'By killing his father and laying the blame at Adam's door, he would keep the inheritance.' She sighed. 'The trouble is, we can't prove a thing.'

'I can be a witness to Adam's birth,' Eleanor pointed out.

'Yes, you can, but no one witnessed the murder, and if we go back to England I am afraid there will be more trouble. It is one of the reasons I delayed so long.'

'If there are no witnesses, how can they prove anything?' Madame Saint-Pierre was far more logical than Maryanne was over it. 'And if someone tries to manufacture evidence, then we must uncover the culprit. If it was Mark, he will be a very frightened man and will give himself away when he learns that we have all returned to England.'

'But *Maman*, we don't know where Adam is. He could be anywhere. He might be wounded and lying in some hospital with no means of telling us. He might even. . .' She gulped hard. 'He might even be dead.'

Maman patted her hand. 'I thought he was dead once but he was alive all the time. Like a cat, he has nine lives.'

Maryanne managed a wry smile. 'Yes, but we do not know how many he has used up.' She stood up and went to the window and watched the rain lashing against the glass. 'I hope he isn't out in this.'

'Come and sit down, my dear. He is not out there.'

'No, but someone is. There are horsemen coming. Do you think it is the French army? Perhaps Bonaparte himself.' Maryanne leaned forward to watch the riders. They were led by a man in white buckskin breeches and a big blue cape. On his head he had a cocked hat worn 'fore and aft'. He was riding perfectly calmly a little ahead of his companions. Maryanne had seen him once before, at Westminster, almost exactly a year ago.

'It's the Duke of Wellington,' she said. 'And he's stopping here.' She craned forward as the Duke dismounted. 'He's coming in. Do you think if we went downstairs we would learn anything of the battle? He doesn't look like a man who has been beaten.'

'I doubt he'll tell you his plans, Maryanne.'

'No, but one of his aides might. I'm going to dress

and go down. I'll pretend I need some more hot water.'
While she spoke, she was scrambling back into her
dress. 'This will have to do; I don't suppose anyone
expects a ballgown, in the circumstances.'

She remembered that comment when she went
downstairs and the first person she saw, coming out of
the inn parlour, was Lord Brandon in evening dress,
with dancing slippers on his feet, but so covered in
mud that it was obvious he had been out in the rain in
them for some time. She stopped on the bottom stair,
wondering if he would recognise her, and, if he did,
whether he would acknowledge it. He was part of
facing up to the world, but she had not expected to
have to do that so soon. She found herself trembling as
he turned towards her.

'I beg your pardon, *mam'selle*,' he said.

She decided to test her courage and made no move
to stand aside. 'It is Madame Saint-Pierre now, my
lord.'

His mouth dropped open. 'Miss Paynter. . .*madame*.
What, in the name of all that's holy, are you doing
here?'

She smiled. 'Taking shelter from the rain.'

'But how did you arrive here? Don't you know you
are in the middle of a battleground?' he said.

'Yes, we had a notion we might be when we heard
the guns. My mother-in-law and I were going to
Brussels and then on to Antwerp to find a boat to
England.'

'England,' he repeated as if his thoughts were miles
away.

'Yes,' she said defiantly. 'Is there any reason we
should not?'

'No, I wish I were going too.' He smiled slowly. 'But
may I offer you some advice. . .?'

She laughed. 'Avoid the Duke of Wiltshire.'

'Oh, that too.' A grin spread across his face and she
found herself warming to him. 'No, this is a personal
matter. When you reach Brussels, find Caroline and

tell her you have seen me. Say I am well and in good spirits and, God willing, I will be with her again soon.'

'Caroline is in Brussels?'

'Yes. She is my wife. We were married in Vienna in February.'

'Congratulations.'

'Thank you. Will you do as I ask?'

'I will try, but will she still be there? I imagine many English people will be anxious to leave. . .'

He laughed. 'Not Caroline.' He took her arm, as if to emphasise what he was saying. 'If events make it necessary, if we are defeated or I am killed, will you take her back to England with you?'

'With me? Is Mark not with her?'

He gave a little grunt. 'He went home long ago, soon after we saw you in Paris. He prefers to have his little wars at home.'

She did not ask him what he meant; it did not seem to matter. 'Have we been beaten? The men we saw on the road seemed to think so.'

He smiled wryly. 'It was hardly a resounding victory, but we stopped the French from taking Quatre Bras. It will give us the respite we need to re-group before the Prussians come to our aid.'

'We thought Napoleon was on our heels; you don't know how relieved we were to see the Duke of Wellington looking so unconcerned.'

He smiled. 'He has that effect on the men too. He can turn a lost battle into a victory just by being there. Have no fear.' He turned as a voice bellowed, 'Brandon!' from the parlour. 'I must go. Please make all haste to leave. I am sorry I cannot escort you, nor provide you with a carriage. We need all the horses we have.'

'I understand. Thank you.' She turned to go back upstairs. 'Where will I find Caroline?'

'We have an apartment in the Rue du Damier, number five.' Lord Brandon paused. 'Tell her I love her.'

Maryanne went back to Eleanor to repack their
belongings and resume a journey which was becoming
more and more exhausting as day followed day. And
to top it all she was committed to finding Caroline and
conveying loving messages. If only someone would
bring her a message, any message at all, so long as it
told her Adam was alive.

In an effort to keep their feet dry, they walked on
the paved road, but even that had its problems because
they frequently had to stand aside to allow troops,
horses and guns to pass, and these threw up so much
mud that they were soon as wet as they had been
before. They hardly noticed the cart draw up beside
them until someone spoke. 'Would you ladies care for
a ride?'

Maryanne turned to see a plump little man sitting on
the driving board of a covered wagon. What surprised
her was not that he seemed to be a civilian in the
middle of all things military, but that his coat and hat
were covered in buttons sewn on haphazardly—cloth
buttons of every colour and size, black and brown
leather buttons, gold and silver and lace buttons.

'I can take you to the next village,' he added.

Gratefully they climbed up beside him. He was, he
told them, a button salesman.

'In the middle of a battlefield!' Maryanne exclaimed.

He chuckled. 'The army always needs buttons. It
would hardly do if a fellow's coat was flapping open or
his breeches fell down just when he was ordered to
charge, would it? Can you imagine the effect that
would have?'

Maryanne laughed. 'For the want of a button the
battle was lost. . . But aren't you afraid?'

'Terrified, ma'am, but I have a living to make.' He
paused. 'What are you doing so far forward? The
baggage train is on the other side of Soignes woods.'

'We are not camp followers,' Maryanne said, muster-
ing her dignity. 'We are simply travellers who have had
our horses confiscated and want to reach Brussels.'

'Then it is as well you met with me, for unless I miss
my guess there will be an unholy row starting before
long.'

They left him at the crossroads at Mont-St-Jean,
pondering whether to go left or right, and set off again
on foot. They passed through the little village of
Waterloo as dusk began to fall, but by unspoken
agreement they did not stop. Further along the woods
on either side of the road were dotted with the camp
fires of the waiting army, eating, preparing their
weapons, trying to sleep. They gratefully accepted an
invitation from one of the women to sit by the fire,
where both dropped asleep.

When they awoke at dawn, cold, cramped and
hungry, the men had gone and only a handful of camp
followers remained. They bade them goodbye and
began walking again, thankful the rain had stopped at
last. They were approaching the gates of Brussels when
they heard the bombardment begin behind them. It
was half-past eleven.

It seemed as though half the population of the city
was on the ramparts as they passed through the Namur
gate. 'What news?' they called down to the travellers.
'Where is Wellington?'

'Back down the road,' shouted a bandaged infantry-
man who had been walking beside Maryanne.

'Is he beaten?'

The man shrugged and Maryanne looked up at the
anxious faces. 'I think he is making a stand,' she said.
'His aide said not to worry.'

'What aide?' A woman suddenly appeared on the
cobbles beside her and grabbed her arm. 'Which aide?
Who was it? Tell me, I must know.'

Maryanne turned towards the speaker, who was
dressed in an Empire gown of blue silk with velvet
ribbon threaded through the high waist. Matching
loops of ribbon and a long plume decorated the crown
of her high-brimmed bonnet. She made Maryanne
conscious of her own disreputable appearance, which

did not make her feel any better about facing her. 'It was Lord Brandon, Caroline,' she said.

Caroline stared at her. 'Maryanne! It can't be. . .'

'Oh, but it is. Your husband spoke to me yesterday. He bade me tell you he was safe and in good spirits.'

'Thank God. Tell me, how did he look? He wasn't wounded, was he? You would tell me if he were?'

'No, he wasn't wounded, and he looked well—in fact just as if he were going to a ball.'

Caroline giggled suddenly as relief swept through her. 'We were at a ball when the alarm was sounded. He rushed off without even changing. We hardly had time to say goodbye. Oh, you don't know how relieved I am.' She paused. 'But how did you come to see him?'

Maryanne took Madame Saint-Pierre's hand, drawing her forward to introduce her, then added, 'We were on our way to Antwerp to find a passage to England.'

'I am afraid you won't be able to do that,' Caroline said. 'The commandant will not issue any passports. He says that running away will demonstrate a lack of faith in our troops and set a bad example to the locals. Some did try to go by barge, but those were all requisitioned to carry the wounded. I would not leave Richard in any event.'

All the time they had been talking the sound of gunfire had been increasing and could not be ignored. Somewhere to the south a terrible battle was taking place, a battle in which men of both sides were dying. Maryanne's thoughts were with Adam. Was he out there, fighting with Napoleon? She felt weary beyond anything she had felt before.

'Excuse me, I must find somewhere for us to stay. We are both excessively tired,' she said.

'Oh, you must stay with me,' Caroline said unexpectedly. 'I have plenty of room and I shall be glad of your company.' She set herself between the two women and took an arm of each. 'Come along. We will wait together.'

Maryanne could hardly contain her surprise. 'I would not want to inconvenience you.'

'Inconvenience! After you have brought me the best piece of news I have had in two long days of waiting. Come along. You shall have baths and clean clothes and then we shall sit down and have a comfortable cose.'

There were, of course, no horses and, therefore, no carriages, so they walked to the Rue du Damier.

'Did you say the Duke was making a stand?' Caroline asked when Maryanne and Eleanor had bathed and changed their clothes and rejoined her in her drawing-room.

'It would seem so. His lordship said they were waiting for the Prussians to come up with them and then they would stand and fight,' Maryanne told her.

'Oh, but the Prussians have been defeated,' Caroline wailed. 'They have fallen back *miles*. For two days now we have had only bad news. Deserters and wounded coming back into the city with the most dreadful tales. A whole regiment of Brunswickers galloped back through the city and rode north as if the hounds of hell were after them.'

'His lordship seemed very confident, Caroline, and the Duke was so calm, you would think he was out for an afternoon's gentle exercise.'

'If anything happens to Richard. . .'

Maryanne hardly knew how to reassure her because her own fears ran along the same lines. Caroline had been unexpectedly friendly and hospitable, but what would she think if she knew Adam was with the enemy? To speak of him would raise all the old enmity, all the old accusations, and Maryanne was too tired and weak to indulge in a private battle in the middle of a conflict which was putting an end to so many thousands of young lives.

It was getting late and still the guns boomed, still they heard the refugees and wounded trudging in, and still they waited. Maryanne persuaded Eleanor to retire, and kept vigil with Caroline, who darted to the window whenever she heard the clop of hoofs on the *pavé*.

'Sit down, Caroline,' she said for the third time. 'It will not bring him any quicker.'

Caroline subsided into a chair. 'You know,' she said slowly, 'I was such a conceited fool before I realised I loved Richard. Do you remember I said I would not marry for love? Oh, no, I wanted money and a title, wardrobes full of gowns and shoes, carriages and horses, everything that is not worth a pin when it comes down to it. I derided you for wanting to fall in love. And then I did exactly that. Richard has only a minor title and little wealth but he is a good man, the best. I cannot eat or sleep for thinking I might lose him. Can you understand that?'

'Yes, of course.'

'Adam?'

Maryanne smiled. 'Who else? He is my husband.'

'Where is he?'

'I do not know. He told me to go back to England if there was trouble. I have been trying to do that.'

'You are very brave, Maryanne. I don't know if I could have done what you did. The scandal after you left was prodigious. I thought it would never die down. If it had not been for Richard, I do not think I could have borne it.'

Maryanne smiled; London and London Society seemed so far away, another world, an ostentatious, shallow, unimportant world. 'Is there a warrant out for our arrest?' she asked.

Caroline laughed. 'No, Mark said while you stayed in France he would do nothing, but——' She jumped up and went to the window as a horseman came galloping through the street, shouting. 'Listen,' she said.

'*Victoire!*' The shout was clear now. '*Victoire!* Boney is routed!'

Caroline rushed out to question the rider, but he had

gone by the time she reached the street. She returned
indoors. 'It's over,' she said. 'He will be home soon.'

'Amen,' Maryanne said fervently.

They sat together until dawn, and although carts full
of wounded rumbled back to the dressing stations and
officers, relieved of their duties, rode back to their
loved ones, Richard was not among them. By six
o'clock Caroline was desperate. 'I'm going to find him,'
she said suddenly.

'How?' Maryanne had been dozing from sheer
exhaustion.

'The officers who came back had horses; I'll borrow
one for each of us. You will come with me, won't you?'

'Where?' Maryanne asked.

'To the battlefield.'

There was no dissuading her, and Maryanne, conscious of the charge Lord Brandon had put on her,
would not let her go alone. They left a note for
Madame Saint-Pierre, who was still asleep, and set off
on horses which were already exhausted. The only
advantage of that, Maryanne decided, was that they
were easy to handle.

They rode silently, each with her own thoughts, each
trying to stifle the fear of what they might find. It
mattered little which side the men fought on; she and
Caroline had something in common—their concern for
their husbands. Among the forest trees, the remnants
of an army had returned to their camp fires to eat and
drink and talk, but, most of all, to sleep. Caroline did
not expect to find Richard among their number, and
they rode on, past the inn and the little chapel at
Waterloo and on to the crossroads where Maryanne
and Eleanor had left the button man. The scene was
worse than either of them could ever have imagined.

Dead and dying men and horses littered the fields,
along with broken guns, uptilted limbers, wood, shreds
of uniform, plumes. The whole area stank to heaven
and the dreadful sounds of muted groans seemed to
issue from the earth itself. Some of the wounded had

dragged themselves to the edge of the road, others lay propped against trees, waiting to be carried off to the surgeon. Orderlies with stretchers were running to and fro, loading them into carts. Women darted in and out among them, looking for their men, crying their names. Some who had found them lay sprawled across their bodies, sobbing out their grief; others stoically went from one motionless form to another, searching with growing desperation.

The battlefield covered several miles from the château of Hougoumont in the south-east to Papelotte over on their left, and they had no idea where to start looking.

'Have you seen Lord Brandon?' Caroline cried, dismounting and dashing up to a stretcher-bearer who was tying off the stump of an arm, before putting its owner on to a stretcher.

'Who?'

'Lord Brandon. He was with the Duke, one of his aides.'

'As far as I know all the Duke's aides fell. It was a miracle he wasn't hit himself.'

'Oh, no! Where? Tell me where,' Caroline pleaded.

The man shrugged. 'Could be anywhere; you will just have to keep looking, or go back and wait for news.'

Caroline would not do that, and they tethered the horses and combed the field, hardening themselves to the terrible sights they saw. They searched all morning, even after the orderlies had left with the last of the wounded. 'There aren't any more,' they were told. 'Those that are left are beyond help. We will come back for them later.'

Maryanne was only half aware of the last cart leaving, for she had come upon a sight which had stopped her in her tracks. Three French soldiers lay, one on top of the other, so that it was difficult to tell which limb belonged to which. One of them had a wide grin on his face as if he had died laughing. It was all she could do to control her heaving stomach, but she could not stop staring at him with her mouth open because she had recognised the uniform of the French Seventh Regiment. Did that mean Adam was dead? She did not want to believe it; she could not believe it. She would know, deep in her heart, she would know, wouldn't she?

She turned away at last and followed Caroline into another field, where the tall corn had been flattened and would never be harvested. The picture was the same, and over at the château of Hougoumont it was even worse. Thousands of men had died in the orchard surrounding it; their bodies were piled everywhere.

Maryanne, looking at the gruesome scene, put her hands to her stomach as she felt the first faint movements of her child. In the midst of death there was life; something sweet and new would come out of all this carnage. She took a deep breath and followed Caroline, who had gone through the gate of the château and was racing across to where a man lay propped against a wall.

'Richard!' she shrieked, falling on her knees beside him. He still wore his dress uniform, which was in tatters, and one of his dancing slippers; the other had disappeared along with the foot which had been wearing it. His face was a uniform grey and his eyes were shut. Caroline put her hand on his heart. 'He's alive!' she said, tears streaming down her face. 'Maryanne, he is alive.' She looked up at Maryanne. 'Oh, what are we to do? We need help, a stretcher, a cart. Oh, why did they all have to leave? We must bind up that foot. I'll do it. You go and find help. Quickly! Quickly!'

Maryanne, dashing off to obey, marvelled at the strength of character Caroline had found to help her do what had to be done. That was what love did for you, she thought wryly.

The road, when she reached it, was empty, except for the button man's wagon, with its tired old horse clop-clopping along, as if driver and animal were both

asleep. She breathed a fervent prayer of thanks and
stood waiting for it to come up to her.

Adam allowed the horse to go at its own pace, too
exhausted to think any more, yet too tired to stop his
thoughts from wandering. Pictures came and went in
front of eyes too deprived of sleep to focus properly.
Maryanne, *Maman*, the father he had never really
known, the man who had taken his place and died so
cruelly. But his death, brutal as it had been, had been
a quick one compared to the suffering of these poor
devils in the last three days. The stench of death filled
the air and unsteadied the horse. 'Easy, old fellow,
easy,' he said. 'Soon have you home and a bag of oats
on your nose.'

He smiled crookedly. Home. Where was home?
Wherever Maryanne was. Pray God she was safe. He
could tell her now, all of it, from the beginning, from
the day in 1810 when he had run into a British patrol
in the mists of Busaco to yesterday when he had
witnessed Napoleon leaving the scene of his defeat in
his blue and gilt carriage, escorted by a handful of his
faithful Old Guard. He could tell her, if he could find
her. He knew she had not gone to England, so where
was she?

The Duke of Wellington must let him go now. He
had done all that had been asked of him and, like his
chief, had come through unscathed. But it had been a
close thing, too close for comfort. Life with the Seventh
had become untenable when one of the men had
challenged his identity, and he had decided that the
time had come to leave them. His usefulness there had
been over in any case; Napoleon had decided to march
on Belgium. He had rejoined his commander-in-chief
and spent the time chasing from one battlefield to
another with dispatches, watching the French movements, infiltrating their ranks and listening to their
gossip.

He had been on his way to Brussels with his intelli-

gence when he had fallen foul of a patrol from the
Seventh who had recognised him, and he had been
obliged to fight his way out of his predicament. He had
killed one, left two others mortally wounded and the
remainder searching the cornfields for him. Evading
them had taken the best part of half a day and, in his
haste to make up for lost time, he had been careless of
his horse; the stallion had fallen and could not rise. He
had put it out of its misery, cursing in at least four
languages, but it had made no difference—he could
not turn the tide; it rolled inexorably on towards the
fields of Waterloo. Afterwards, returning to the British
lines on foot, he had come across the wagon under a
tree, with its button-covered owner dead across the
seat; it was better than walking.

The last hundred days might have solved Europe's
problems but they had done nothing to solve his. He
could no longer live in France, where those still loyal
to the Emperor might seek revenge, but neither was he
sure England was the answer. Even if he was not
indicted for murder, there would still be the scandal;
ought he to subject Maryanne to that? And, more to
the point, could he stand by and let Mark Danbury
usurp his title and say nothing? But he was tired of
fighting. All he wanted was to live in peace; surely,
somewhere, there was a haven for the two of them?

He smiled slowly, painting pictures in his mind's eye.
Maryanne at Castle Cedars, young and fearful of the
future, even more fearful of the past; Maryanne helping a chubby little doctor dig a bullet out of his
shoulder—how the damp weather made that ache!—
Maryanne laughing, Maryanne angry, Maryanne sad.
He saw her dressed for a ball in a pure white gown,
wreathed in greenery, and Maryanne in rags, covered
in mud and blood, her hair hanging damply about her
face, her eyes wide with anxiety. The vision was so real
that he pulled on the reins and the horse stopped with
an abruptness which nearly threw him off the driving

seat. Was it a vision, a ghost come to haunt him for neglecting her?

'Maryanne,' he croaked. 'Maryanne.'

'Adam!' She reached up tentatively to touch his thigh. 'Adam, can it really be you?'

He blinked and slid down from the seat. Her hand was warm in his, her eyes were vibrant and alive. Real tears were sliding down her face, making channels in the dirt. He took her in his arms and held her close against his chest, feeling the warmth of her, the trembling of her, felt her heartbeat under his hand, tasted her lips, gently lest she disappear like the apparition he had believed her to be.

She wanted to stay in the security of his arms, but the urgency of her errand forced her to be practical. 'Come,' she said, scrambling up on to the driver's seat and picking up the reins. 'Come quickly. Lord Brandon has had his foot blown off. Caroline is with him. They are up at the château. We need the cart.'

He looked up at her in a daze, still bemused by her sudden appearance, unable to believe she was real. He climbed up beside her and took the reins from her. 'How did you come to be here?' he asked. 'And where is *Maman*? You look as though you had been in a battle yourself.'

'I very nearly was.' She laughed. 'But I'll tell you about that later. We left *Maman* fast asleep in Brussels; she is perfectly safe and well. Now we must get Lord Brandon back there where he will be looked after. He and Caroline are married; did you know? No, of course, you didn't. . .'

He let her prattle on. Time enough later to tell her the wedding had been the talk of Vienna when he had been there in February; time enough to talk and make plans for the future. He guided the cart into the courtyard and towards the spot where Caroline sat with her husband's head in her lap, waiting for them.

The rest of the day was a blur of activity. Maryanne's senses were heightened by the fact that Adam was at her side, but there was no chance to speak of personal matters. They took Lord Brandon to the hospital on the cart and comforted Caroline who, understandably, burst into tears as soon as her husband had been delivered to the surgeon. She insisted on staying with him, but begged Adam and Maryanne to make themselves at home in her apartment.

Madame Saint-Pierre's joy at seeing Adam soon dispelled her annoyance at being left behind and she gave orders for an early supper to be served and a bed to be made up.

By the time Maryanne had bathed and changed her filthy clothes, and sat down to their meal, she was too tired to eat. She wanted to be alone with her husband, wanted to be held in his arms, to know their quarrel was forgotten. She begged to be excused and went up to their bedroom. Adam followed her, shutting the door behind him.

She turned towards him with a smile, but it faded when he kissed her and then held her out at arm's length to look into her face. 'Now, madam,' he said severely. 'An explanation, if you please.'

CHAPTER TWELVE

ALL day Maryanne had been looking forward to being alone with her husband, to feel his kisses on her lips and know that the rift between them had been healed. And all he could do was continue their quarrel as if there had been no interruption!

'Explanation?' she retorted. 'You are asking *me* for an explanation?'

'Yes. I expect my wife to obey me. I sent you to Paris with instructions to go back to London. Robert and Jeannie were expecting you. How do you think I felt when Robert wrote to say you had not arrived and when I went to Paris you were not there either?'

'No worse than I felt when you disappeared.' She failed to see the twinkle of amusement in his eye. 'And how could Robert write to you, when no one knew where you were?'

'He knew I could be reached through the Duke.'

'Which Duke?'

'Wellington, of course.'

'It seems to me,' she said tartly, 'I am the one requiring an explanation.'

He burst out laughing. 'I knew we should fight but I did not imagine it would be so soon.'

'I believe you enjoy it.' She was bewildered and angry at his behaviour. 'You deliberately provoke me.'

'And you rise to the bait every time, my darling.' He pulled her towards him to kiss her. 'There will be time for explanations later. Now I want to make love to my wife.'

He drew her down on to the bed beside him and she melted under his caresses, forgetting the past, the unbelievably long day, all the things which divided them, giving herself up to her undenied and undeniable love. He took his time undressing her, kissing her lips, her neck, her shoulders and arms, letting his mouth roam down her body to her stomach with its tiny bulge. 'Maryanne,' he said suddenly, sitting up to look down at her, naked and glowing with a kind of iridescent beauty which made him ache with love. 'Are you. . .?'

She laughed at the expression on his face—delight, concern, wonder. 'Yes, I am increasing,' she said.

'Then should we. . .?'

Her answer was to wind her hands round his neck and pull him down on to her. 'He is only very tiny,' she whispered. 'You will not hurt him.'

He smothered her with kisses, forgetting his intention to savour their lovemaking slowly. She would not have let him do that in any case; her passion was as great as his and they were carried away on a cloud of rapture which took them to paradise.

It was some time later when he murmured dreamily, 'You said "he".'

'Isn't that what you want, a son and heir?' she asked.

'An heir,' he repeated. 'Heir to what? I cannot go back to France, and returning to England means. . .'

'I know what it means,' she said. 'It is why I delayed so long—I was too cowardly to face it alone.'

'You are not alone now.'

'No, but how long before you disappear again? How can I ever be sure of you? You have so many secrets. Why didn't you tell me you were James's heir? I had to learn it from *Maman*,' Maryanne told him.

'When could I have told you? When we first met? Should I have said, when you fled from Castle Cedars and threw yourself into my arms, "By the way, I am the Viscount's son"? Should I have told you at the ball? Do you know, I very nearly did? That was why I asked you to meet me in the conservatory but, as always, we misunderstood each other and I let it pass. And later, when you announced your engagement to Mark, was I supposed to step in and spoil your happiness by throwing a cat among the pigeons? I fully intended to return to France without speaking to my father, but I could not leave before the curricle race because that would have been construed as cowardice. After that everything was taken out of my hands by events I could not control. And the longer we have been together since, the more difficult it has become.'

'Try now. From the beginning.'

He put his arm around her and drew her head on to his shoulder. 'The beginning. I suppose it began with the Revolution, the Terror and the execution of the man I had always known as my father. Before he went to the guillotine, he told me to go to England and find Mr Rudge—Robert's father—who would look after me. I set out and reached Paris, but there I stayed. I had neither the means nor the inclination to go further. As far as I was concerned, *Maman* and *Papa* had been my parents, and if I felt anything at all it was anger at the callous behaviour of a father who did not care about the child he had brought into the world.'

His grip tightened as he remembered. 'I became *Le Choucas*, the Jackdaw, the thief. I would have slit your throat for a few sous. I forgot my loving home, I forgot my birthright; my only thought was to stay alive and out of the dungeons of Paris. At sixteen I was a man you would not have liked.'

'But how could you forget all your adopted mother had taught you, to live like that?'

He laughed. 'You still do not understand, do you? That was the way I wanted to be. I wanted to deny my background because then it did not hurt so much, and if I could damage someone in authority, if only in a small way, then I was avenging *Papa*. And later, when I enlisted in the army, it was not to fight for my country, not from any sense of patriotism, but simply to stay alive. I had no axe to grind for Bonaparte; in fact as the years went by I became more and more disillusioned.'

He paused to kiss the top of her head. 'One day, in Portugal, I was out with a patrol when we missed our way in the fog and were captured. The others, including the Compte de Challac, who was a captain at the time, were marched off to spend the remainder of the war on the hulks in Portsmouth Sound, but because I spoke English I was taken to see Viscount Wellington. We had a long talk and at the end he said, "An Englishman in a French uniform is just the article I need. Will you go back for me?".'

She lifted her head to look into his face. 'And you agreed?'

'Yes. He convinced me I could do most good by returning to the French lines.'

'What happened when you went back?' she asked.

'I pretended I had escaped. The false information I had been provided with ensured my welcome.' He paused, smiling. 'And, in the absence of the Count, my promotion.'

'Didn't you feel like a traitor?'

'Any qualms of conscience were soon stilled when I thought about what Bonaparte was doing to Europe—the devastation, the looting. He had no care for the casualties he inflicted, not only on those who resisted him, but on his own troops. He once admitted a million lives meant nothing to him. I lost many a friend to his fanaticism, Jeannie's husband among them. And, even though I had grown up in France, I knew myself to be English, and it was the French who had executed my adoptive parents.' He paused. 'If I had known *Maman* was still alive, I might have behaved differently, but I don't think so.'

'So you became a spy?' Maryanne demanded.

He grinned. 'I prefer to say intelligence officer. I was Captain Choucas to the French and Sir Peter Adams to the English. When the British army entered France, I could neither stay with the French nor march with Wellington, so I decided, duty done, to go to England as Adam Saint-Pierre. I had been forced to take Michel into my confidence early on and he had risked his life on more than one occasion to help me. I had promised him I would look after Jeannie, and she wanted to return to London. It was from Robert I learned who my real father was.'

'Were you shocked?' Maryanne asked.

He smiled. '*Maman* had hinted that he was well born, but I had no idea who he was. I had already planned to go to Portsmouth to expedite the release of the Count, and curiosity took me to Beckford and Castle Cedars. I found myself wanting to meet my father, but as he had acquired a second family, who obviously did not know of my existence, I was hesitant, especially as I had no proof of my identity.'

'How did Mark find out?'

'My father spotted me at the Duke's funeral and asked me to call on him.'

'He knew who you were?'

'Yes, he had made his own enquiries after you told him my name. He thought we had all died in the Terror, and said if he had known I had survived he would have done his best to trace me. Far from forgetting me, he found I was always in his thoughts. I don't know why I went—perhaps because I was beginning to revise my ill opinion of him, perhaps because I hoped I would see you again. I wanted to tell you everything then, but you had gone to Beckford with Mark.'

'That was when I decided I could not marry him,' Maryanne said.

'My father talked to me about the family and the estate and how he had not wanted to inherit the dukedom. He said he would have preferred to remain Viscount Danbury and Squire of Beckford. He spoke about the villagers and their grievances, and told me he was afraid Mark would ruin the estate and hurt the people. He also mentioned his suspicion that Mark had engineered the curricle accident. Those men had been paid to upset the logs.'

'Not by you?' she exclaimed.

'*Mon Dieu*! Did you think that?' He was almost angry again.

'I heard Lady Markham say you needed more than luck. . .'

'She meant I needed advice on a good rig and plenty of practice.'

'Oh, I've been such a fool. Can you ever forgive me?' she cried.

He kissed her. 'Does that answer your question?'

She wriggled comfortably in his arms and he went on, 'Mark came in while we were talking and, before I could stop him, my father told him who I was. You can imagine his reaction. He raved and threatened, and because I had no intention of coming between them I left. And then, foolish, foolish girl, you decided to take matters into your own hands. . .'

'And my timing, as always, was terrible.'

'It was catastrophic.'

'You did not want me with you?'

'I wanted it more than anything in the world, my love, but not that way, not fleeing the country followed by accusation and scandal. Mark believes you know the truth, that you saw what happened, which is why, when Robert told me of the murder, I had to take you with me.'

'Why didn't you tell me?'

He smiled ruefully. 'I learned in a very hard school not to confide in anyone, however close they seemed. Ever since I was twelve, I have had to solve my own problems, and it did not come easy after all that time to find I had an accomplice, willing or unwilling.'

'I was. . .am your willing hostage,' she said softly.

'I was never sure if you came as friend or foe. One day I thought one thing and the next I was convinced of the opposite.'

'You are a fine one,' she said, scrambling to a sitting position so that she could look down on him. 'You expected me to know you were innocent without being told, but you could not dispel your own doubts about me. Why, in heaven's name, did you think I came with you? For a jaunt? I can tell you it has been no jaunt. Curiosity? Not even I am as curious as that. And why have I stayed? I could have left you at the inn by the river and gone back with the fishermen. When we were in Montmartre, I could have gone to the British Embassy for help, and when I saw Mark in Paris I could have thrown myself on his mercy and told him I had been held against my will. Even when you sent me home, I stayed. I did it because I love you. Oh, Adam, can you not see what is under your nose?'

'A very pretty little mouth,' he said, pulling her down and rolling over so that he was above her. 'Don't you know I love you more than life?'

'You only ever said it once and it did not stop you from going to war again, did it?' She ran her hands over his muscular torso, making desire well up again. 'I was furious with you.'

'I did not want to go, believe me, but when the Duke heard I was going to Challac he asked me to send him reports of Napoleon's movements and I could not refuse him. It was why I was away from home so much. That last time, when I was gone so long, I went to Vienna to report in person. His Grace convinced me it was my duty to re-enlist. He said he still needed an Englishman in a French uniform. Before I could return and tell you about it, we were ordered to Challac. You can have no idea of what went through my mind.'

'I was angry,' Maryanne said.

'So was I, but not with you—with myself.'

She lifted her head to kiss his cheek. 'What happened after I left?'

'Nothing—that is the irony of it. The regiment went over to the Emperor without firing a shot.' He smiled wryly. 'When Napoleon marched on Belgium, my usefulness seemed over and I deserted, went back to Paris. . .'

'And I had left.'

'Yes. Now, if you please, I will have that explanation. Why did you decide to ignore my instructions?'

'I didn't ignore them, I simply delayed obeying them. We kept hoping, *Maman* and I, that you would come back. When we finally decided to leave, there was only one way we could go.'

'Oh, my impetuous duchess, when I think of what could have happened. . .'

She was thoughtful. 'Adam, don't you think we should put that behind us? The inheritance, I mean.'

'Is that what you want?'

'I. . . I don't know. I simply want to be at peace with everyone. I don't want to stir up old enmity, especially as Caroline seems to have changed so much. We could be friends.'

'Our quarrel is not with Caroline, Maryanne.'

'No, but she will always be loyal to her brother.'

'I am also her brother, my darling.'

'Half-brother.'

'So? What would you have me do? Hide away for the rest of my life? If I do, you will soon tire of it, I can tell you. We should fight, until one or other of us was completely subdued and, because I am a strong-willed man, it would be you. I would make you miserable. Is that the home life you want for our child?'

'Oh, Adam, I do not know.'

'Then let me decide what is to be done. I have to go to London.' He smiled. 'Robert and Jeannie are to be married. I have been asked to give the bride away. While I am there, I will ask his advice.' He stroked her face gently, kissing her forehead, murmuring endearments, soothing her. 'You may go back to Challac and wait for me there, if you wish.'

'Oh, no! I will not be left behind. We go together or not at all.'

'Very well,' he said, cradling her head back into his shoulder and smiling to himself; the last thing he wanted was to be parted from her again. 'Go to sleep now,' he said softly. 'All will be well.'

It had been a long, long day, full of horror and despair, but out of it had come reunion with Adam and a new understanding. There was no longer any need for her to be mindful of her responsibility towards Madame Saint-Pierre, to be strong and forceful, to decide which road to take, when to eat, when to take shelter, to be cheeful when she felt like crying, to pretend she was well when she felt sick. She could relax. She slept, leaving him to stare up into the darkness, wide-eyed and awake.

It was ten days before they were given permission to leave, and by that time Richard was judged well enough to travel. He had to use crutches but was amazingly cheerful and full of plans for the future. The two couples went together.

England, when they reached it, was jubilantly celebrating all over again, with bells ringing, flags and banners flying, music and fairs, but Maryanne was more concerned with wondering what she would do if they were arrested than with the festivities. She saw constables round every corner and imagined they were being followed by the two henchmen Mark had sent after them before.

Once in London, Richard and Caroline left for their estate in Hampshire, not far from Castle Cedars, while Adam, Maryanne and Madame Saint-Pierre went to Adelphi Terrace. Robert and Jeannie, who cared not a pin about scandal, made them welcome, insisting they stay with them.

'Unless you plan to take over Wiltshire House,' Robert laughed as he led them into the drawing-room they had left so suddenly the year before. 'Danbury has put it up for sale.'

'Oh?' Adam raised an eyebrow. 'Why is he selling?'

Robert gave orders for a meal to be prepared and beds to be made up, before replying. 'Gambling debts. He is on his uppers. He has already sold almost everything of value at Beckford Hall. The Dowager died last month, so it will not be long before he begins emptying Castle Cedars of its treasures too.'

'But he can't do that,' *Maman* said. 'They are not his to dispose of.'

Robert smiled at Adam. 'Well, my friend, what do you propose to do about it?'

'What can I do?'

'Come out into the open. Force his hand.'

'No,' Maryanne said quickly. 'It is too risky.'

'Doubts, Maryanne?' Adam queried with a half-smile that lifted the scar on his brow.

It was an expression which meant he would do exactly as he pleased. She wished Robert would not encourage him, and *Maman* too. In some ways, she wished they had not returned to England. She wanted her child to be born in her homeland, but not at the price of Adam's life. If he were convicted of murder. . . Oh, if they could only prove his innocence!

'No, of course not,' she said hastily. 'But Mark holds all the cards.'

Adam chuckled. 'But we have just been told what a poor gambler he is.' He turned to Robert. 'Tell me, what cards do we hold?'

Robert shrugged. 'Madame Saint-Pierre can prove who you are.'

'But we cannot prove who killed James,' Maryanne said. 'Until we can, I think Adam should do nothing.'

A servant announced that supper was served, and they went in to the dining-room, and for a little while the conversation was of other things—their adventures, what had been happening England, the latest gossip, food prices, anything but the subject which was most on their minds. Afterwards, the ladies went back to the drawing-room to talk of weddings and clothes and babies, leaving the two men to a more serious discussion over port and cigars.

'You know, Adam, even without the accusations of murder there was enough gossip about you before, but to return and do nothing to silence it. . .' Robert paused, but Adam did not interrupt. 'And you and Maryanne are not the only ones to consider. You will have an heir one day. . .'

'Very soon,' Adam murmured. 'The end of October, I am led to believe.'

Robert smiled and lifted his glass in a toast. 'Congratulations. But all the more reason to fight. If you do not, the estate will be broken up, furniture, pictures, valuable heirlooms all scattered. It is already happening. And it is not just your family who will suffer, but the estate workers and villagers who depend on the landowner for a livelihood. Your half-brother has already put up a bill to enclose the common land at Beckford. When it is done, he will sell at a good profit, no matter what hardship it causes others. Adam, you have a responsibility to those people; you cannot let him do it.'

'And if I am arrested?'

'Then I will do my best to defend you,' Robert replied.

Adam smiled wryly. 'Thank you, my friend. But I am not at all sure I am brave enough to face my wife's wrath if I go against her wishes.'

Robert smiled. 'I am sure you can think of a way round that. You must have done it before.'

Adam threw back his head and laughed. 'It will be a battle royal.'

He was right. Maryanne was adamant; if he insisted on putting his head in a noose, then she would accompany him, and nothing he could say would dissuade her. Knowing she was quite capable of riding after him and risking not only her baby's life but her own as well, he gave up his intention of riding to Wiltshire and ordered a post chaise.

'But you will stay in the carriage,' he said, facing her across the breakfast table. 'I shall see him alone. I mean to give him the opportunity to retract his accusation. If he does, I'll help him to go abroad and stay there. There will be no need to make the reason for his going public.'

She laughed. 'One more Danbury scandal is neither here nor there and he will never agree.'

'We will see,' he said.

They arrived at Castle Cedars in the middle of the morning three days later, having spent the previous night at an inn a few miles short of their destination. The gate was opened for them by the young son of the gatekeeper, who told them that the Duke had gone out in his carriage not ten minutes before.

Adam cursed under his breath. He wanted the confrontation over and done with. It was like going into battle; the plans had been made, the ground chosen, the dispositions of the troops set, and all that remained was the order to charge. The waiting always keyed him up, made his stomach churn, killed his appetite, made him restless and sharp-tempered, and the only cure was action. As soon as he was in the thick of it, his nerves disappeared.

'I reckon there'll be trouble. . .' the boy said, pocketing the coin Adam had given him.

'Trouble?'

'At Beckford. The villagers are up in arms about the enclosure. I heard they were marching today. His Grace will be off to fetch the militia. . .'

'Beckford!' Adam shouted up to their driver. 'And make haste.'

They could hear the noise before the bend in the road brought the cause of it into view. Beckford Common was packed with villagers milling about and shouting threats. Maryanne was appalled to see men and women she had hitherto thought of as law-abiding and peace-loving carrying pitchforks and rakes and other implements as weapons, brandishing them as if they meant to use them.

'What are they going to do?' Maryanne asked as they pulled up under an oak whose leafy shadow helped to conceal them.

'I don't know. They are shouting against the Duke,' Adam replied.

No one paid them the slightest attention because they had seen the Danbury carriage coming down the hill and were surging towards it. It was forced to a stop as they surrounded it.

'We want the Duke!' they yelled. 'Where is the black-hearted devil?'

They wrenched open the door of the coach and pulled Mark out. It looked as though they intended to lynch him.

Adam could remain still no longer. Bidding Maryanne stay in the coach, he pushed his way through to the front of the crowd. 'Stop this madness!' he roared. His powerful voice carried across the heads of the mob like a roll of thunder before a storm. 'Don't you know rioting is a serious offence? Listen to reason!'

In the sudden silence that followed Mark looked up and realised who had caused it. His eyes lit with sadistic pleasure. 'What have we here?' he said, ignoring the villagers, although he was still firmly held by two of them. 'Has my patience been rewarded? Has the spider caught the fly?'

'Go back to your work and your homes,' Adam said, ignoring him and addressing the villagers. 'And I will guarantee you have your grazing land back.'

Mark laughed harshly. 'Are you going to listen to the empty promises of a dead man?' he shouted. 'You know this man is wanted for the murder of the late Duke of Wiltshire—he is not in a position to guarantee anything. I'll give ten guineas to anyone coming to my aid!'

The rioters looked at each other doubtfully. Ten guineas was a great deal of money, and might, in some measure, compensate them for the loss of their grazing land.

'I will overlook your behaviour today,' Mark went on. 'I will send the militia away. All you have to do is seize that man.' His arms were firmly held; he indicated Adam with a nod of his head.

Maryanne, fearful for the man she loved, forced her way through the mob to his side. 'He is innocent,' she cried. 'Do not turn against him.'

For a moment she quailed at the look of annoyance Adam gave her, but then smiled up at him defiantly. 'I told you before, where you go, I go,' she said.

'How touching!' Mark sneered. 'And are you prepared to preach at Tyburn Cross along with him?' He turned to address the villagers. 'This woman, whom you once took into your midst out of the goodness of your hearts, is his accomplice. I am a magistrate, empowered to take them into custody, and I have the right to insist on assistance. Seize them both and bring them to the Hall.'

Maryanne moved closer to Adam, trying to shield him with her own small body. Knowing and liking her, the villagers looked unsure of what to do. One of them took her arm, but whether in obedience to Mark or as a gesture of reassurance she could not tell. Another took a pace or two towards Adam. He dodged and went to stand beside his half-brother.

'His Grace and I have a great deal to talk about and it were better done in private,' he said to the crowd, then, turning to Mark, 'I will come with you, provided my wife is allowed to go free.' To Maryanne he said, 'Go back to the coach.'

'I will not,' she answered promptly. 'I am coming too.'

Mark's mocking grin of triumph sent trickles of ice running down her back. 'Fetch the constable from wherever he is,' he ordered the blacksmith. 'Bring him to the Hall.' Then, as the man hurried away, he called after him, 'There is no need for haste—the prisoners will be safe in my keeping.'

Adam's behaviour was anything but that of a prisoner as he handed Maryanne up into the Danbury coach before climbing in himself.

No one spoke on the journey to the house, and when they arrived Maryanne was shocked by the change in the place. It had a forlorn air, as if it knew the loving care that had been lavished on it by its previous owner was no more. And when they went inside she realised that Robert had not been exaggerating. It was easy to see where the pictures had been taken from the walls, and there was only the barest minimum of furniture and that not the best of what had once been there. The library was bereft of books and held only a small desk against one wall and a few chairs. She was reminded of the day she had entered this room for the first time, when James had asked her to go to Castle Cedars with him. What would she have said if someone had told her then that she would come back one day to be accused of being an accomplice to his murder? She would have laughed at the absurdity of it.

'Coming back to England was a very foolhardy thing to do,' Mark said, locking the door and turning to face them. 'And coming to Beckford was madness—you must have known you would be arrested, so why return?'

'To prove my innocence and your guilt,' Adam said.

Mark laughed. 'There can be no proof, you know that. As far as the world is concerned, you murdered my father.'

'*Our* father,' Adam corrected him. 'And it was you who did the killing. Having caused the death of the fifth Duke and got away with it, you became even more ambitious. With Father dead, no one would know the truth except me, and if I were hanged for murder there would be no one to dispute your claim. You would inherit an impoverished dukedom and Maryanne would provide the capital when she came into her inheritance.'

'Now, I wonder who would be believed if you were brought to court?' Mark sneered. 'A rough soldier—and a Frenchman at that—or a respected peer of the realm whose antecedents are without question? Everyone knows the late Duke of Wiltshire was a faithful husband and a good father, and Caroline and I are his only children. . .'

'You are very confident,' Adam said coolly. 'How can you be so sure my story will not be believed? I have proof of my birth, and in wedlock too. Your mother was not our father's first wife. I may not have wanted my inheritance before, but I am claiming it now. I suggest you withdraw with a good grace. Leave the country and I will see you want for nothing.'

'Where is this proof?' Mark demanded.

'My lawyer will provide it,' Adam told him.

'You bluff,' Mark said. 'You have no proof and no hope of being believed. Your foster-parents are both dead, that much I know. . .'

'You are wrong. Madame Saint-Pierre is alive and well and in London at this moment with my lawyer,' Adam informed him.

'You lie,' Mark said, going over to the drawer of the desk and taking out a small pistol. 'I have captured a wanted murderer and no one would blame me if I took revenge for my father's death.'

'No! No!' Maryanne shrieked, flinging herself between them. 'You can't kill him, you must not.'

'I can and I will, and you too, just as I did that old miser, our father,' Mark stated.

'Stand aside, Maryanne,' Adam said quietly, putting her from him. 'Move away.'

'The constable will be here soon,' she said, more out of desperation than conviction. Now she knew why Mark had told the blacksmith not to hurry.

'And he will find both prisoners dead, killed while trying to escape. I shall, of course, be sorry that I had not been able to take you alive, but I had to defend myself.' He took aim very deliberately and squeezed the trigger.

Adam, ignoring the gun, hurled himself at his half-brother and the shot went wild. They struggled together for possession of the weapon while Maryanne stood with her fist in her mouth and her heart beating wildly. They were well-matched in size and weight and neither was prepared to give an inch.

Maryanne skirted round them and stooped to pick up the poker from the fireplace. It could only have been seconds, but it seemed like hours, before she had a clear view and then she brought the poker down on Mark's head as hard as she could. He slid to the floor and Adam turned and took a pace towards her, smiling. 'Good girl!' he exclaimed. The next moment he had crumpled at her feet and she realised the shot had found its target after all.

'Adam!' She stared at him in disbelieving horror and then threw herself down beside him, cradling his head in her lap. 'Adam,' she said over and over again, ignoring the sound of people shouting and banging on the locked door. 'Oh, Adam.'

'Adam! Adam! For God's sake, man, if you are all right, open the door!' She heard, and yet did not hear, someone throw his weight against it. She was numb with shock. Her heart had cracked into a thousand pieces, dissolved and left a hollow space, a void, a numbness, a dryness which could produce no tears. There was nothing there to feel with, no emotion, only emptiness. She could only sit there, stroking Adam's face with a blood-covered hand in an unthinking gesture, as if doing so would let him know how much she had loved him. She looked up with unseeing eyes when the glass of the window shattered and Robert Rudge and the constable climbed over the sill into the room.

Robert ran to crouch beside her. 'Maryanne, what happened?'

'He shot Adam,' she said dully, nodding towards Mark, lying across the hearth where he had fallen, with the blood-stained poker beside him. 'He didn't want either of us to live. I had to stop him.' Her voice was flat, toneless; all life had been drained from her.

Robert left her to unlock the door. A crowd of noisy people invaded the room and began talking and asking questions, and she could find no voice to answer. She clung to Adam, refusing to leave him.

'Fetch the doctor,' Robert said to someone behind him as he returned to Maryanne's side.

'Oh, why did Adam have to come here today?' she asked. 'I told him! I told him it was too risky. . .' She looked up at Robert as if seeing him for the first time. 'How did you get here?'

He smiled. 'When Jeannie found out that I had given in to Adam and allowed you to come alone, she was furious. She sent me post-haste after you.'

'If only you had arrived sooner, you might. . .' Still she could not cry. 'You might have prevented this. . .' She looked round the room. It was a scene of chaos; there was blood everywhere. The housekeeper had fetched blankets and cushions from the servants' quarters to make Adam comfortable and others were doing the same for Mark, whose head was a mess of blood. He was moaning softly.

'What happened?' Robert asked.

'He said we must die, just as his father had died. He took the gun out of the drawer and. . .' She took a deep breath. 'He killed Adam.'

He had put his hand on Adam's chest and smiled suddenly. 'You despair too soon, my dear. He is not dead, though very close to it.'

'Are you sure?'

He placed her hand on Adam's heart. 'Feel it?'

'Yes! Yes!' What a fool she was! She had seen enough of the carnage after the battle of Waterloo to know that a man did not necessarily die of a bullet wound. The relief did something that her grief could not—it brought on the tears. They flowed down her face as if a dam had burst.

'I am sorry, Maryanne.'

Maryanne raised brimming eyes to look up at Caroline, still too shocked to show surprise. 'You here too?' she gasped.

'I was on my way to visit my brother when I saw Mr

Rudge. Oh, Maryanne, I just wish I had spoken up before. I've been thinking about it ever since Richard and I left London. He said I should come and see Mark, sort something out. . .'

'Sort what out?'

'What I had seen. The night Papa was. . .was killed. After you had gone to up to your room, I went into the hall. I saw Adam leave and Papa was still alive then because I heard him and Mark quarrelling. I had never before heard Papa raise his voice in anger, and it frightened me. And Mark was shouting too. Then I heard a scuffle and it all went quiet. When Mark came out of the library, I dashed up the stairs to my room.'

'You could have proved Adam did not kill James? You could have saved all this. . .' Maryanne was too numb with shock to sound angry. 'Why did you say nothing before?'

'I didn't want to believe it; I kept hoping I had misunderstood what I saw and there was a simple explanation. I kept telling myself that Adam must have returned later. And you had disappeared too. Mark said he had seen you running upstairs afterwards; he believed you knew exactly what happened, but it was not you he saw, but me.'

She knelt down beside Maryanne and took her hand, gripping it tightly. 'When you were so good to me in Brussels, I realised how wrong I had been. I could not banish it from my mind, so I told Richard and he told me to make a clean breast of it. I came here to tell Mark what I was going to do. Maryanne, can you ever forgive me?'

'If Adam. . . No, I will not think such thoughts,' Maryanne added, as the doctor arrived. He knelt to pull open Adam's coat and revealed a shirt soaked in blood; it seemed to give the lie to Robert's statement that her husband was still alive.

'Come away,' Caroline said, helping her to rise. 'He is in good hands now.'

She allowed herself to be led to the window, where

they sat in silence, watching the doctor, aided by Robert, administer to his patients. When he had almost finished Maryanne murmured her excuses and hurried over to kneel beside her husband and take his hand.

'I have done all that can be done,' the doctor said. 'Now all we can do is pray.'

'But he will live?' Maryanne asked.

'With careful nursing.' He turned to address two menservants who had arrived with a stretcher. 'I think it is safe to move His Grace now.'

It was a moment or two before she realised he was referring to Adam and not Mark. She smiled and reluctantly released Adam's hand, so that he could be put on the stretcher and taken upstairs to one of the few rooms which were still properly furnished. She followed and stood waiting as the men put him to bed and left the room.

'Adam,' she whispered, taking his hand and raising it to her cheek. 'Everything is going to be all right. You are going to get well.' She thought she felt his grip tighten and went on, 'Adam, can you hear me?'

She watched his face, almost afraid to hope, then she let her breath out in a long sigh of relief when his brown eyes opened and a quirk of a smile appeared.

'I hear,' he whispered. He was in a great deal of pain and the morphia the doctor had given him was making him drowsy, but he had the strength to tug on her hand and draw her towards him. 'I do not suppose you will ever be a dutiful wife,' he added.

'Would you love me half as much if I were?'

'Now, there's a question!'

Outside, they could hear the sound of cheering, as the estate workers, the villagers and a now redundant troop of militia crowded on the drive in front of the house below the bedroom. 'Tell them they can have their grazing land,' he went on, though speaking was an effort. 'And find Robert. . .'

'He is here. So is Caroline. There is nothing for you to worry about, nothing at all,' she assured him.

'Come nearer.'

She bent over to kiss him. It was the gentlest of kisses, a foretaste of all the joy to come, and she was overwhelmed with happiness. It would, she knew, be a slow process, his return to full health, but there was no doubt in her mind that it would happen, because they had so much to look forward to, so much to do, so many friends wishing them well. Now instead of following him she would be beside him, always.

A fire burned in the bedroom grate, casting a pink glow over the polished furniture and the silk-draped cradle. Beside it, Adam shifted his gaze from the study of the little miracle it contained to his wife. Motherhood had made her even more beautiful; she glowed with contentment. But inside she was just the same as she had always been—a girl in love, a girl prepared to go through fire and water to stay at the side of the man she adored. And now she had been doubly blessed.

She smiled. 'Pick him up, he is not made of eggshells.'

'Him?'

'James, Marquis of Beckford.'

He laughed and lifted the child, ignoring the nurse twittering in the background. 'James.' He smiled as he laid the child in her arms and watched as she prepared to feed him. 'James Louis.'

It was a little over three months since the library at Beckford Hall had been the scene of so much greed and hate, and yet out of it had come an unshakeable love, a love which had spread to everyone around.

From his sick-bed, Adam had been able to direct his representatives to repair the ravages his half-brother had caused on the estate, to restore the villagers' grazing land and to make sure their wages were sufficient to support them. Since his recovery he had refurnished Beckford Hall for Madame Saint-Pierre, and she lived there now, adored by the servants and the villagers. The law had taken care of Mark's crime; Adam had spoken on his behalf and he had not paid the ultimate penalty. Instead he had been sent to one of the penal colonies and would never return.

'Thank you, Betty,' Maryanne said, trying not to smile in the face of the girl's disapproval. 'I will send for you when I need you.'

Betty, who could not accustom herself to the unconventional ways of the Duke and the Duchess, looked as though she was about to protest, but changed her mind and, clucking disapproval at parents who employed nursemaids and then looked after the children themselves, bobbed a curtsy and left.

Maryanne reached across the baby's head and put her hand into Adam's. He smiled as he put her palm to his lips.

Outside, the old house, reflecting the light of the setting sun, seemed to glow with a life of its own, as if the happiness of its inmates extended to the bricks and mortar. The ancient cedars, tall and strong, cast long shadows across a home no scandal could touch because inside there was trust and hope and an abiding love.

The other exciting

MASQUERADE *Historical*

available this month is:

AN ANGEL'S TOUCH
Elizabeth Bailey

Miss Verity Lambourn found she had no choice about
accompanying elderly Lady Crossens to Tunbridge
Wells, but she didn't mind. Far from husband hunting,
Verity had other plans in mind which would make full
use of her vivid imagination! But dreaming didn't stop
her impetuous rescue of two small children, nor cause
her to back down from their stern father. When she
discovered his identity she did consider she ought to
have been more circumspect, not knowing her
refreshing candour drew both children and father. . .

Look out for the two intriguing

MASQUERADE *Historical*

Romances coming next month

REBEL HARVEST
Pauline Bentley

The Jacobite uprising of 1715 had engendered suspicion
everywhere, even in Sussex, and Katherine Winters was sure
her younger brother Paul had been lured into planning
insurgence by Viscount St Clere.

When Luke Ryder brought his dragoons into the area,
concealing Paul's idiocy was Katherine's abiding concern,
despite the fact that she and Luke struck sparks whenever
they met. With the cards stacked against them, could she
keep her brother safe, yet still have the man she knew she
loved?

BREATH OF SCANDAL
Elizabeth Lowther

Cassie Haydon had always wanted to go to Austria, her
grandmother's home, but not until the death of her mother
was she free to do so. A liberated woman, after all, this was
1904, Cassie had no qualms about accepting a post working
at the Kurhaus in Bad Adler.

Unfortunately, the first person she encountered was Count
Petransky, who was convinced she would be delighted to be
his mistress! His behaviour ruined her chances of a happy
working life, for the Kurhaus director, Dr Anton Sommer,
disliked the count and believed Cassie was a loose woman.
How was she to make Anton see the truth?

Available in January

Experience the thrill of 2 Masquerade Historical Romances Absolutely Free!

*Experience the passions of bygone days
in 2 gripping Masquerade Romances - absolutely free!
Enjoy these tales of tempestuous love from
the illustrious past.
Then, if you wish, look forward to a regular supply of
Masquerade, delivered to your door!
Turn the page for details of 2 extra FREE gifts,
and how to apply.*

An irresistible offer for you

Here at Reader Service we would love you to become a regular reader of Masquerade. And to welcome you, we'd like you to have two books, a cuddly teddy and a MYSTERY GIFT - ABSOLUTELY FREE and without obligation.

Then, every two months you could look forward to receiving 4 more brand-new Masquerade Romances for just £2.25 each, delivered to your door, postage and packing is free. Plus our free newsletter featuring competitions, author news, special offers offering some great prizes, and lots more!

This invitation comes with no strings attached. You can cancel or suspend your subscription at any time, and still keep your free books and gifts.

Its so easy. Send no money now. Simply fill in the coupon below at once and post it to - Reader Service, FREEPOST, PO Box 236, Croydon, Surrey CR9 9EL.

- ■ NO STAMP REQUIRED ■ →

Yes! Please rush me my 2 Free Masquerade Romances and 2 Free Gifts! Please also reserve me a Reader Service Subscription. If I decide to subscribe, I can look forward to receiving 4 brand new Masquerade Romances every two months for just £9.00, delivered direct to my door. Post and packing is free, and there's a free Newsletter. If I choose not to subscribe I shall write to you within 10 days - I can keep the books and gifts whatever I decide. I can cancel or suspend my subscription at any time. I am over 18.

Mrs/Miss/Ms/Mr _____ EP30M

Address _____

_____

_____ Postcode _____

Signature _____

The right is reserved to refuse an application and change the terms of this offer. Offer expires 28th February 1993. Readers in Southern Africa write to Book Services International Ltd, P.O. Box 41654, Craighall, Transvaal 2024. Other Overseas and Eire, send for details. You may be mailed with other offers from Mills & Boon and other reputable companies as a result of this application. If you would prefer not to share in this opportunity, please tick box. ☐

mps MAILING PREFERENCE SERVICE